Praise for *D*

'With fabulous world-build[...]
could bounce a quarter o[...] *...... Lullaby* is a
Handmaid's Tale for the modern world, about the ways
our human need for love can serve as both society's
salvation, and its undoing.'
Sarah Langan, author of *Good Neighbors*

'This gripping thriller has everything: beautiful writing,
shedloads of tension, family drama. It made me grateful
for my fragile freedoms.'
Emily Koch, author of *If I Die Before I Wake*

'*Dark Lullaby* is hard-hitting, mournful and deeply
affecting, reading like the offspring of *Never Let Me Go*
and *1984*, and it addresses universal fears about early
parenthood without providing easy answers. I raced
through it and when I'd finished, it made me hug my
own children tight.'
Tim Major, author of *Hope Island*

'A heart-wrenching and beautifully told novel, absolutely
compelling, and scarily plausible. This is the best kind
of speculative fiction: thoughtful, committed, alert to
the outlines of a possible near-future, that inhabits your
mind long after reading. One of the most important
books to be published this year.'
Marian Womack, author of *The Golden Key*

'An expertly crafted exploration of love and loss, with a truly haunting conclusion. Intimate, often poetic prose shines bright through the encroaching dread. Bleak, beautiful and bittersweet at every turn. I loved it.'
Martyn Ford, author of *Every Missing Thing*

'Polly Ho-Yen masterfully balances eerie, dream-like prose with a distressingly realistic portrayal of a world where reproductive right has become reproductive responsibility. To be a parent is to live with your heart outside your body and, through smart world-building, memorable characters and sharp insight, *Dark Lullaby* perfectly encapsulates the power and terror of that love.'
Dave Rudden, author of *The Wintertime Paradox*

'*Dark Lullaby* is a gripping story of love and desperation, of intimate and social structures, of sisterhood and motherhood that rings true as a bell. I devoured it.'
Deirdre Sullivan, author of *Perfectly Preventable Deaths*

DARK LULLABY

POLLY HO-YEN

TITAN BOOKS

Dark Lullaby
Print edition ISBN: 9781789094251
E-book edition ISBN: 9781789094268

Published by Titan Books
A division of Titan Publishing Group Ltd
144 Southwark Street, London SE1 0UP
www.titanbooks.com

First edition: March 2021
10 9 8 7 6 5 4 3 2 1

This is a work of fiction. All of the characters, organizations, and events portrayed in this novel are either products of the author's imagination or are used fictitiously. Any resemblance to actual persons, living or dead (except for satirical purposes), is entirely coincidental.

Polly Ho-Yen asserts the moral right to be identified as the author of this work.

A CIP catalogue record for this title is available from the British Library.

Printed and bound by LSC Communications, Harrisonburg

To Dan

I scarce believe my love to be so pure
As I had thought it was,
Because it doth endure
Vicissitude, and season, as the grass;
Methinks I lied all winter when I swore
My love was infinite, if spring make it more.

from 'Love's Growth' by John Donne

OSIP stands for the Office of Standards in Parenting.

IPS refers to an 'insufficient parenting standard'.

Induction is the process of fertility treatments a woman undertakes to conceive a child.

Extraction is the process of a child being removed from the care of their biological parent or parents if the standard of care is deemed insufficient by OSIP.

Out is an unofficial term referring to a person viewed as one of 'OSIP's Un-Tapped'.

THEN

The last time that I saw Mimi she was almost one.

We decided to celebrate her birthday early, just Thomas and myself, along with Thomas's mother Santa, the only parent we had left between us.

I'd made a cake out of little more than pure oats, butter and maple syrup; Mimi had just been diagnosed with an intolerance to gluten and I was now vigilant to the point of obsessive over any crumb that passed her lips since I had received the last IPS.

I suppose that as we sat down around our small table that night in November we were thinking of how little time we had left with her. We did not speak of it. We simply lost ourselves in my pathetic, flattened offering of a cake, with the electric candle that Thomas had bought especially sitting crookedly on top.

There was a part of me that knew then.

That very morning, I'd buried my face into the wispy fuzz that settled on the crown of her head after she napped. 'Her little halo,' Thomas called it, bouncing a hand upon its golden springiness. I knew it then, at that moment: *We don't have long left together*. But it was such an awful thought, one so singed with pain, so full of blackness, an emptiness like no other, that I didn't dare examine it. I shoved it away desperately and whispered, 'Happy birthday, darling girl,' into the silkiness of her tiny ear.

We gathered closer together as we began to sing 'Happy Birthday', pulled towards each other as though the little hard light from the candle's bulb gave off something like warmth. We sounded weary. The words no longer bore any promise; they only seemed to spell out our shortcomings. *Happy birthday, dear Mimi.*

Santa's singing rang out louder than Thomas and I combined, the off-key notes covering our faltering voices. She was dressed in her usual style, a gold and orange scarf hanging loosely off her shoulders, a skirt that matched her lips in its ruddiness, her dark hair flecked with a few errant silver strands pulled back from her face with a printed headscarf. Thomas and I were like shadows in comparison: grey, blurred, just behind her.

Her rose-red smile was fixed upon her beloved and only granddaughter. I remember thinking that she was making the most of these last moments, filling them with colour and light in the same way that she approached her canvases, her life. She had dressed that day with especial care, in the richer hues of her wardrobe, to offset the gloom, the sadness that had flooded through our life and carried us along with it. I tried to fix a smile on my face but I could feel it hanging there, a slipping mask.

Hap – py Birth – day to – you. Why does the tune slow as you sing it? The last few notes stretched on, awkwardly, until Santa started clapping, which made us all join in too. I looked at my daughter, at the centre of us, and wondered what I always wondered: had we created a world in which she was happy, in which she was safe?

Mimi sat perfectly straight in her chair. It had grown with her through her first year, being some sort of elegant Nordic-inspired design that could be made smaller or bigger depending on its sitter's proportions. I insisted on it when I was pregnant with her, had coveted it in one of the OHs, the 'Outstanding Homes', which we had visited during the induction, despite myself.

Before we visited the OHs, Thomas and I had a frank conversation about money and how having stuff would not make us better parents. Love was the answer, we told ourselves, not stuff. And yet, as soon as I saw the chair, its honey-coloured wood and gently curving lines, I vowed to have it for her. I could already picture our daughter sitting upon it at dinnertime, completing the triangle. It was hers before her eyes were open, before she felt the breath of the world upon her skin, and long before she was ready to sit up or feed herself.

'Blow it out, Meems!' Santa bellowed. 'Make a wish!'

Mimi was entranced by the candlelight – but then her eyes darted to me.

'Blow it out, my darling!' I said and I leant in close to her. 'This is what we do on our birthdays.' I ballooned my cheeks comically.

Then Thomas joined in too and in those moments, as we clowned and laughed and pretended to blow out the candle together, I think we forgot. I think we forgot what had brought us together a full twenty-two days before the date of her first birthday.

Mimi studied our faces and for a moment it looked like she was going to copy us and fill her bud-like cheeks and blow down on the plastic stump of light.

'You can do it, Mimi!' I called out in a burst. I was reminded of a long-distant memory of myself sitting in Mimi's place, my sister Evie next to me. A birthday cake directly ahead, safe and sure in my absolute belief in everything that my sister did and told me. 'Make a wish! You can do it, Kit!' she'd yelled to me, desperately, as I had to Mimi, as though she could not contain it. I remembered thinking that I must do it because Evie had told me to; that it must come true for she had told me it would. But in those few moments I'd already blown the candle out and forgotten to wish for anything.

Mimi's mouth unfolded into an open grin, and there, right there in her eyes, I saw it.

Pure delight.

Her brown eyes seemed to blossom, grow larger, and the light of the candle danced in her pupils. Or was it a light from within her? I let myself revel in it and I thought for that moment: *Yes. Yes, my daughter is happy. Yes, all is right in the world. And no, there is nothing, not any one thing that I would ask for more than this single moment of her happiness.*

She leant towards the blinking light of the LED candle as though she really did understand that she should blow it out.

'Switch it off,' I hissed. For a second longer that it should have, its bulb remained obstinately bright. I was mildly aware of Thomas's panic beside me; he had been pressing and was now striking the remote that controlled the candle. Quite suddenly, the bulb went out.

I remembered again the candle that I'd blown out on the birthday when I'd forgotten to make a wish. Its wavering flame glowed and as I blew, it bent away from me until it diminished to nothing. Its smoke had streamed from the wick and the scent of it, though acrid and sharp, I'd liked and savoured. But I dismissed the memory: it wasn't worth the risk to give Mimi a real candle on her birthday cake, however soft the light it cast.

I reached a hand out towards Thomas, feeling for the first time that day waves of contentment inside me. As though he'd had just the same thought, his hand was swinging towards mine and our fingers met in mid-air and clasped together fiercely. Mimi was triumphant now, toothy and innocent; her mouth gaped open with the thrill of it all.

It was then, just then, that we heard the rapping at the door.

NOW

There's a knock on the car window; it jolts me awake.

I notice the crick in my neck from sleeping with my head to one side, the blaring lights of the charging station, the slight hum of activity tracing the air.

Thomas's face shifts into focus, his eyes wide and searching. He mouths a question to me through the window: *Want anything?*

I shake my head and he turns away. I watch the quick rhythm of his steps as he crosses the forecourt. We can't stop here for long.

I'm still not quite awake and for those few moments I forget what we've done, forget why we're here. Then I turn to the back seat, suddenly, viciously. I whip my head round so that it jars, even though I know what I will find when I look back there.

The grey seats are empty; the seatbelts hang redundant.

I turn back to the front, deflated. I can see the top of Thomas's head past the buckets of half-dead flowers, the glowing Spheres that revolve above. He's eyeing something on one of the shelves as though he is about to pick it up but then he straightens, turns towards the sign for the toilets and disappears from view.

A car pulls up in the bay beside us. A man driving, a woman sitting in the back. I sense some unease between them; he wrings his hands as they speak, then rubs his temples in long upward sweeps. She's crouched over, curved like the branch of an old tree. Then I glimpse the outline of the car seat next to her. That's why she's sitting in the back.

I crane my neck to see if I can spot the baby. We haven't seen any children since we left home and I realise right then that I'm holding on to a hunger to see one. A tiny, new face slumped over in sleep, a toddler taking tottering steps; I'm flooded with an urgent need to see proof of their existence before me.

The woman catches my eye and I turn away quickly, pretending instead to be watching the Spheres as they change over. When I glance back, she is still staring at me, as is the man. They wonder what interest I have in them. They suspect perhaps that I'm not merely looking at them but watching them, inspecting them, judging them.

In the next moment, they pull away without charging their vehicle. Their car moves forwards in lurching jolts, taking the corner a little too sharply, a little too quickly. I wish I could tell them there's no need for them to go but there's another part of me that's glad they're suspicious, that wants to urge them to be on their guard, always.

I hunch my shoulders, my back stiff from travelling for so long. I want to release it, this pain that lines my spine, but I carry it with me, it is ingrained.

The Spheres turn over again. They crackle with another

news story and I scan them, wanting to be distracted from myself, from my own thoughts that also revolve and rotate in an endless cycle. I yawn noisily, my eyelids beginning to droop.

That's when I see it.

I am branded by it. I feel it, like a pressure on my chest that's increasing, a heavy lump in my throat that grows and engorges. Everything I thought I knew drops away.

I see it, over and over, after the Spheres have changed again and moved on to quoting statistics.

I see it as Thomas walks back towards the car and I flick my eyes closed and let my head loll back, as though I've fallen back into a dream.

I see it as I hear the rustle of something he bought being stashed in the glove compartment.

He traces a finger across my cheek, believing me asleep again.

His kiss brushes the side of my head.

I hear him say, 'I love you.'

But I don't react. I pretend I'm asleep; I play dead.

All I can think of is what I have just seen.

There's nothing left for him.

THEN

I t was at Jakob's naming ceremony where we first met.

An extended group of family and friends filled Evie and Seb's narrow strip of garden, drinking a particularly sharp homemade lemonade and waiting for the barbecue to be lit.

Jakob was wearing a babygrow printed with orange lions and had spent the entire afternoon asleep in Evie's arms. Each time Evie and Jakob walked down the garden, Seb just behind them, always close by, the crowd automatically parted to let them through, their voices dipping to a respectful silence. It gave an odd solemnity to the informal gathering.

He didn't quite fill the babygrow. At four weeks old, he still seemed so small that I wondered why they'd planned the naming ceremony for so soon after the birth, until Evie had told me that OSIP could use public engagements as a tool to assess how new parents were coping. There was a balance to be met, she explained to me, between social isolation and protective isolation, for the physical health of the baby.

Whispers crept around me as I weaved through the crowd.

She's looking well, isn't she – considering what she went through…

How many inductions did they do in the end?
I heard she almost didn't make it.

I could only half hear them and when I turned, I couldn't see who had been speaking. An image of Evie flashed in my mind, pale and lost, almost disappearing into the hospital bed that held her. I shook my head, dispelling the image.

An older woman who I didn't recognise kept staring at Jakob long after they had passed her. She didn't seem to realise that her arms were reaching towards them, as though she were imagining she was cradling him. But in the following moment, the man next to her started speaking in a loud, braying voice and her arms collapsed to her sides.

'I mean, who could have predicted it?' he said. 'We used to worry about nuclear weapons, overpopulation, climate change... but not this. Not infertility. And still no one can explain why it's happened.'

'I heard something the other day about it being down to pollution, a theory about microplastics,' the older woman replied. She spoke quite slowly, as though wearied just by putting the sentence together.

'But if it were something like that, wouldn't it have got better now that pollution has dropped? We've been at 99.98 per cent infertility rate for years now.'

'It was just something I heard,' she replied, in the same tired tone.

Dad stood a little back from everyone else, hunched over, inspecting the flowerbeds, one hand in his pocket, the other holding on to his glass awkwardly. He was wearing a coat even though everyone around him was in T-shirts and thin cotton shirts. I knew he felt particularly uncomfortable when the talk turned to infertility, which it often did. He might bolt at any moment. I made my way over but before I could reach him, I was halted by the soft chiming sound of a glass struck with a spoon.

Seb stood in front of us all, his drink raised, ready. He nodded to someone at the back, easily able to see over the crowd, he was so much taller than anyone else there. His hair had grown just a tiny bit too long. I imagined Evie trying to tame it before the party began.

'Just a couple of words,' he started to say. He smiled easily, raising his shoulders and spreading his arms out as if to say that it couldn't be helped. 'I'm not going to be long, I promised Evie that.'

They exchanged a conspiratorial look, Evie's eyes flashing dark with affection.

'I just wanted to say, when Evie and I decided to start induction together, we had no idea how it might all end.'

I couldn't stop my attention drifting from Seb to Evie, as he spoke. She stood a little stiffly next to him, holding Jakob closely to her but I imagined that if her hands were free, her fingers would be lightly fidgeting with the fabric of her dress. I could tell she didn't really want Seb to give a speech.

I saw her flinch slightly as he said, 'induction', and she stared determinedly down at Jakob, as though she could lose herself in his face. We'd known the word from an early age, we were taught it at school; I could still hear the faceless voice from the videos we were shown, word for word, in my ear: 'Induction is the only way to narrow in on that tiny band of still viable eggs and sperm.' My head would swim with the diagrams of ovaries and embryos and phrases like 'intensive egg harvesting' which had sounded frightening even then, before I truly understood what it would mean for us.

I remember Evie and I, as teenagers, trying to make sense of it, in that piecemeal way when what you're trying to grasp feels just too big, too alien, to comprehend. It only dawned on me slowly that this was about our own bodies, that those distant-looking diagrams were in fact part of us.

As we grew older, Evie spoke about induction with increasing authority but when she was actually going through it, her expertise turned jaded. 'It's just a numbers game,' she said to me wearily as she came to the end of yet another failed cycle and was about to start another. She didn't want to talk about how the drug combinations that were used to stimulate ovaries could often cause them to over-respond, causing blood clots, permanent organ damage, heart attacks. I didn't remember that detail from school. When Evie started induction, I had looked it up for myself; I'd read her drug notes when she wasn't looking. Seeing the facts in an innocuous little font had made me feel entirely numb. I didn't want to believe that it could be true. I'd buried it inside and a sick feeling, an uneasiness, had not left me since. I forced myself to look back to Seb as though I could dispel the shadow from my mind.

'But I always, always – and I didn't even tell Evie this – had a picture in my mind of us together sharing our child with the people who mean the most to us in the world. However tough things got, it was that picture that always kept me going. And now, being here, introducing you to Jakob, our beautiful son, right now, it's a dream come—'

Suddenly, Seb's voice was lost, cut off.

At first it appeared like he was laughing. There were a few nervous giggles as we watched his shoulders start to shake, his face creasing. But then he didn't, or couldn't, stop the silent quaking. We took in how his body dropped as though the strings that had been holding him upright and expansive had been severed in one cruel slash. Evie rushed towards him, concern set in lines across her face, and as she reached him we heard the unmistakable sound of a sob. It didn't possibly sound like it could have come from the same man who'd begun the toast just moments before.

As if in echo, there was a collective moan, a united lament, in the garden. It almost sounded like disappointment. This was not how this was meant to end, it seemed to say. There was a rush of people who crowded in towards him behind Evie, while the rest of us hung back, awkwardly, trying not to stare but unable to stop our eyes from finding Seb's tear-stricken face.

'I'm all right, I'm all right.' His words were almost lost in the noise of well-wishing and reassurances that surrounded him.

Someone, I can't remember now who, raised his glass and shouted out, 'To Evie and Seb, and to little Jakob!' but those around shushed him. 'Not now!' I heard a vicious whisper. Everyone chatted in subdued voices afterwards as though anything louder than a staged whisper might be deemed inappropriate.

I went from group to group, refilling glasses, offering around bowls of crisps that everyone refused. Seb was so happy to be a father that he couldn't keep control of his emotions was the party line. They were sleep-deprived with a newborn. Who is able to keep a handle on their emotions when you haven't slept for longer than two hours at a stretch?

'It won't be long till the food's ready,' Evie trilled when the first of the guests appeared before her to say their goodbyes. The only person she'd let leave without a word was Dad, who'd made his exit almost as soon as Seb had spoken. Tears always had that effect on him.

Evie stood in front of the barbeque; holding a large silver kitchen knife in her hand that she was using to cut into the plastic packets of raw, pink sausages. It looked far too big, too murderous, for the job. She'd handed Jakob to an old work friend of hers, a matronly woman called Deborah, who sat in a deckchair not far away. Jakob slept without stirring on Deborah's chest, although Evie's eyes kept flitting back to him. I went to take the knife from her but before I could, a man I had never met before, with very short dark hair, put his hand over hers and gently took it.

Evie relinquished the job gratefully. She stepped away and peered around the crowded garden, searching for something or someone she could not find.

'Are you okay?' I asked her. 'Can I do anything?'

Evie saw it was me and let her smile waver, falter.

'It's okay. I'm okay. It's probably nothing…'

'Tell me,' I said simply, with a sisterly directness.

'It's Jakob. We got a warning from OSIP. Not an actual IPS, just a warning. But it shook us up. Especially Seb.'

'When? What happened?' OSIP had been around for as long as inductions had been implemented. Officers of OSIP, enforcers, monitored parenting, ensuring that the needs of every child born were met to the highest standard. The stories of neglect and abuse of the past were consigned to history; enforcers had far greater powers and reach than the Social Services that had preceded them. Now parents everywhere lived in fear of enforcers issuing them an IPS and ultimately extracting their child from their care.

'It was nothing. We were just putting him back into the car after shopping for the food for today. Seb was getting the seat ready, I was holding Jakey, and then Seb said he was ready and so I passed Jakey to him and maybe because of the way Seb was standing, half in the car, he didn't have him properly... that was when it happened.'

'Did he drop him?'

'No! Nothing like that. He just wasn't supporting his neck fully. That was what the enforcer said.'

'That's nothing,' I agreed. 'Did you think it was okay?'

'Well...' Evie hesitated. 'I suppose so. Until the enforcer came running up and pointed it out. I mean, I guess he could have been supporting his neck more.'

'Put it out of your head,' I said. 'It was a one-off.'

'I hope so,' Evie said. 'Seb blames himself, but like I said to him, I hadn't noticed either. It was just as much my fault. The enforcer said that to me too. That I had been – what was the word she used? – *complicit*.'

'What was she like – the enforcer?'

'She looked like someone you would just walk past in the street, just like anybody else. Shortish hair, no make-up. A little bit... a little bit frumpy. I used to imagine that they would all wear suits and dark glasses, so you could see when one was close by, but you would have just walked straight past her. She was just normal, average.'

'Imagine doing that job.' I shivered. 'Why would anyone do it?'

'That was the thing. She was very worthy about it all. I could sense she really felt she was helping us when she pointed out how Seb was holding him. It was as though she was pleased with herself for noticing. Like she was doing us a favour.'

'I suppose if it was just a warning and nothing will come of it, maybe she was, in a way. Now you know that you need to be super vigilant.'

'Yes,' Evie said and she smiled in a sad sort of way. 'It's going to be harder than I thought.'

'You'll be fine,' I reassured her.

'Maybe,' Evie said. 'Maybe not.' She fiercely brushed away a tear that had started to trail down one of her cheeks.

'Don't think like that. Remember the inductions, everything you've learnt, everything you've been through. You're a wonderful mum. And Seb's so good with him. Jakey's a lucky little boy.'

Evie swallowed hard. Her face flushed pink from trying to stop crying. There was the beginning of a rash visible upon her neck, creeping over her collarbone.

'Stop it, you,' she said gently.

'Why don't you go find Seb? I'll help with the food.' I gestured towards the dark-haired man who had taken the knife from her. He had emptied all the sausages out of their packets and made a rough pyramid with them on a plate and was now breaking up the foamy white block of a firelighter over the charcoal. 'We'll get these people fed. Who's that guy at the barbecue?'

'He works with Seb,' Evie said. 'Thomas.'

She looked like she was going to say something else but then thought better of it and instead a sound left her; a deflation, a sigh, a space.

NOW

Thomas sleeps next to me.

He lies on his side, facing the blank, white wall, a framed print of a blurry watercolour of a garden its only decoration. If he opened his eyes now, the first thing that he would see would be that painting.

Its shapes run into one another, dozy, green bushes that become flowers that become a person – a gardener wearing oversized boots and a floppy hat so that their face is obscured. It was chosen for being bland, innocuous, for its bleached-out colours, and wavering lines, but it offends me.

As though it is urging me to see life that way, through a haze, with soft edges. Out of focus and out of shape. To forget its prickle, stab and sting.

Thomas breathes steadily. I am sure he is sleeping deeply, although earlier I was also sure, until I moved and he shifted and turned and reached for me. We're in the early hours of the morning but it could be the depths of the night. When we got here it was almost midnight, and then it took time for Thomas to settle. He wanted to talk and then took a while to drop off; he moved restlessly, kept turning over, his feet kicking out against the covers as though he were trying to escape it. Only now am I convinced that he is truly asleep.

I stretch one leg out of the bed and, when Thomas does not stir, ease the rest of me from under the white sheets. They are just a little scratchy from not being washed very often. I tread slowly out of the bedroom and on to the landing. Only when I am downstairs do I let myself take a breath.

These rooms are new to me, though I have planned this route in my head so many times since we arrived that I feel I know them well: I have turned the corner, tiptoed down the stairs and edged open the sitting-room door slowly again and again as I lie silently in bed, waiting for the right time to leave.

When we arrived last night in darkness, Thomas explored every inch of the maisonette, throwing on light switch after light switch as he went, as though he could make it more welcoming and familiar. It's another from the list of safe houses we've been to and each one has been as soulless as the last. A little too tidy, stiff sheets pulled across the bed sharply; none of the indents of life or character of love.

If I'd had a choice, I wouldn't have left the festering heap of bedclothes in our bedroom at home. There, our curtains are lined with dust. Little, silvery moths circle the air, breeding somewhere, making a home in my stagnancy.

But now we are in this white, bright place.

Rooms with no memories.

Walls with no photographs.

I made a wall of photographs of our families when I was pregnant. Mimi squirmed and hiccupped inside me as I drilled holes, hung frames and dug out old photographs of Mum, Dad and Evie I'd forgotten I'd ever had. I couldn't find any of Maia, my little sister who'd died as a young baby, although I have a memory of seeing one once – a tiny, wrinkled face, a bundle of white blanket. There was a recent one of Santa and Thomas; they were not looking at the camera but caught unawares, laughing, their heads dipped towards each other.

Our family was unusual in having both Evie and me; siblings were something of an anomaly. My parents, in an unbelievable lottery, happened to fall into that very rare sliver of the population who could conceive naturally. Only a few years before Evie was born, the infertility cases had begun to rise and by the time Mum was pregnant with us, almost everyone was undergoing induction if they wanted to have children.

Evie and I were atypical in that there were two of us but we were extraordinary in that we had been conceived naturally. I can't remember when I first learnt the truth of it, although I have a memory of Dad telling us we shouldn't talk about it. It made other people uncomfortable, he said.

Uncomfortable. I remember parroting the word back at him, stumbling over its syllables. I can't recall how old I was at the time.

Pregnant with Mimi, I would stand by that wall of family photographs and trace a finger over the faces of my mother and father, hand in hand on their wedding day. They were so like any other newly married couple amongst their confetti petals, so remarkable and yet unremarkable in their joy. You would not be able to tell from that photograph the miracle that would befall them – that somehow, they would be able to conceive without help.

Then I would turn to the other pictures, telling Mimi who

they were and what they were like. It became a constant in our day from when she was a newborn, standing by that wall and me repeating the same things to her, in a sing-song voice that I could not stop using even when I tried.

I can imagine those photographs clearly before me now as I stand before the beige blankness of the walls of this transitory place. And, as if by magic, I can see it all, I can transform this soulless room into the home Thomas and I made together. I can picture the view from the nursery window that faced out on to the mulberry tree we planted when we first moved in. We spent time, Mimi and I, examining its spindly branches that resembled long, thin fingers, beckoning to us. There was the quilted playmat with its jewel-coloured squares, which lay scattered with whatever toys held her interest at that time. My dad's chair. Paintings by Thomas and Santa. All those little pieces that fitted together to make up our home, now abandoned.

Here, everything that we own is out of place. The bread and bananas and box of tea that Thomas bought in a fit of organisation sit in an uneasy pile on the polished, flecked worktop. The carton of milk stands in the middle of an empty fridge at a rakish angle as though trying to take up some more space, just because it can. My coat lies slung across the plumped, cherry-red sofa where I discarded it, crumpled and tatty against the furnishings.

I reach for my coat without thinking and button it securely over the T-shirt and worn-soft pyjama bottoms I'm wearing. With each button, I'm a little more together, a little more like a person who is standing in the morning, a day in front of them to do with as they choose.

With the last button done, I am covered, protected.

I shove my shoes on to my bare feet and pluck the car keys from where Thomas dropped them, scattered next to a fruit bowl that holds no fruit.

The day is mine.

And I am leaving.

THEN

He was standing slightly hunched, leaning intently over the barbeque.

Though we had never met, I found myself reaching out towards him, resting one of my hands gently upon the back of one of his shoulders.

The cotton of his shirt was cool beneath my palm.

'Thomas?'

He turned slowly towards me and for a beat longer than it should have lasted, we stood there, wordless, our eyes searching each other's faces as though they were landscapes to be viewed.

'I'm Evie's sister,' I said, suddenly ridiculously, unaccountably, shy. 'Kit,' I managed to say, conscious as I always was of that word, *sister*. *Sister, brother*; words that were gradually becoming obsolete.

'Kit,' he repeated quietly as though committing the name to memory.

'I've come to help – with the barbeque.'

'Great, all I've managed to achieve so far is make a tower

of sausages. And blindly hope I can get the coals lit before the crowd turns feral from hunger.'

'Well there are two of us now. We can beat them back with…' I surveyed the instruments before me and brandished the long metal tongs with a flourish.

'I'll take…' Thomas peered over the detritus upon the table and selected a wooden spoon. 'This could do a lot of damage – if wielded correctly.'

'Well, time will tell if we have to use them.' I glanced towards the people gathered in the garden, speaking sedately in small groups. 'They look like a harmless bunch.'

Just then, voices carried towards us from the group closest to us.

'Should have been done a long time ago,' a small greying man said. I recognised him as an old family friend of Seb's. He leant forwards as he spoke, in juddering, jittery movements. 'The custodians realised we were headed towards this – they should have got on with it far sooner. If Torrent hadn't died when he did, we would be in a far better position.'

I saw Thomas glance towards them.

'Here we go,' I murmured, without thinking.

The man continued to bellow.

'If they'd brought in these measures say ten, fifteen years ago…'

'But I'm not actually sure how many will want to start though. Young women—' Evie's work friend Deborah started to say, but he carried on talking regardless.

I had an impulse out of nowhere to interrupt him, to cut him short as he had done to Deborah. I wanted to say something clear and meaningful that would stop his overbearing tirade but when I opened my mouth to speak, there was nothing there. I had no answers.

It had been happening more and more, I'd noticed, when conversations turned to politics. There was something inside me, vehement and sure, wanting to escape and be heard but I simply couldn't put words to it. I felt gagged although I was not entirely sure why.

I told myself that I didn't know enough, which had some truth in it. I'd thought when I was younger that I could just ignore it all. I'd only ever known life under the custodians, their vision for how we would solve the problem of our rapidly shrinking population. I'd caught scraps here and there from my father about what it was like before – the elections and referendums, the debates and the polling. He always looked troubled when he mentioned it, like he still couldn't quite grasp how we ended up here – a one-party state, a totalitarian government.

'This could go on for a while,' Thomas whispered back.

'Do you think... what do you think... about the custodians?'

He turned to me. 'Generally? That's a big question. I'm afraid I don't really have an answer. Maybe because there's so much noise around it all.' He frowned.

'I feel like that,' I admitted. 'I want to say something about what's happening – something that I actually believe, not just repeating someone else.'

'That's difficult when all we hear is the Spheres and the people talking about what they've heard on the Spheres.'

I nodded and then found myself opening up. 'I don't think I like the way they've handled things, but then I sort of understand it was an almost impossible problem. That we had to do something.'

I felt so acutely aware of how clumsy my words were, how vague, but Thomas nodded gently.

'You can think both, though, can't you?' he said back quietly.

'So many people seem so sure that they are what we needed, what we still need. I hear more from people talking about wanting them to go further. Like our friend over there.' I motioned towards Seb's family friend who was still trumpeting on.

'We're past encouraging now,' he was saying. 'Obligatory inductions will be next on the cards, mark my words. And it will go younger still. It has to, doesn't it?'

Some heads bobbed in response and murmured in agreement. The woman who I'd watched reach out for Jakob stayed still, her lips sealed shut.

'Did you hear the news?' Thomas asked me in a low voice.

I nodded. That morning while I was running around my flat trying to get a stain out of the dress I wanted to wear, my workSphere had stirred and began blaring out a new announcement. I'd turned the hot tap to maximum hoping the sound of the water would drown out the words, but they reached me nonetheless. The minimum age for induction treatment had dropped from eighteen to sixteen. Girls aged sixteen would now be permitted, encouraged, to undergo fertility treatment. There'd been a graph showing the expected decrease in population if the number of inductions did not rise. The fall in production would mean shortages and expensive imports. A custodian spokesperson gave the short briefing, his features haggard, his face in folds.

'It doesn't feel right,' I said and again was struck by the ineptitude of my remark. It didn't run to how deeply I feared what this meant. Seb's family friend was right; we were another step closer to inductions becoming obligatory for everyone. I felt it like a shadow falling around me that I could not possibly outrun.

Just then, a woman Evie and Seb had met at induction approached us. She cleared her throat quietly, impatiently.

'Is the barbeque lit yet?' she asked, pointedly eyeing the pile of sooty briquettes that were as cold as the stones on the ground. She had neat, bobbed hair, a staged look of concern mingled with annoyance.

I saw, out of the corner of my eye, Thomas raise his wooden spoon in readiness, and suppressing a giggle, I met the woman's gaze levelly.

'If it's not lit are you planning on leaving?'

'Well, no, of course not. I was just wondering because…' She trailed off.

'Because you're hungry?' I finished for her.

'No, it's not—'

'Because you want to know what is happening?'

'I just wondered… if I could help?'

'The more the merrier!' I exclaimed. 'In fact, I was just about to get the salads out of the fridge for the table. Could you do that? It's Jacqui, isn't it? I'm Kit, Evie's sister. And this is Thomas. Together, we are team food.'

Jacqui gave a shy sort of smile, that seemed to surprise even her, and turned towards the kitchen. Then she turned back again, 'Anything else we need?'

'Napkins,' I said. 'If you can find any. I think they are

in one of the drawers in the middle of the dresser. Try the bottom one.'

'Wow,' Thomas said, as Jacqui disappeared purposefully into the house. 'You have a gift. You bring out the best in people.'

I shrugged. 'I don't know about that. But most people want to help, given the opportunity. Actually,' I confessed, 'I was a little too hard on her. I didn't mean to be, to be so... so sharp. It just came out, before I could stop myself.'

It was a part of me that I didn't like to examine too closely, the way I could turn words into pointed claws that could leave a mark, a scar. I hadn't been able to admit that to anyone else before and yet it felt good, right even, to confide.

'You were just sharp enough. She was quite rude.'

'Maybe. But I need to watch myself sometimes.'

'Doesn't everybody?'

'Also, she probably hasn't had the easiest ride. Her inductions didn't—' I stopped myself abruptly and busied myself with placing the cubes of firelighters amongst the ovals of charcoal. My fingertips quickly dusted with black.

'Do you know her, then?' Thomas reached for the box of matches.

'Not really, but Evie's told me about her. She's still going through it. Her sister, she has a sister who... has a son.'

I'd almost said 'still has her son'.

'How old?' Thomas asked quickly.

'He's three, thereabouts.'

'Out of the danger zone, then.' He winced as the words left his mouth. Extractions were far more likely to happen when children were babies. If you passed through that stage, though extraction could still technically happen, your child would most likely remain with you. OSIP cited that early standards were a strong predicator of future parenting.

I tried to clean my fingers of the black of the charcoal, rubbing my hands together briskly, but it only made the dark grey stain more set. Another memory of Evie returned to me: crying, crumpled, after another failed induction. It made my head swim and I felt the weight of tears build just behind my own eyes.

'Are you OK?' Thomas asked.

I nodded but didn't meet his gaze.

Thomas paused and then asked, 'Do you think then that people have a right to be more rude depending on what has happened to them?'

I looked up at him then. 'Well, yes – maybe they do.'

'What about those people who've had, you know, a load of shit, and they are still cordial… pleasant to others.'

'Those people are called saints.'

'I disagree. We have a terrible tolerance for rude behaviour. It's a choice when people act that way. They don't have to. That's why you're my hero. You don't stand for it.'

I wasn't sure what to say but at that moment Thomas lit the match and the firelighters caught.

Half orange, half invisible flames licked their way round the coals and the warmth they cast off reached me.

NOW

Thomas won't be able to ring me.

I left my phone, along with my wallet, in my bag back at the apartment, in my rush to leave. When we rid ourselves of our goSpheres, Thomas bought us old mobile phones so we would still have a way of contacting each other if we got separated. We were told that they would be able to trace us through our goSpheres and so they had to go.

Though he has no way of reaching me, and no way to follow, my eyes keep darting to the mirror, to the road that grows behind me.

I only remembered I left my bag behind as I kicked the car into gear and started to reverse away. I slammed down on the brakes as soon as I realised, my mind flashing to the bundles of cash stored within it. The door of the maisonette remained closed. Thomas was not running out after me. I could go back in, quietly, retrieve my bag and leave again. But something stopped me. Just the thought that Thomas might wake, that he might talk me out of what I was about to do. We'd recharged the phones the night before, the power level is still at the maximum. I reached into my coat pocket and found a few notes folded into rectangles there – enough money to fill up again if needed, enough not to risk me running into Thomas. I drove on, leaving my bag and its contents behind.

It's very early in the morning and I haven't seen another car but I can't shift the idea of Thomas pursuing me. He won't let me go easily.

He could tell the police to look for me. He might say to them that I haven't been in my 'right mind of late' – a distant sort of phrase that I've heard pass his lips when he thinks I'm not listening. He could tell them about the bottles of pills on the small glass shelf in the bathroom. Another extension of me I have left behind.

I would have to change cars if that happened. Change my appearance – hack off my hair that's grown longer than it's been since I was a child. Bleach it brassy in a public toilet? Find some dark glasses that dwarf my cheeks and shield my eyes?

But he won't contact the police. He can't. They will already be searching for us.

I push my foot down harder on the accelerator and the car speeds up, the landscape blurs as it races past me.

I savour being alone. I turn to the passenger seat next to me – steel-coloured and empty – and experience something like a rush of happiness, though it is not so uncomplicated, that no one's there.

Part of it's down to wanting to be able to remember freely. For too long, I didn't realise that Thomas noticed when I was remembering. I didn't know that my arms were moving, rearranging themselves to hold her in an empty embrace.

I would murmur sentences under my breath. I'd tilt my face to the side as I did when I used to speak to her.

'Stop it, Kit,' he said one day when I was quite lost in a memory.

'Stop what?'

'Doing what you're doing. Pretending she is still here.'

I wasn't pretending, though; I knew that she was gone. What I was doing was remembering, reliving something that happened so keenly that my body literally went through the motions. The whole of me ached for her. My breasts became swollen with milk, solid and hard. Each time I pumped to keep up my supply, I tried to block out the rhythmic drone of the breast pump and imagined I was feeding Mimi. It's advice I was given to help me produce more milk – to think of your baby – but in fact it was impossible for me not to imagine her as the bottle would fill, drop by drop, like tears falling. I had to tip it all away, the milk that was still warm from my body. I would pour it into the sink, run the taps and watch it drain down the plughole in a diluted white swirl.

My breasts grow heavier as I drive; it's almost as though they could become separate entities to me. I've left my pump behind and so I will have to hand express before they become engorged, before the burn of pain sets in. Part of me likes this, this physicality of being a mother that I carry with me; a memory of Mimi that lives on in my body – tangible and real.

In those first empty moments after they took her, I poured over all the photos and videos I had of her stored on my goSphere. I trawled through the gallery, greedily swiping at the next image, the next clip, until Thomas told me it was time to go. I knew that I had to leave the goSphere behind but I hadn't quite prepared myself for not being able to take those digital albums we'd made of her with us. After that, I would spend time lost in my own imagination, conjuring her from memory to recreate moments we had once shared together.

I often thought back to a particular rainy day. It was so wet I had dressed her in some puffy waterproof all-in-one suit and by the time I had finished and pulled up the hood, all I could see was a tiny circle of her face. Only the very top of her mouth, her nose and eyes were visible.

I would remember reaching out with one finger and pressing the red tip of her nose and making a silly sound, something like a trumpet or a horn or a beep. That was what Thomas had seen me doing: reaching out with a pointed finger to touch the air in front of me, to touch her nose as if she was still before me, the faint sound of a trumpet lingering on my lips.

'I wasn't doing anything,' I said.

'Kit,' Thomas said, with a sigh. 'Your face changes. You're imagining her again.'

I didn't have any rebuke, but from then on, I always made sure that when I wanted to remember Mimi, I was alone.

Now, in the car, I luxuriate in the absence of others. It makes me realise how long it's been since I've been truly alone. Thomas has always been within reach since she went.

Maybe he is afraid of what I would do if I was left alone.

Maybe I am, too.

THEN

They had a name for people like me.

Outs, they'd call us.

OSIP's UnTapped. Women who chose not to go through induction. There was no name or stigma for men who chose not to become fathers.

Of course to undergo induction, I didn't have to be in a couple. OSIP supported single women alongside homosexual couples, heterosexual couples, all with the same zeal.

From time to time, there'd be a piece about the sorry state of the outs cropping up over the Spheres. It usually centred on an interview, riddled with regret, with a woman who did not, and now could not, have children.

Typically, they ended with computer-generated images of chubby, unsmiling toddlers: projections of what the woman's children would look like if they'd ever existed. Whilst there was some likeness to their 'mothers', these imaginary casts were always given the same eyes: doleful, beseeching stares that followed you around the room.

Then there were the more factual pieces about outs; the higher tax rates you faced if you elected not to go through induction, they grew year on year from when a woman reached twenty and kept on rising. This, coupled with the growing salary restrictions meant it would be almost impossible to sustain being an out if the figures continued in the same trend. Housing credits were minimal and so the choice of where to live within the narrow bands of areas available was reduced even further. Men did not face these same penalties; enough sperm was donated voluntarily that there wasn't a shortage, there was no demand on their bodies.

I prickled with rage each month as I struggled to get by on my paltry salary in my dank flat. Protests were met with the same resolute message: only women could go through induction and those who did deserved to be rewarded; they didn't care that the penalties for opting out felt more like a punishment than rewards for opting in.

Then there were the opinion pieces and films that labelled all outs as 'selfish, egoistic maniacs, who are sabotaging the survival of our species,' as one reporter put it.

But the items about outs were in fact just a fraction of what they produced. OSIP filled the Spheres with stories and articles, case studies and statistics. There were many, many articles dedicated to the joy and benefits of having children, details of how you could claim financial incentives if you signed up, new developments coming every day in their fertility treatments. OSIP did everything they could to force women down the path of induction. Though it wasn't illegal to be an out, it felt that way a lot of the time.

'Can't you turn that thing off?' Dad would say each time the films started up. He didn't come round to visit me that often. We both found it difficult. His face would crumple with disgust at my workSphere as though he had just tasted milk that was sour.

'You know I can't,' I'd say, through clenched teeth, quietly so only I could hear the words reverberating around my own head.

'How do you stand it?' my father would continue. He'd turn his back to my workSphere, or leave the room if he could. I didn't tell him that you got used to it after a while, that over time you stopped hearing the voices.

He avoided them by rarely going out other than to his allotment. The Spheres were found in public places only, though by that I mean every place: train stations and bus stops, cafes and parks, shops and cinemas, gyms and swimming pools. Anywhere that was not a home. They had not made it into every one of those. Yet.

There appeared to be more each day as though they were living creatures, reproducing at a rate that we could never keep up with. The globular balls of information that never shut down, that you could approach from any angle, from any direction and its screen would align with your eyeline. They had no back, they had no end.

Evie and I had elected to have the workSpheres in our homes and the goSpheres that we carried with us at all times. Most people did. They were so much more advanced than any other computer that it wasn't really a choice, but a necessity.

'You should get rid of it,' Dad would persist, ignoring the fact that I had not responded. 'It's not healthy having it start up like this. It's like giving someone a key to your front door – they could walk in at any time.'

It was the same back-and-forth we always had when he came round. We'd repeated it so often, I would find myself waiting for the moment when he would start to complain about the workSphere, my shoulders tensing before he'd even spoken.

'I'd never have one,' he'd gripe.

Dad never questioned me about being an out. Not like Evie.

She made a point of raising it with me, circling the issue each time before going in for the kill.

'You shouldn't close yourself off to it, Kit.'

'Off to what?'

'Induction,' Evie replied quickly, making the word sound smaller than it was.

We were lying on the carpet, side by side, in her sitting room. Dinner plates discarded, half-drunk wine glasses within reach.

This was before. Before Jakob. Before any of it.

We lay next to each other as we did when we were younger, when Dad started letting us sleep in the same bedroom. After our mother died, when I was three and Evie five, it was almost every night. Mum had died very suddenly from a brain tumour not long after our youngest sister, Maia, had passed away when she was still a baby. There'd been complications since Maia was born although I didn't know the details; Dad didn't like to talk about Mum or Maia. In truth, I couldn't recall either of them clearly; Evie was what I remembered.

We'd always lay out our sleeping bags on the floor next to

each other when we became too big to fit in a single bed side by side, talking into the night.

I stared up at the ceiling as we spoke, the shadows blurred in the warm half-light cast by the lamp. I realised when I was older that I found it difficult to confide in people when I was looking directly at them because I was so used to those night-time talks with Evie. Words flowed easily between us when we stared at the space of the ceiling above us.

'Don't you want to be a mum?' I didn't need to see Evie's face to picture her heart-shaped face lighting up as she spoke. She was a careful, practical person, one who took care of every part of her appearance: her nails were always cut in neat squares and polished, her dark hair shiny, brushed and parted just to one side, but beneath the layers of sensibility, she was a dreamer.

Women were encouraged to go through induction as many times as they could and Evie had seriously considered going through it alone when she was twenty-two. I hadn't tried to hide my relief when she told me she'd changed her mind and decided to wait to find a partner to parent with. In the years since then, she'd been dating continuously through the OSIP Partner Centres to try to find her mate. Dating through the Partner Centres could be lucrative; there were financial incentives attached if you signed up to them and an even bigger payout if you did conceive with a Partner Centre match.

'I'm just not sure I could do it,' I replied. I'd seen the way it had already taken over my sister's life before she'd even properly begun the process. As Evie was registered to start induction as soon as she found a suitable partner, she regularly had gynaecological appointments and medical examinations. On top of the Partner Centre matches, her life rotated around induction already.

'Of course you could,' Evie said. 'And then you could finally afford to move out of your building.' The population had shrunk so much that we lived in concentrated sections in the remaining cities and where you lived within a quarter depended on your salary and housing credits. I was predictably in the lower bracket for both.

'I don't mind living there.'

'That's not what I heard you say to Dad the other day.' Though I tried to downplay it to Evie, for the very reason that she would bring up induction, my flat was tiny, falling apart and fetid, no matter how much I cleaned or tended to it. Mould spread over the walls during the winter, and in the summer, it was like living in an airless tank. I'd never been able to get rid of the mice that scampered from flat to flat, finding holes upon holes within the walls in their own private labyrinth. But I didn't have the credits needed to move and I'd resigned myself to it.

'And, you know, induction's much, much safer than it was,' Evie parroted. 'I saw a piece this morning on the Spheres...'

Her voice dropped as I stood and started to clatter our plates and glasses into a pile.

'Kit. If you can't talk to me to me about this, who can you?'

'It's not just about the induction, though, is it?'

We never had an idea of the actual number of children that were extracted. It simply wasn't spoken about in those terms. OSIP released statistics annually which flooded the Spheres with figures concerning children's welfare and well-being –

'a 21 per cent rise in children's safety at home with a 15 per cent rise in safety out of the home.' But there was nothing on how many families had their children taken from them.

And induction didn't work for more and more women. However OSIP spun it, however many studies they released, they couldn't hide the danger. The cocktail of drugs you had to take made most women very sick and to some was fatal. Evie's friend from school, Tola, died when she underwent induction just before she turned twenty. I'd gone with Evie to her funeral. It had been as awful as I imagined it would be. The service had been crowded, people standing in the aisles because there weren't enough seats. Her parents, white-faced throughout it all, seemed unable to speak to anyone there. Evie had grasped my hand so tightly I wondered if she was worried she might fall.

Not even a year later, we heard that Flo, another member of Evie's class had died through induction. And six months after that, it was Connie. I remember that it was the second time Connie had been through it, her first child had been extracted early on.

They were not the last funerals we'd go to.

Sometimes when I remembered Tola or when I'd spot an old school photo of Evie's that Dad still had pinned up on his board, a mass of smiling faces, I'd question how it was that we were able to bear such loss. I'd wonder at the numbness I felt hardening within me when the same thing happened to someone I went to school with, or dad's neighbours' daughter, or the cousin of a friend. The list grew and grew. And so when I'd hear about another OSIP requirement coming out, there'd be a part of me that would think, fair enough, it made sense that OSIP monitored each child's welfare so strictly. Every child born had been fought for, every child was precious. It was almost as though I could see the shadows of all those women who had sacrificed everything when I saw any child. And so if parenting standards weren't met, extraction of the child for their own protection was the next logical step. I knew that.

It didn't stop people going through induction and becoming parents, but not everyone, like me, signed up for it.

NOW

I start to feel cold. My hands are numb from clenching the steering wheel. If I take them off the wheel then they will stay in the same shape: hunched, useless claws.

But I can't stop driving. I've learnt the route, the roads to take, the ones to avoid, and so I can almost see the journey criss-crossing in front of me, as though I have already made it before. You didn't hear about people being on the run like we were, not on the Spheres. The man we met with told us that. He was small, bald, older than us, not someone that I would have ever expected to be part of any kind of resistance. He wouldn't have seemed out of place in a pulpit.

The custodians didn't want it getting out, he told me, that people were trying to escape OSIP. But OSIP will be looking for you, of course. It can be done, though, he said. It can be done. It's all a matter of preparation.

I reported our conversation back to Thomas and I saw him mouthing those words as though he were trying to convince himself.

I try not to notice the bare skin where my wristband for Mimi once sat. It highlights the permanent sensation that I am forgetting something. I feel naked, exposed, without it. We'd had to leave the house as soon as they'd removed our bands; it was the last thing that happened before we'd walked out of the front door, stumbling over our own footsteps as though we couldn't move quickly enough.

Just over an hour after Mimi had gone, we left too. An enforcer might have dropped in that weekend and realised we had fled. Or perhaps, we hoped, OSIP would not realise we had gone until Thomas's unexplained absence from work was noted.

918.

I say the number aloud. I picture them: metallic, silver and screwed on to a door. It helps, it makes me feel a little more whole.

Then the postcode: *NNW 1HW.* I remember the bald man telling me that I couldn't write it down anywhere. I'd not hidden my scorn – I would never consider writing it down, not only because of the risk, but because I would never forget it. I say it aloud and then again, with the number.

NNW 1HW. 918.

The numbers and letters merge in my mind, oscillating, growing and revolving; for a moment they are all I can see. That's when the sharp, strident boom of a horn cuts through me.

It's a lorry. It's passing me, coming in the opposite direction, but it's impossibly close; our sides seem sure to scrape against each other. I am too close to the middle of the road. I brace myself for a deafening clash and crunch and twist of metal, I am so certain we will hit.

I swerve away violently. My car climbs the grassy bank

and I hit the brakes, throwing myself forwards as the car screeches to a halt. There's another horn now, the car behind has had to swerve too, to avoid me. It zips past me angrily. I don't see the face of the driver; I can only stare at my hands, still clasped around the steering wheel, still claws.

My breath comes ragged, in wheezes.

I want to cry, I want to scream.

I can't bear that I still have so far to go.

I have doubts, worm-like, carnivorous doubts, that I will make it. I wonder if I am actually able to do this. I remember Thomas' insistence that I try the medication that Santa offered me, the bottles of pills that he lined up like soldiers going into battle. She'd pulled them out of a box stashed at the back of a cupboard, as though they were treasure she'd been hoarding.

918. NNW 1HW.

They come again. The numbers and letters. And then I see a face – a tiny, newborn face that yawns and puckers its lips, eyelids flickering slightly as though dreaming.

It doesn't belong to Mimi, though. That dark hair can only be Jakob's.

THEN

I happened to be meeting Evie and Seb for dinner after their first induction session.

I was flustered, askew, at the thought of them starting, and my day had been off-kilter, like it had not properly begun but was passing me by anyway.

There was a rainstorm that lasted for hours. It flashed up on the Spheres as a possible flood warning and so I wondered if the dinner we had planned would be cancelled. But in the end, the downpour came to a stop; there was no flood.

I tried to concentrate on work but the words were just out of reach. Stubborn, furtive, they resisted my melding. I worked remotely, as most people did, through my workSphere. I was a life documenter, which meant I wrote biographies for people who lived more exciting lives than most; 'exciting' meaning that they made more money than most of us would ever see in our lifetime.

I never met my clients. They may as well have lived in a different universe to the rest of us. While we clustered in the quarters around the last of the cities, my clients resided in gated communities or in remote luxury dwellings built in bucolic idylls. Even so, sometimes I felt I knew their faces, the cadence of their voices, their particular turn of phrase, far better than my own family. I would be there through their lives, not just viewing their public media, but privy to anything private they opted in for. Life documenting encouraged them to share almost everything; it was a huge volume of data that never stopped growing.

I was recruited in my final months of university through one of my professors. Before I really knew what I was doing or why I was doing it, lured by a salary and an advance of a sizable amount, I'd signed a contract with them. The very next day, files of content arrived on my workSphere and so without ever really considering what job I actually wanted to do, I was plunged into work.

I'd reached a cap now in how much I could earn because of my out status, so there was little reason for me to switch career for monetary gain, and I found that I did in fact like the work. Much of the time, I barely wrote but spent hours untangling sense from the phone calls, home videos, emails, messages and articles that amassed on my workSphere. The subject of the life document, of course, never knew who I was, or that my job even existed.

Clients preferred to believe that their life document was written by a computer, rather than a person. A stranger out there, a voyeur, some silent passenger always alongside them – it was so obviously unappealing, even by our standards. But human writers composed the best life documents.

Biographies written by algorithm failed to capture the essence of a person. AI could not linger on the important events long enough, it was unable to add the necessary embellishments, trim the grey to create the perfect memories our clients so dearly wanted to capture and leave behind them. And so the company behind life documenting let them believe that there was a computer programme that was good enough and wrote contracts so obscure that the truth was hidden beneath clauses, assurances and promises.

Life documenters like me had to sign so many legal agreements about confidentiality that it would have taken me months and months to read them through properly – but it was basically about agreeing never to disclose the nature of our work to other parties. Clients got their life documents. Life documenters got paid. Everyone was happy. The time would come when they had tinkered with the algorithm enough to replace me but, back then, I didn't waste time worrying about that. I had too much work to be getting on with.

On that day, I left the paragraph I'd been struggling with mid-sentence and started working through some phone calls from three years before from one of my older clients. Jonah was reaching seventy and he'd already approved the draft I had completed, but life documents were only considered finished when they included the circumstances of a client's death.

I listened to him talking to his daughter. She sounded like she had something she wanted to tell him but there were so many noises in the background that I couldn't decipher what they were saying. Their voices had dropped low, too, something which I noticed Jonah and Genevieve did when they had long conversations together. They were close, they always had been.

Most life document subjects had not had their families

through induction but, like Jonah, had paid for an XC. I would have been a toddler at the time when XCs were first introduced but we'd learnt about it at school. Year on year, we were fed just a little more information. When I was in primary school, we were told you could have children through induction or by having an XC, although I didn't fully understand either term back then. I can't remember exactly which year at secondary school I was in when we were taught about the artificial wombs that would house the XC foetuses in specially-designed laboratories. After that, we learnt how manufactured eggs and sperm were created from a mix of genetic material, not solely that of their parents, and so the mother did not have to undergo induction. That lesson, I remember. I remember learning that.

It was a hot summer afternoon where the thick air slowed your thoughts and the post-lunch fogginess hung over us like heavy capes. Our teacher had started playing a film about XCs and then sat back on her chair, staring into the distance as though she was struck with the same lethargy as us. I was sure that one of my classmates had actually fallen asleep. They'd laid their head down on their arms on the table and were completely still. Diagrams and images flashed before us on the screen, I thought it was just a repeat of what I already knew, but then came the line the about mothers not having to go through induction.

At the time I'd been trying to understand the feelings I had around knowing that Evie and I had been born naturally, not through induction. Dad had warned us not to tell people, and I was at the fringes of understanding why that was now. It marked me out. I was aware that I was holding onto a guilt around it, knowing that our family had not had to suffer like so many others.

'Any questions?' the teacher had asked when the film had finished.

A girl named Morag who I remember as usually quite quiet, sat up taller in her chair and raised her hand. She had such long, thick hair it looked like it could aptly be described as a mane. I remember I was looking at it, at the way it stuck out, untamed by her ponytail, when she asked: 'Why doesn't everyone have XC children? Instead of going through induction?'

'Well, that's a good question actually Morag. I believe when the XC programme was developed that was the initial plan. But essentially it was not as successful in addressing infertility as was hoped. XC children have the same infertility issues as any other person nowadays. And, well, it's an expensive process.'

'Do you have to be rich?' Morag asked. 'You have to be rich to do it.'

'Yes,' the teacher said.

'But that's not fair,' Morag said.

'Be that as it may,' our teacher replied.

'What does that even mean?' Morag said back, her voice rising higher, close to breaking. At that moment, the bell had rung and most of the class slumped from the class, seemingly unaware of Morag's distress.

I'd learnt later both her aunts had died during induction.

Genevieve was in fact one of the first XCs. It had been in the early days of the science and she'd become unwell as a toddler from a metabolic genetic disorder that had not been picked up in the initial screening for genetic abnormalities – something that, according to the Spheres at least, didn't happen any more. Sometimes I would find myself replaying the footage of her returning home from hospital. She'd clung on to Jonah's hand, taking faltering steps, but just a few days later, she was running with abandon. Her ease of movement was reflected in Jonah's expression, his face was flooded with a relief that she was well again; it was almost as if a warm light was emanating from within him. His wife had contracted cancer when Genevieve was only a few months old and died before she turned one; his daughter was everything to him.

I played the call again but even after listening to it a few times, I couldn't make out what Genevieve was telling her dad. But then Jonah had ended the call very quickly, all in a rush. I couldn't work out what it was that Genevieve had said that made him react in that way.

One of the background noises was the sound of the puppy Genevieve had bought recently, skittering back and forth across the floor. I isolated the sound of the dog paws and then cleaned the file of it. But there was something else, too, clouding their voices.

Cleaning up files so you could hear what people are saying was a large part of the job. I liked doing it. There was something satisfying about being able to scrub a call that at first was mumbled and lost and make it into something coherent and meaningful. The most tender and significant utterances were made quietly, just under the breath. That was another reason why I was doing the job instead of a computer programme; I could sense when it was worth the trouble to clean up a file.

I recognised the repeated static and whir of a workSphere and removed that from the audio too. But it was still not quite clear enough.

In the end, noticing the time, I logged it into the file I'd compiled on Genevieve to return to later.

Evie and Seb had arrived ahead of me. I saw them before they saw me, waiting at a table in the busy restaurant, not talking, not touching. 'How was it?' I asked, kissing Evie on the cheek. She took a little too long to react, as though she were waking from sleep. Evie had blue shadows under her eyes, reminding me of the way a bruise blooms, and Seb sat stiffly, his shoulders hunched, his neck cramped.

Neither of them answered. Evie gave a little sigh. Almost like a moan. But it was lost in the noise of the diners around us, and then Evie smiled, kissing me back, squeezing my hand. Her lips were perfectly red, as though she had just applied lipstick. The ruby mouth, alongside her dark hair that sat in waves just above her shoulders, gave her the air of old-time movie star, beautiful, pale and fragile.

'Hi, Seb.'

'Good to see you, Kit. How's things?'

'Oh, you know. Fine. Good. Nothing to report, really.'

'Work going well?' Seb asked, and I was struck for a moment by the thought that when Evie had gained a partner, I had gained a watchful, concerned older brother.

'Yeah, busy. Good.' As none of them knew the details of life documenting, Dad, Evie and Seb believed that I was a writer for one of the Spheres' news pages.

'Great.' Seb smiled tightly, as though his face wouldn't let him relax into a grin.

Evie was fiddling with her napkin.

'Are you okay? Is there something...?' I said slowly.

I let the question dwindle and die. Evie reached for Seb's hand, I saw how tightly they clung to one another.

'Just a hard day,' Evie said, whilst looking to Seb for something. Comfort? Reassurance?

'Do you want to talk about it?'

'Oh no,' Evie said. 'Let's not. How's work going?' she asked brightly, too brightly, oblivious to Seb's question only moments before.

I had my cue. I'd become inventive over the years and had added characters and back story to my fictional work life. I told them about Ted, 'my editor.' I imagined him near bald but with a whisper of ginger hair, and a paunch that he was almost proud of. I created an imaginary tussle we'd had over the stories that I'd worked on. Ted featured so much when I told my family about work that sometimes I wished that he did exist. I'd painted him as a mentor and a friend, one that irritated me with his directness sometimes.

We were in safe territory now, talking about my job. It was somewhere we didn't want to leave in a hurry. Seb visibly relaxed into his chair as he told us a story about his first boss, who he was still in touch with. Colour returned to Evie's cheeks as her husband became animated.

Only later, when Seb had left the table, and after she'd consumed a large portion of the red wine we had ordered by the bottle, did Evie lean across the table conspiratorially, her elbows knocking against the dessert plates.

'It was awful, Kit. Today. Just awful.'

I squeezed her hand. 'I'm sorry. What happened?'

'Seb says we just got off to a bad start. We're trying to put it behind us.'

'That's a good idea, I'm sure you're right. Don't be too hard on yourselves.'

'He didn't want me to tell you. He doesn't want to tell anyone.'

I paused, sensing Evie wanted to talk.

'He doesn't want us to be negative about it and if we start telling people about it then we won't be able to help it.'

'Well, I suppose he's got a point,' I said. 'But it's not great if you can't talk about it, get it out of your system. Vent.'

'That's what I think,' Evie said, her voice rising indignantly.

'What happened?' I asked again.

'Well, they did lots of tests, took bloods, that kind of thing. Examinations. I mean we have to get that all done, you know, it wasn't that bad. They talked about the first lot of drugs I have to take. There could be all kinds of different side effects but I was expecting that. I mean it sounds a lot when you hear it all at once but...'

Evie let her voice trail off for a moment. I knew she was downplaying what the effects of the drugs might be.

'And they talked about the training we'd need to undertake too, to minimise the chance of extraction. I mean the information is all really useful. Some of it's going to be quite practical, like about feeding and sleep patterns and then there's more moral and ethical stuff about how our behaviour as parents affects our children's development. There'll be lots about language acquisition, that sort of thing. It's kind of fascinating.'

'Sounds... good.'

'Yes, the content is good. And the way they presented it made me feel that we could do it, you know, avoid extraction, it really gave me hope.'

At just that moment, as though they were listening in on our conversation, the Spheres in the restaurant stirred into action and an OSIP film began to play out.

Extractions are for the good of everyone, the text appeared across the screens in bold, blue letters. Then the film turned to an animation of child walking away from the dark outlines of their parental figures down a path of light, towards a vision of other children, smiling and care-free. More words darted across the screen amongst the faces of the children, almost subliminally: *Highest standard of living, Forward-thinking education, Opportunities for all.*

Our elite compounds for extracted children give them the best possible future in this changing world. The film closed and the Spheres whirred down to dormancy. Most of other diners had been oblivious to the film but neither Evie nor I could be drawn away from it while it played.

Evie paled and swallowed hard.

'They talked about the compounds too, today,' she said. 'Not for long but they went into why they were so special – all the statistics that showed how hugely beneficial they were to child development – mentally, emotionally, physically. They really do give a child a better chance, more opportunities.'

I grappled for words. 'But… a moment ago you said that the information they gave you meant you could avoid extraction.'

'Well, yes. It did seem a bit like that. But then I said something, I said…'

Evie bit her lip, shuddering slightly at the memory of it.

'I said – I was joking, I mean, I was just joking – that we'd be sure to mess them up, even if we tried not to. It was just stupid. We were talking through the parental influences and it just slipped out. The group leader just pounced on me. She asked me if I thought I had no control. And then the whole group started this massive debate on responsibility and I could just sense everyone else... they were just... desperate, desperate to distance themselves from me, us. Everyone just started attacking what I said. And then when I said I was just joking, it just started them off again. *Do you think this is something to joke over?* That kind of thing. It was horrible, just horrible.

'I never want to go back, which, of course, is not an option. I just wish we could start again. Like I could rewind time and begin the session again. And keep my stupid mouth shut.'

'Hey, that's my sister you're talking about.'

'I just wish—' Evie stopped herself abruptly as Seb appeared back at the table. She smiled up at him, falsely cheerful.

'All okay?' he asked.

'Good, good,' Evie said perkily although I saw the way her fingers twisted and tensed around the stem of her wine glass.

'We were just talking about Dad's gardening,' I covered. 'He's spending more time at the allotment than at home.'

Seb looked relieved. 'Last time we spoke he was telling me that he has found some kind of new super compost. Wouldn't say what it was though.'

'Now that would be telling,' I said. 'I honestly think that he believes his phone is tapped and he is worried one of the allotment cronies will steal his ideas.'

'They're all so competitive,' Evie joined in and we talked about Dad and his beans and the war he had declared on all slugs because it was easy. Far easier than talking about what we were actually all thinking.

NOW

Evie. I think of Evie.

Her eyes gleaming when she was happy; the way they looked like dull pennies when she was not.

Her tiny, narrow wrists that most bracelets would slip off. She was always losing bracelets.

The dark of her hair smelling only ever of shampoo.

The time that has passed since we saw each other has been the longest period we have ever been apart. I try to think of her only in small details. Otherwise, I lose her. I remember where we are now and I can't look back on the years and years we stood side by side, united. I think of the last months. I think of those final few taut conversations that spiked, that turned us into strangers.

THEN

I'd seen Marie and Leo bring Tia home, carrying her delicately in a nest of blankets. A tiny, sleep-filled face amidst a cushion of white. They lived in the same building as me, on the floor above mine. The sounds of her crying filled the empty spaces, sinking through walls, creeping around corners.

'Just look at her!' Elizabeth, the red-haired woman from the fourth floor, exclaimed as the lift doors closed. Marie, wearing Tia in a sling, had walked out past us as we were getting in. Elizabeth was in her fifties. She had pale skin untouched by the sun, and half-closed, heavy-lidded eyes that made her appear either very bored or very tired or both. 'Such a wee thing. I just can't believe we have a child in our building!'

I smiled back at her but my jaw was tight, in anticipation of what might be coming.

'They'll probably be moving out soon,' she continued. 'This isn't the best place to raise a child. They'll be able to afford somewhere better than this now.' Her hand lightly touched the tatty wall of the lift. Our building was mostly populated with Outs, and a few older people like Elizabeth who I'd heard had tried induction only once but not again.

I murmured a nondescript answer.

'Are you going through induction?' she asked. The question came swiftly, deftly. 'You're the right age for it.' Elizabeth narrowed her eyes.

'I'm... I'm not,' I said back with more confidence than I felt. More and more, I was being questioned like this and though I thought I could handle it, the truth was that I was finding it harder and harder each time I was challenged. It was like I was being unpeeled with every criticism.

'You're *not*?' she punctuated.

I smiled back at her again, even more tightly, and gave a small but definite shake of my head.

'That's an odd choice to make nowadays, if you don't mind me saying. I mean, not even trying. It doesn't work for all of us – but not even trying.' I saw Elizabeth's hand come to rest on her abdomen. She spotted me noticing and quickly dusted down her skirt unnecessarily.

An answer formed on my lips; I was ready to lash out, asking her what had happened to her, why she'd not had more inductions, why it was she was living here amongst us Outs – us outcasts. But I swallowed it down. She must have either become so ill that she couldn't go through it again, or losing a child through extraction was too painful for her to be able to repeat it. She would have slipped back financially if she didn't try again and again. This was why, I told myself, she was calling me out on it with such vehemence; it was all just too close to her.

'It's a...' Elizabeth paused for a moment, as if casting

around for a word, but the one she came out with was the same as always – the word that had been bandied around the Spheres as the catch-all label for Outs, '*selfish* decision, really, isn't it? The state the world's in.' She shook her head, her voice dwindling out in disapproval, but there was something else building in her eyes, a sunk-in shame that made me wonder how many times she'd been told this herself.

'Some people think that,' I replied shortly.

The lift doors started to open and I squeezed through the gap sideways to escape her. I could hear her still talking behind me but I hurried away, into the safety of my flat. I leant against the door that I'd closed behind me, needing to feel the physicality of a barrier between me and the outside world.

I saw Marie and Leo from time to time in the days following that. In the lobby, the lift or close by to the building. On one of those occasions when it was just Marie pushing Tia in her pram, I thought she was crying but when I looked again, I couldn't be sure. The next day, though, I spotted her sitting alone on a park bench in one of the little areas of green close to our building. This time, there was no mistaking the tears that carved down her face, shining her cheeks.

Maybe it was because Evie and Seb had just started induction, even though I barely knew the couple, I couldn't let it pass me by.

I knocked on their door that evening. I heard a muttered conversation from inside and something else, a cry, not from a baby, of anguish. Or anger.

I stepped backwards a little and wondered if I had made a mistake and briefly, whether I could just walk away, when the lock turned. The door opened.

It was Leo. His dark, dishevelled hair stuck up in peaks, making him appear even taller than his beanstalk-thin frame. His face was set, grim as though he had just been given bad news seconds before, but when he saw me standing there, an awkward smile painted upon my face, his expression turned quickly to surprise and then relief.

'Hi,' I said. 'I'm Kit. From downstairs. We've not met properly but I just wanted to say hi. Like I've already said. Sorry.' I stopped myself. 'I'm not making much sense.'

'It's okay,' Leo said. I noticed him glancing down the corridor. When he saw there was no one there, he asked, 'Would you like to come in?'

'Oh. No. I mean... I don't mean to intrude. It's just that—'

'It's fine,' Leo said and opened the door to me.

'If you're sure.'

'Please.'

As soon as I stepped in, the smell hit me. A mixture of stale milk and the full nappy bags that were discarded in a pile by the door.

'Sorry about the smell,' Leo apologised as he took in my slight grimace, though I tried to hide it. He tried to open one of the windows but it jammed almost immediately and only stayed open a crack.

'Oh, I'm sorry,' I said, uselessly.

He shut the door, pressing against it securely and then stuffed a towel into the small crack at its bottom. I couldn't help but watch him and as he saw me, he straightened.

'We've been having some complaints. About the noise.' He gestured towards the next room and the sound of Tia crying. 'It won't help much, we're all on top of each other in this building, but it's something. Everyone said we should move before the baby came but we were waiting for this house, the perfect place, and it fell through. We'll move as soon as we can, though… this place is really—' He stopped himself abruptly, remembering that I lived here too.

'Who's there?' came a voice from the bedroom. Marie.

'Hi there, it's just me,' I said ridiculously. 'Kit,' I added, feebly.

'Oh. Hi,' said Marie blankly, appearing at the doorway, holding Tia in her arms. She was petite, much shorter than Leo, only reaching his chest in height, and so standing next to him made her appear smaller still. She looked pale and tired, as though just carrying Tia was exhausting her. Tia was bleating and red-faced, squirming and arching her back with a strength that seemed more than her small body could possess.

'It's Marie, right? I'm Kit,' I said again. I suddenly had the feeling that I was in a play and had forgotten my lines, or I had missed my cue somewhere along the way, but I couldn't rely on anyone to prompt me.

'Yes, we've met before,' Marie said and I remembered then that we had. Properly. Not just passing in the corridor or sticking an arm out to stop the lift doors closing for one another. It was at one of those apartment building meetings where nothing gets decided on really but if you don't happen to go then something awful, like a motion to turn the communal garden into more parking spaces, gets passed – since that had happened I have never missed one. Marie had arrived late and had to knock past the knees of everyone on our row to get to the only spare seat – which was next to me.

She had worn her hair cut short around her neck back then, graduating down longer around her cheeks. It was sleek and hung straight, like a curtain falling around the frame of a window. Her lips were glossy and she wore eyeliner in a stylish flick, upwards slanting black lines painted on with the fine brush of an artist. She looked out of place amongst us other tenants; there were none as polished or glamorous as her.

The meeting had begun predictably with a number of complaints being raised that set almost everyone's head nodding in agreement. I drank a glass of tepid wine that tasted vinegary and coated my mouth unpleasantly, but taking birdlike sips was the only thing I could do to stop my mind from wandering.

'It's disgusting, isn't it?' Marie muttered to me when the chairman was consulting with another neighbour about some trivial matter.

'Awful,' I agreed taking another sip and grimacing.

'Not the wine!' she said playfully. 'The hypocrisy of it all. Of *them* all.'

Before I could reply we were called to vote on the shade of blue that maintenance were going to paint the walls of the corridors. The seriousness, the ceremony of the vote, overtook all else.

'*This* is important?' Marie had said to me before she was shushed by our neighbour who was taking the meeting notes.

Now, Marie pulled on a strand of hair unnecessarily; it had turned wavy, its ends were dry and frizzy, and so it would not stay in the place where she had tucked it.

Just then Tia's bleats turned to wails that grew louder and

louder with each cry. There was a moment where no one moved. Leo looked to Marie and then at me and then back at Marie again.

Marie jigged Tia in her arms a bit; I noticed how scrawny she was and how in some way, her newborn crying baby seemed plumper, had more life force than she did.

'I'll nurse her in the bedroom,' Marie said. She turned to close the door behind her but with both hands holding Tia, she had to kick out with her foot to shut it. It closed with a slam.

'Sorry,' Leo said. He put his hands in his pockets as though he was not sure what to with them. 'It's been—' He thought better of finishing the sentence.

'You don't need to apologise for anything.'

'No, it's just... it's just been hard... so much harder than...' He looked around him in a daze as if he were trying to find someone, something, to blame the difficulty on.

'I can't imagine, I really can't. That's why I came round. I wondered if I could do anything, something to help. Shopping maybe – anything you need.'

'Oh, that's so kind, that'd be great,' Leo said in a rush. 'We could do with some help. Our families don't live close by and,' he dropped his voice low, 'Marie needs to see other people. People other than just me and—'

'Leo!' Marie called from the other room. 'Leo, come here, would you?'

He started and rushed to the bedroom. Their living room was the same size as mine but it felt much smaller with all the baby paraphernalia that decorated the room – the muslins, the heap of baby-grows, the piles of rubbish and nappy sacks, the changing mat and nappies that were spread over the floor.

I waited for them to come back through from the bedroom for longer than was comfortable. I considered leaving, even glanced around for a scrap of paper and a pen and so I could leave a note and slip out without disturbing them.

When Leo walked back in, he seemed at first to have forgotten that I was still there, almost surprised to see me standing there.

'Sorry,' he said again. 'Feeding. It's been – again – well, a minefield.'

'It's fine – sorry – I didn't want to disturb you or...'

Leo's disjointed way of speaking was catching.

Marie wandered back in too then, cradling Tia to her shoulder. Her eyes took me in blankly. I smiled towards her but her expression did not change.

'Marie,' Leo said a little too loudly. 'Kit said she could help out with shopping and stuff. That would be good, wouldn't it?'

She opened her mouth as though to speak but instead, her shoulders shook, she began to cry.

'Oh, Rie!' Leo rushed to her. 'It's okay, it's okay.' He tried to hug her but because she was holding Tia he could only pat her on her back awkwardly.

'I'll come back another time,' I said quickly. 'But the offer's there, whenever you need anything. I'm at number 227.'

'Please don't go,' Leo said. 'I'll make some tea.'

'No, no, it's okay, honestly. I could come back though. If that's okay?' I said to Marie.

She nodded ever so slightly.

We agreed on a routine whereby Marie would slip a list of things that she needed under my door and I would take them round the next day, around noon. Leo said it was a good time because it broke up the day while he was at work and that it helped to have routines.

'Don't worry about the time too much,' he added politely.

But I felt sure that the timing had come from Marie as a way of her preparing for a visitor and decided I must abide by it.

NOW

There's a sign for a service station and I pull in and run from the car as soon as I've parked. When I am at the entrance, I stop abruptly in front of the Spheres. Someone who had paused to let me pass makes a sound of surprise.

I wait there for a few revolutions of articles, hearing the Spheres' drone, but there is nothing more about what I heard last night.

After five minutes or so, I dash back to the car and drive away as rapidly as I dare. I thought I saw someone approaching me as I walked across the car park. Though I couldn't be sure, it made me hurry on.

I chide myself for stopping, for wasting time, although I know that if I can prepare myself at all for what I'll be walking into, then it won't have been futile.

In fact I find it hard not to pull over at the next services but I make myself wait until I've driven more miles before I let myself stop again. I pass a sign for a town that has been decommissioned; the name has been spray-painted over. Roadblocks sealing off the exit squat on the tarmac. The redistribution of the population was met with some opposition but the custodians pushed it through with the simple fact that the country could not support so many areas of residence.

I can't ignore any longer the dense weight of the milk building in my breasts and stop at the next charging station I come to. In the toilets, I knead them until the dripping milk turns to fine jets. I am bovine, I am plentiful. My breath steadies as the pressure releases and fades, releases and fades. It feels like a heartbeat. I only stop when there's give in my breasts again, when I've turned them once more to jelly. I am empty again.

Then I stand in front of the Spheres as everyone else passes me by. They pay the orbs no attention; it's as if they do not see them. There're stories about the new, consolidated townships in the North, an interview with Theon Brand, the current leader of the custodians that has been edited heavily so he sounds like he could be talking about anything.

An older couple walking past me start to mutter something about what Brand is saying but then they notice me standing there and fall silent.

My head jerks when I see the faces of children fill the domed screen, but it's just an OSIP film, another one about reformed outs and the children they now have living together in something resembling a commune.

I turn away.

THEN

The first time I found a list from Marie under my door, I had trouble reading it. I deciphered 'nappies', 'detergent' and what I decided in the end was 'dinner', but this was the start of only more questions. What size of nappies were needed and was a special detergent needed for baby clothes? I strained to remember Evie mentioning something about it. And dinner – I did not know if there was anything that they didn't especially like, if they were vegetarian – but surely Marie would have mentioned it?

After taking too long at the shops deciding to buy a range of nappy sizes and reading the backs of detergent bottles, I had to rush to get back for midday. This time, I could hear Tia through the door, not crying but making babbling hums and the sound of Marie's voice, coaxing and low.

I knocked and pushed the strands of hair from my sweaty face, trying to appear more presentable than I felt. Marie suddenly fell silent.

'It's me,' I said. I corrected myself: 'It's Kit. I've brought the shopping.'

For a moment I wondered if Marie might tell me to leave

it outside but then the lock scraped and she pulled the door open.

'Hi,' I said. 'Here you go.' I passed the bags over. Her eyes widened a little when she saw how many there were.

'I wasn't sure what to get exactly and so I brought you a few options,' I said in way of explanation.

'I'm sorry. I didn't tell you the size of nappy... or anything, did I?' she said, peering into one of the bags. 'And, pizza? And chicken, salad? I don't even remember writing any of this down. I'm so tired, but how could I forget that?'

'For dinner?' I ventured. 'I had to take a bit of a punt on what you would like but most people like chicken. I got pizza as well in case you were vegetarian. Unless – well, you don't – sorry, I can get something else. I had to guess...'

Marie took the crumpled list that I held out. She read it and then she began to laugh. The laughter rose up in her chest and she started to wheeze from the exertion, reminding me of an accordion being squeezed.

'Olives!' she managed to say at last, when she could speak again. 'I meant to write olives. But you're right, it does read like I was asking you to get dinner for us. I'm sorry. I must give you some money for all this.'

'No, there's no need – Leo gave me some to cover it already.'

'Really? Well, thank you. This will keep us going.'

Just then, Tia gave a slightly louder gurgle, as though she were in agreement.

'How is she?' I asked.

Marie gave a tiny smile at her daughter.

'Do you want to come in?' she asked, but then her forehead

furrowed a little. I wasn't entirely sure if she regretted asking as soon as she had said it.

'Um, well, maybe – just for a moment.'

We peered over at Tia on her playmat. She was kicking her legs now and again, concentration etched into her face.

'We're having a good day,' Marie said quietly and then she leant into her daughter and brushed her fingers against the downy soft of her cheek. She said again, 'We're having a good day, aren't we, my little love?'

Tia's face relaxed at the sound of her mother's voice and, as she felt her touch, she seemed to smile and look towards her.

'She's smiling!' I said.

'Oh no, I think that she's too young to smile. It's probably wind or something,' Marie said quickly.

'No, it was when you spoke to her and touched her face, just then, I'm sure of it.'

'Do you think so?'

Marie spoke to Tia again: 'Are you smiling, little one?' she asked. 'Have you learnt how to smile?' She reached for her cheek again and this time there was no denying it – Tia's face blossomed into a wonky little grin that lit up and was reflected back to her in Marie.

'She did!' Marie said. 'She did smile, you're right! Clever girl, aren't you, you little smiler.' She leant into Tia again until they were nose to nose. 'She did it again!' Marie looked up at me, any trace of worry and doubt she had before had gone.

I let myself out shortly after that and forced myself to continue working for the rest of the day, although I could not shift the memory from my mind – of Tia's newly smiling face and her mother's delighted smile back at her.

I sensed that Marie both ached and was reluctant for company and so often when dropping the shopping off, I would bring other things with me for us to share, a couple of decaffeinated coffees, a bag of pastries, excuses for us to spend a few moments together. After the first few times I did this, I could see that she was expecting it. She might have a teapot brewing or be grinding coffee beans, ready for when I dropped off the bags. Over time, we spent longer and longer together.

We came to trust one another.

We told each other things that we tried to hide from others.

'Sometimes I feel like I am playing being a mother,' she admitted to me one day. Tia was gurgling to herself on her playmat just to the side of us, reaching out for one of the fabric toys that hung above her, batting it to the side and making it spin. 'Like it's not really real, you know? It's a sort of game. I mean I didn't think I would ever get through induction. I never thought that I would actually do it, in fact. I was an out. It's why we're living here.'

She shifted uncomfortably. We'd never spoken about my situation before.

'I'm not sure I ever want to do it,' I admitted, filling the silence that had built up between us.

'That's just how I felt,' Marie said. 'But I was working for a conglomerate and I couldn't go any higher even though I knew that I could do a far better job than all of the men that were being promoted above me. I was good at it. I even started doing more work for the same money – just because I wanted to, because I knew that I could do it well. I'd reached the ceiling for out income. And then… well, they started giving me the worst work, the work that no one else could be bothered to do. My boss was completely incompetent. Most of the time I was just trying to cover for him. Leo encouraged me to leave, to try anything else. And so I did. I started over in a different company. And basically the same thing happened again. I couldn't keep doing it over and over.

'This time, Leo suggested we start induction. I didn't want to do it at first. But then I had no other choice. I mean, that came out wrong, it wasn't that Leo forced me into it. I just… I couldn't see another way.'

I felt my breath grow tight in my chest. What Marie was saying was too close to the thoughts that would spiral through my mind in the early mornings when sleep seemed impossible. Though I didn't want to have a child, what with the cap on my earnings and my low housing credits, the mutterings and pointed remarks, I was starting to feel more and more pressure. We were often told on the Spheres about how different inductions were in the UK compared to the rest of the world. About pubescent girls, children themselves, forced into induction camps abroad. Or women dying after mandatory induction after induction. Here, we still had to opt in. The custodians claimed that because women can choose, our induction rate is supposedly one of the highest in the world. And yet, the reality was it didn't feel like a choice at all. It felt like we were all slowly being pushed down this route, whether we wanted to or not.

I forced my thoughts back to Marie; words continued to spill from her as though it were a relief or some kind of confession.

'We started. And then it was like before I knew what was happening, we were in the middle of it. It was a bit like a dream that I couldn't wake up from.

'Suddenly things were moving so fast. I'd started on the drugs, I was barely able to function when I was taking them. I couldn't see to the other end of it, even what it was that we were doing it for. Sounds crazy, doesn't it, with everything we see on the Spheres? And now that we're here, now that we actually made it, I'm not doing it very well. I'm just playing at being a mum, pretending – it's not for real.'

'It must be incredibly overwhelming. I've had the same sort of feeling in the past, that I'm pretending to be something. A lot of people do. What's that thing that people say – fake it till you make it. There's truth in that, I think.'

'But I see other mothers in the street. They seem so put together. They're always so certain, so sure of what they are doing. I'd rather not see anyone but it's discouraged. I've heard you can get an IPS for being too socially isolated and so I force myself to go to this playgroup every week. Everyone there is just so confident. And it's like they could smell it on me that I was unsure, one of them started sprouting all this advice. She insisted on taking my goSphere and sending me all these articles. I'm sure she meant well but it just made me feel completely inadequate and also angry, you know. Everyone else is more than coping, they're excelling.'

'Are they, though? Remember you are just seeing the outside view, not what they are thinking or feeling. And that woman who started giving you advice like that – she sounds like she was overcompensating to me. Maybe everyone is hiding how they really feel.'

'I'm trying my best. But what if it's not enough? I'm just so sure…' Marie began to cry. She let the tears roll down her cheeks unchecked. Then she sat up straighter and wiped her face. She stared hard into the distance and I was reminded of the woman that I first met at the building meeting all those months before. 'I'm sure they are going to take her.'

'You don't know that. You're doing so well. You all are.' But Marie crumpled as though a great weight was bearing down on her. 'We're only one away from extraction, Kit,' Marie said. 'Just one IPS.' Marie and Leo had received several already. They'd come in a flurry, starting on the day I'd seen Marie crying in the park. 'But then – oh God, I can't believe I'm telling you this – sometimes I think that it would be better for her if she was extracted. They would take better care of her in the compounds. I've heard, I've heard…'

Marie looked around the room as though she were checking that we were alone, and then down to her daughter.

'I've heard that some families will try to get an IPS on purpose. When they know that they have made a mistake. When they realise that they can't cope – they can't handle being parents. They know that the compounds would be a better place for them.'

'On purpose?'

'For the good of their child. Before the child gets hurt. To give them a better life,' Marie stared hard at Tia. 'It makes sense, doesn't it? It's actually a selfless act.'

Although I'd seen the compounds in countless films on the Spheres, I realised that I'd never actually met anyone who'd grown up in one. I wondered if in fact I had but that they chose to keep that part of themselves hidden. Maybe they weren't the best places for extracted children despite everything we'd been told. I wondered about asking Marie what she knew about them but I could see that there was something more she wanted to tell me.

'Sometimes I have a thought, like a whisper in my ear – what would happen if I dropped her right now? What would happen if I just stopped feeding her, if I just let her scream? I don't actually do it, but I think it, Kit, I think it. That's not right, is it? And when I think about that I know that I deserve the IPSs. We got them because we aren't good enough. We shouldn't have become parents.'

'I don't believe that,' I said. 'I see the way you are with her. You love her, she loves you. No one can love her like you and Leo do. Those thoughts that you are having – they are something else. They are depression or tiredness or working so hard to be as good as you can be. And you haven't acted on them, have you? That's the important part.'

Marie started to speak but was interrupted by a sudden knock on the door.

It was so loud and so sudden that when it stopped, I wondered if we had imagined it.

But then it came again, a fierce drumming that shook the door.

'Are you expecting—?' I started to ask.

But Marie clenched my arm tightly in alarm. 'It's them,' she said. 'They've come to take her.'

The knock came again.

'What do I do? I didn't mean what I said. I don't want them to take her, I don't—' Her voice was twisting and shrill.

'Of course – I know that.'

'What do I do, Kit? What do I do?' Her grip on my arm tightened; I didn't realise she had such strength.

A hundred scenarios played through my head. The person knocking at the door was actually just Elizabeth from the building. Or it was the enforcers but we barricaded the door and so Marie and Tia managed to escape by going through the window and miraculously not injuring themselves in the fall. Or the knocking would stop and we would continue sipping our tea while Tia giggled to herself on her playmat, safe in our watch.

But none of these came to pass.

NOW

My eyes flicker closed for a moment longer than a blink: I picture a playmat, I hear the sound of a light giggle. I wrench my head upwards. The movement wakes me.

I see the road, hard and unforgiving ahead of me and I try to sit up straighter, open my eyes wider. I try not to think of the hours that I have already driven this morning and the hours that I still need to drive.

The man we met said that it would be possible. You could avoid being caught if you stayed away from main roads, if you moved evasively across the county from quarter to quarter. It could be done. There would not be a wide alert out for us on the Spheres because they didn't want it to be news that there was a family on the run from OSIP. Of course there was always the risk that they would catch up to us but we were prepared, we learnt the routes, we changed vehicles, we didn't leave a trail. We had been told which municipalities had low resources and so there was less chance of spot checks.

I can't let all that preparation be wasted because I fall asleep at the wheel.

I must stay awake. Or I must rest.

There's a turn-off approaching and I take it. I drive down unused roads, weeds sprouting through the tarmac. There are empty car parks and silent buildings that, for just that moment, are beautiful and inviting, lit up by bleached golden sunshine. It's an old shopping centre, the faded signs are still in place although they appear fragile, as though they might fall if anyone disturbed them. It's late morning now, a Saturday, and I wonder for a moment what this place would have been like before, packed with cars and people and bustle.

I swing into one of the spaces and park, ignoring the signs that tell me I can't.

There's a way to make my seat go down so it becomes almost level but I can't find the lever. I push the thought from my mind that Thomas would be able to do it instantly. Instead, I crawl across the back seat. I press my feet against the car door because there isn't room to stretch out my legs properly and, uncomfortable as it sounds, I fall asleep quickly.

I don't dream. Or I forget my dreams.

I have no way of setting an alarm. I hope that my body will rest for only as long as it needs and that I will wake soon. I do not want to waste time here. It is a race, I feel it as one, but if I have an accident when I am driving, I might never get to the end.

My mind has made me sleep. Shut me down, closed me for business. This way, I don't have to think of Thomas. I don't linger through the hours of the day imagining what he's doing, now that he's found me gone. I don't imagine his anxiety growing when I do not return. I do not think about him at lunchtime, pacing the apartment, wondering if he should go out, whether it's the right thing to do because then I might come back to no one there.

Thomas will search for a note, some word of what I am doing. He will re-examine how I acted yesterday: was there anything particularly out of the ordinary about me the night before, something that he can pin this on? But he didn't see the headlines on the Spheres at the charging station; he's oblivious to what I know.

THEN

Marie turned to me, gripping my arm so tightly I could feel my arteries throb.

I heard her words again: 'What do I do, Kit?'

I froze, panicked; I didn't have an answer, couldn't conjure a plan.

Marie rose unsteadily to answer the door.

'Are you Marie Rachel Trevers, mother of Tia Lola Trevers-White?' said a female voice. It wavered slightly, as though unused to speaking in this manner.

I wanted to do something, anything that I could, much in the same way as I had first reached out to Marie and Leo, and so I slid out of my chair down to the floor so I was beside Tia. She was steadily examining the toy sheep that dangled over her. Then I shouted in a loud voice to Marie, 'Tia's fine, Marie. I'm watching her.'

'Is there someone here with you?' said the voice.

'My friend is here,' said Marie and she glanced over at me as though she were checking that I was not a hallucination.

'What is she doing?'

'She's looking after Tia with me.'

'Right,' said the voice, sounding a little annoyed. 'So there is supervision with the baby while you have answered the door to us?'

'Yes,' said Marie. 'Of course.'

'We will enter now.' The waver had gone and I saw the voice belonged to an older lady, who was wearing glasses and holding a clipboard. She peered around the flat suspiciously. If it weren't for the circumstances, she looked wholly unthreatening, someone you would pass on the street without a double glance. Behind her were two more enforcers, both wearing a uniform I had never seen before. Young men with the sort of physical fitness that they wore conspicuously, like a badge of honour. Though one of them was much taller than the other, the similarity between them made me think they could have been brothers.

'Who are you?' the woman asked me.

'I'm Kit Moss. A friend. And neighbour.' The woman nodded at me as she made a note on her clipboard. 'Who are you?' I asked.

'I'm sorry?' Her tone was almost amused.

'I asked who you are. You haven't introduced yourself to me, or to my friend Marie.'

'It's quite obvious who we are.' She flicked the card that hung around her neck. It read *OSIP* in blue stark letters.

'No, I meant, I'm Kit and this is Marie, what is your name?'

'Unnecessary,' she said. It was as though she had slapped me.

'Excuse me?' I said.

Marie brought her hand to mine and pleaded, 'Kit, don't.'

'I am an enforcer of OSIP, my identity is irrelevant to

this…' she looked from the flat to Marie to Tia with barely disguised disgust – 'situation. Now Mrs Trevers, as I am sure you are aware, you have received six IPSs in the last five months and your child is being closely monitored for extraction. As you are so close to the accepted limit, we have labelled your child as RCS, "requiring continual surveillance". As such, you can expect these drop-in visits at any time of the day or night.'

'A drop-in?'

'A full sweep of your home, which my colleagues are undertaking, an examination of the subject, and an interview with an enforcer, the latter of which will commence now. Can you tell me when the baby was last fed?'

Marie looked at me, wide-eyed. Bangs and thumps came from the bedroom where the men had started their search. Marie started to speak, stumbling on her words.

'I last fed her, her last feed was, it was…'

The enforcer started writing on her clipboard.

'It was just when I arrived, wasn't it, Marie? I'm always here at—' I managed to get out before I was interrupted by a shriek.

'This interview is for parents only. I'll ask you to wait in the other room, Miss…' She checked her clipboard for confirmation. 'Miss Moss.'

For a moment I didn't move. The enforcer called towards the other room. 'Please escort Miss Moss into the bedroom.'

'It's all right, I'm going,' I said and started to move towards the bedroom.

I heard Marie say as I walked away, 'Midday. Her last feed was midday. She is due another in just under an hour.'

I waited in the bedroom as the two men stood by the bedroom door as though they were guarding it, me or Marie, I couldn't work out which.

I felt suddenly very cold standing there in Marie and Leo's bedroom. I could hear the rise and fall of voices from next door but nothing of what was being said. It went on interminably and though I wished with all my might that Marie could find the answers that she needed, I already knew it was over. I knew it from the moment they arrived. They were taking Tia with them; this was decided long before they took a step into the flat, before they had knocked on the door. This visit was just a cover for them doing what had already been decided.

I heard Marie's sobs coming through the wall and I asked the men if I could go to her.

'We've told you before. Parents only.'

'What about Tia's father? Surely he should be here for this? His work is only twenty minutes away. Shouldn't he be contacted?'

I could see I had struck a nerve. They looked at each other, furtively almost, as though some sort of secret message passed between them. The shorter one said to the other, 'Well, you ask her, then.'

The other man knocked on the sitting-room door and when there was no answer he knocked again. Finally, the command came. 'Come.'

He left the door open behind him and so I could hear the rasps of Marie's sobs and some of what she was saying.

'We'll do whatever you want,' she was saying. 'Please don't do this,' but the words were broken by gulps and more sobs.

Then there were the quiet murmurings of the enforcers talking, so quietly I imagined him at her ear, and above everything else, the light sound of Tia's babbles, oblivious to what she was witnessing.

Too soon, he was back and confronted my questioning face with a blank look.

'Well? Shall I ring Leo?' I reached into my bag to feel for the solid shape of my goSphere. I clenched it in my palm tightly.

'No,' he said, sneering slightly as he did, but he leant in to his co-worker with two words: 'New regulations.'

After a while, the men were called back into the living room and left me there, standing by the bed. Then I heard the shouts. There was no one to stop me now. I ran into the living room and saw them both restraining Marie by the arms and the woman reaching down to pluck Tia from her playmat.

'Take off her band,' she told the man, and passed them a scanner. They flashed it towards Marie's wrist; the bracelet she had worn since the day that Tia was born, the one that identified her as Tia's mother, dropped open to the floor.

'Is there any particular toy that Tia is attached to that she can take with her today?' the enforcer asked.

Marie looked up and was suddenly still. Then she looked around the room desperately.

'Her bunny. Take her bunny.'

The enforcer picked up a small grey rabbit lying to one side of the playmat. It had soft plush fur and flowery fabric lining its ears.

'This one?'

Marie nodded, biting her lip, tears streaming down her face.

Then, without saying another word, the enforcer left the flat, with Tia staring over her shoulder. I could just make out the baby's small face, bewildered perhaps. Her bottom lip protruded just a fraction. It gave a little wobble, and then, as though Tia realised what was happening, her face collapsed into a cry; her mouth pulled downwards, her cheeks puffed, her eyes glistened with despair. And then she disappeared through the doorway and was gone.

The men held Marie back for the next twenty minutes or so until she relented and became very quiet, her body sinking into a ball on the floor. Only when she was unmoving, all the fight gone from her, did they leave.

I called Leo as soon as they'd gone. He arrived not long after that and I left them there, both sunk on to the floor as though they were stuck to it, as if chairs and sofas were far too comforting, too civilised, for them now. I staggered back to my flat and collapsed upon my bed, but not before I had seen the message on my goSphere from Evie.

She had started the induction drugs.

NOW

Being a parent means eating with one hand. It means eating furiously in the few moments you have. Eating is something I can't get used to now that Mimi's gone.

My stomach turns on itself. I try to remember when I ate last and if there's anything to eat in the car.

Thomas bought something last night, I remember now, and open the glove compartment to find two bars of chocolate stashed there.

I unwrap one of them and take bites that are too large so they jut from my cheeks in angles. The bar is filled with nougat and I have to chew vigorously, work hard, to make it palatable. It coats my mouth in a furry sweetness. I cast around in the foot wells of the backseats, remembering a discarded, half drunk bottle of water that had been rolling around back there. When my hand closes around it, I am oddly triumphant; I sip slowly, it's not fresh, but then I'm glugging at it thirstily until it's empty.

The car door opens with a creak as though it is, like me, only just waking up. A rush of fresh air greets me. It's only early afternoon; I did not sleep for too long.

My legs move stiffly in small steps after being constrained. I stretch but my coat stops me from being able to move easily. I want to take it off but I've only my pyjamas underneath. They are cloying, soft against my skin and suddenly wearing them feels grotty, unbearable. I can smell the slightly stale odour of me that comes from a night and day of wearing the same clothes.

I start the engine and rejoin the road. I make up for the lost time I slept, overtaking cars, pushing down the accelerator so the engine roars. It sounds like it is straining, like there is something wrong with it, but I push on nonetheless.

918. NNW 1HW.

When I get so far I recall that I can't stay on this road; there'll almost certainly be city border patrols. I weave through smaller roads, single lanes that are patchy with potholes, narrow from overgrown shrubbery. Not many people use them any more. I haven't driven down roads like this before. I was almost surprised when we were told that using them would be a way to escape OSIP. We always knew that there was a risk that we could still be caught, but it's worked for us so far and right now it takes me just a little further.

The charge gauge edges lower as I drive on. I calculate that I will have enough to get me there and a little further still before I'll need to recharge. I have the money in my pocket if I need it. I'm taking another risk but it makes me calmer to run over the logistics.

918. NNW 1HW.

It feels as though it is far longer than hours since I stole away from Thomas – that could have happened a month ago or longer. Unbelievably it is the same day. Apart from stopping to check the Spheres, the quick nap, all I have done is drive. I've urged myself forwards, propelled myself in a sharp, climbing diagonal line across the country.

918. NNW 1HW.

It is settling into the afternoon when I see the sign for a city I have never been to. The turn-off is approaching and my breath catches as I read it.

It's a gasp, not of surprise, but like I am caught out by a pain that stabs me, that leaves a deep wound.

THEN

The next day, I woke with a hollow, stiff pain in my stomach that made me walk crouched over, my back arched.

I returned to Marie and Leo's flat as soon as I could but I didn't bring anything with me, nothing that could suggest that the mood could be brightened, just myself. They didn't answer the door, though I could hear movements inside. After almost an hour of hoping I would catch them, defeated, I returned to my flat.

There was a pad of writing paper I couldn't remember buying in a desk drawer and I started to write to them. I told them, as I had that first day, that I would do what I could to help – whatever that was. *I hoped*, I wrote, but then my words ran into emptiness. I could not offer them hope. There were other things that I could say, things I'd imbibed from the Spheres, about how they could try again. That there was research to show that the extraction of one child could often lead to more successful parenting of another; there was plenty of evidence to encourage repeated inductions. An extraction did not rule out keeping subsequent children.

But I threw the letter away and wrote another that was

much briefer: I was thinking of them and if I could help in any way, I told them, they only needed to call. I shoved the letter under their door and waited for a while to see if anyone would pick it up. I left alone.

Then the week after that, it was Elizabeth, the flame-haired neighbour I'd met in the lift, who told me that they had moved on.

'I heard that she was extracted. And they can't bear to be in the same place any more. Did you see anything?'

Rather than refute or corroborate, I looked directly at her.

She peered right back at me from beneath her large, sunken lids. I'd not noticed before that her hands never lost a slight tremor or how small she was. Her skin stretched tightly across the small frame of her skeleton. Behind her inquisitive glare, there was a well of something tender, something like sadness.

'I was there,' I told her. 'I was with Marie when they took Tia.'

'I'd heard that you'd been helping them out.'

I met her stare once more.

'It was... awful.'

'It always is.' Her words hung in the air like the thread of a cobweb, swaying and fragile, almost imperceptible. She must have spoken without thinking because in her next breath she said in a rush, 'Of course, if the standards are not being met, there's no better place than the compounds. The facilities they have, the access to education, it's best for the child. It really is. There's no getting round it. Every child born these days absolutely has to have the very best start. Where do they say they are located these days?'

I shrugged and let Elizabeth run on. It wasn't known where

the compounds were, although I'd heard a rumour that the Isle of Wight had been especially repurposed.

'Plenty of green space wherever they are. Just the best of the best. Well, I hope they try again,' she continued. 'The next time, it could, it could... stick.' She shook her head a little as she landed clumsily on the word.

We spent the rest of our lift ride in silence.

I wondered about trying to find out where they had gone. I thought of ways that I could trace them, but as quickly as I did, I dismissed the ideas. What would I say, what could I say, that would make it any better? Maybe it was better to do as they had done, to move on. What good could come from speaking about it any more?

Evie was the one who recognised that something was bothering me. She dropped in to see me after visiting the doctor for a check-up.

'Are you okay?' she asked, her eyebrows raised slightly.

She had gained weight since I had seen her last. Her skin was a shade paler and she couldn't stop a hand from resting on her stomach, which bulged out slightly from the loose trousers I'd never seen her wear before. She had started the induction drugs, and they would have begun to affect her by now, but when I asked her how she was doing, she waved away my concerns and turned the questions instead towards me.

I quickly pulled off the sweater I had worn for the last week, noticing a stain on its front.

'I'll make some coffee,' I said, turning away to the kitchen.

'Have you got any fresh mint? I'm off caffeine now.'

'Of course. Erm, no, but I have some peppermint teabags somewhere.'

I rummaged in the cupboard and then swore loudly when I spilled a bag of open rice on to the floor.

'Let me,' Evie said. 'I'm the one who is making you turn everything upside down.' She went to bend down but gave a small gasp as she did and her hand flew to her stomach once more.

'Are you sure you're all right? Maybe you should sit down.'

'It's fine,' Evie said, but she spoke through gritted teeth. 'The doctor said I should expect this. If it gets worse, I'll go back. Let me help.'

'No, I'll do it. It's my mess.'

Evie didn't answer and instead reached out a hand towards me. It was cool, soft and perfumed in mine and we stood for a few moments like that, holding hands, swinging them gently, just as we had done as children together.

'What's going on?' Evie said.

My eyes filled with tears. I had decided as soon as I heard her elated message telling me that she had started taking the induction drugs that I was not going to tell them what had happened to Leo, Marie and Tia.

I shook my head.

'Come on, Kit. You have to tell me. I'm getting worried now.'

'You don't need to, it's nothing, nothing's wrong with me,' I started to say but I couldn't finish the sentence.

'Oh Kit, what is it?' Evie cried as she wrapped me up in such a close hug that for just a moment we were one being, united again, made whole finally. I didn't want to let her go.

'Please tell me what's making you so upset.'

I gave her the briefest outline of what had gone on but Evie pushed me until I told her every gory detail: the enforcers' impersonal brutality, Marie's pain and desperation.

'I didn't want to tell you, what with all you're going through. And it won't be like this for you, I know it won't,' I said fiercely.

'Kit,' Evie said slowly. 'It might be.'

The act of saying those words seemed to exhaust her.

'It might happen to us. We know that it's a possibility. We always have. Everyone does. You wish, you work hard and do everything you possibly can to make it not so, but there's always a chance. In the world we are in,' she finished.

'I just didn't want you to start off hearing this, though.'

'Honestly, Kit, if we hadn't heard this from you, it would have been someone else.'

'But no one talks about it, do they? I mean the only reason that we are talking about it is because we are alone and we are sisters and because you bullied it out of me.' Evie laughed then but I could see there were tears in her eyes too.

'Listen, extractions happen. That's it. There's nothing that you or I can do to change that. I'm just so sorry for your friends.'

'Do you... have you ever heard about children coming back after an extraction?' I asked. I looked up expectantly, although I already knew the answer.

'Returning to their parents? I... well... There's been some stuff on the Spheres about it. But the compounds do give the children the highest standard of living—'

She hugged me again so she did not have to say the word.

For ever. After an extraction, children don't come back.

'Ugh. I wish I could have a drink,' she said.

'I have some whisky.'

'It's no drinking for me for quite a while now.'

'It'll be worth it,' I said, with a faint smile.

'Yes, it will be. Whatever happens. We'll be ready for it, because of you and Dad and Seb's family. That's what it's all about, isn't it? Family.'

I bowed my head in agreement. Then the moment was over and we cleared up the spilt rice and drank the tea that Evie had come for in the first place.

For months and months afterwards, I would still find an odd grain of rice in some crevice of my kitchen. In the end, I stopped picking them up.

NOW

I walk past two women who are hunkered around the navy dome of a pram. Their bodies stiffen as I pass them, and with every wail of their baby, they lean in a little closer to it.

I look away from them and gaze across the parked cars. I have finally arrived.

It's just as it was described – a large grey block of a building that looms in front of me – and that fact both comforts and disturbs me. It's real; I am close, now.

Inside, it's a maze. The flats are numbered and each zone is given a separate letter but the signs all give different information to each other. It's either that or I'm reading them wrong. I walk down long corridors, tube-like and narrow, right to their end, until I realise I've gone in the wrong direction.

I swear to myself and turn down another corridor, breaking into a run.

918.

918.

Thomas and I promised each other that we would never

come here. That was what we first agreed to, a month ago. Time has stretched since then and in those days a whole new lifetime has somehow fitted into those few months. The adjustment to Mimi's absence has leaked into my whole body, it has changed the way I see, how I feel. The pain has caused me to stoop, the stress has made my skin flaky and red as though it is angered.

I keep walking, peering over my shoulder each time I hear a sound. I am sure that Thomas will come here too once he's accepted that I have gone. He will know that this is where I'll come. That was why I had to race, why I was reluctant to sleep, or break at all. If he'd found me before I got here, he would have tried to stop me.

He will stop me not because he doesn't love me, and not because he loves her any less than me but because, as he has told me over and over, he believes we are going through this now for the greater good. We live in agony now so we can live without it in our future.

I've tried to explain to him that I see the future as shadows, that I don't believe in it, I don't believe it will work. His face hardens when I speak like that. He believes that my lack of certainty is a lack of courage.

Perhaps he's right. There is something elemental within me that cannot be without her, that knows with a cement certainty that if Mimi is with me then I can protect her.

It's a ridiculous notion. Thomas has reminded me that Marie watched Tia being taken, he has retold the night we spent with Evie and Seb, but despite all of that hard memory, there is nothing firmer than my belief that I should be with my daughter.

Thomas would not believe me if I told him about what I saw on the Spheres when we stopped to recharge last night.

He'll think that I've given myself an excuse to find her.

A part of me knows that I had to do this by myself because I can't bear to face his disbelief.

THEN

'I don't miss it,' Evie told me, wiping the edges of her mouth carefully with a balled-up tissue. Evie had left work since she had begun taking the induction drugs.

'That's good,' I said. It was all I could say because she didn't have any choice in the matter. Once you started induction, it became your full time job.

She had been vomiting for the last week. Not from morning sickness; she wasn't pregnant. It was the induction drugs that were turning her stomach. She was on the second round of fertility drugs now after being admitted to hospital following the first. The stomach pains she'd felt the day she'd come to visit me had worsened quickly and she'd been at risk of developing a blood clot.

She sipped on a glass of orange squash, something I hadn't seen her drink since we were children.

'Mmm,' she said. 'That's better.' She was doing such a good job of not showing how much she was suffering. 'Drinking this always reminds me of Mum. She'd make us squash if we were sick.'

'Did she?' I asked hungrily. Evie remembered so much more about her than I did.

'Yes, and toast cut into triangles.'

'I can make you some if you like.'

'Oh, no thanks,' Evie replied, paling at the thought of food.

'How do you feel about not going back?' I asked, trying to distract her and take her back to what we had been speaking about. Even though she was not pregnant, her mind was busy preparing for the eventuality that she would be. Evie had worked so hard to get to where she was in her law firm, it was almost unbelievable that if she did get pregnant that she wouldn't go back to it.

'Oh, you know, it'll be fine. I mean, I suppose it is a bit weird. I keep thinking that I'm just taking a break and I'll be back again but... well, hopefully that won't happen.'

'How are you generally?' I pressed.

'Not... great. But I'm fine. Really, I am.'

Her eyes dulled as she spoke.

'Where are you at in the induction cycle?'

Evie reeled off dates and other drugs that she had to start taking on top of what she was on now. There would be more waiting, more tests and scans. I felt as though I was lost in a maze, following her around sharp corners and disappearing bends, as she explained all that was to come.

'Anyway,' she finished, 'it's good to have all the learning to do to take your mind off the medical stuff.'

Their house had been taken over by induction manuals, and pages upon pages of notes both in Evie's spidery letters and Seb's more precise block capitals. Their Spheres were set to OSIP-approved documentaries that filled the rooms with the same monotone, bored-sounding voice.

Their living-room walls were postered with revision notes, all in different colours, intricate diagrams in places. Some parts were underlined heavily, other words highlighted angrily so that they screamed from the wall.

'You can't say you're not committing to it,' I said.

Evie nodded but then she doubled over, her body collapsing in on itself, and she ran to the bathroom.

NOW

The man gave us a number and a postcode: 918, NNW 1HW.

I took care to cover my tracks when I looked up the postcode. I used a workSphere in a shop to find the address, then I traced it on an old map that belonged to Dad and memorised its location. I'd found out the best route to avoid city border patrols, just in case. I don't know whether Thomas did the same; I don't believe he did. If he hasn't, that might slow him down a little.

I say the number to myself whenever I'm anxious, when I cannot sleep.

NNW 1HW. 918. The digits loom in my mind unbidden now as they have throughout today, they are so etched upon me.

I am in front of 918 now, the numbers stuck on a grey door in diagonal dull silver shapes. I almost walked past it – each door's so much like the one before it and the one after. This whole building is made up of so many identical flats, they remind me of the hexagons of a beehive.

I wish I could say that I was drawn to the door, that there

was something magnetic about the bond with my child that led me here. But it's just because this was the number that we'd been told, that I counted it out as I stalked through the corridor.

I raise my hand to the door, and knock. I've arrived.

THEN

Jakob Luke Maybury-Moss arrived at two o'clock on a Friday afternoon in mid-May.

Evie had revealed to me that she felt cumbersome and uncomfortable but mostly she hid this beneath a stoic sensibility. 'I can't complain,' was her mantra in those days. She ran her fingers over the dome of her belly as though to remind herself.

OSIP monitored her nutritional intake during pregnancy. She had had to log each meal, every snack, through her goSphere as well as a daily walk and relaxation exercises. She had to drink a certain amount of water each day so she filled two canisters in the morning and slowly emptied them, sip by sip, as the day wore on. It was overwhelming to me, that every morsel that passed her lips, the number of steps that she took in a day, were all watched over by OSIP. Every move she made was rigorously scrutinised; was it the right thing to do, was it safe for the baby? And what more could she do more that would be of benefit?

Physiological births were much preferred, caesareans performed only in an emergency. Evie told me that she'd learnt that this was because vaginal births had health advantages for the baby. She was constantly monitoring her posture to help the baby get into the best position for birth and this, on top of her new, growing body shape meant she moved with a sort of hunched anxiety that never left her.

She'd been told there was a 30 per cent chance of the induction being successful and that on average women could go through the process eight to nine times. I had to clamp my lips together to stop myself from asking the obvious: what percentage of those babies are extracted? We were never told those figures.

In the months Evie was pregnant a report revolved around the Spheres about a spike in the number of miscarriages. Evie pounced upon it. She wondered aloud if it was something the mother was or wasn't doing; was it linked to food consumption, level of stress, amount of exercise, or lack of it. She darted from one to the other as though to pick apart the problem and when I gently suggested that none of those things caused miscarriages, it was as though I had not spoken.

We didn't speak of the number of induction cycles they had been through, the pain she had endured to get to this point. It was better to concentrate on where she was now, that she was actually pregnant, that her baby was coming. Although the pregnancy was so fraught with Evie trying to 'do the right thing' that at times it was as if she was slipping away somehow, lost in the numbers and statistics, submerged in the advice and the monitoring. I wondered if she felt this way too.

Her life was punctuated with midwife appointments and OSIP checks. She saw different midwives at first but by the middle of the pregnancy, she was assigned a midwife who would see her to the birth. I asked what she was like, and when Evie didn't meet my eye and mumbled something generic about them being fine, I was sure that it was a bigger problem than she was letting on. I asked Seb once when she was out of the room and his face flushed.

'It's not a big deal. Evie thinks,' his voice lowered, 'that the midwife doesn't like her. But she's being oversensitive. It's OK, really it is.'

I tried to ask Evie about it again but she wouldn't be drawn into talking about it.

We were all living close to the edge. Dad rang me most days leading up to the due date, not to talk about anything in particular, just to make contact. We would chat about his allotment for a few moments before the conversation turned inevitably to Evie and the unborn baby. I couldn't remember us ever speaking so much in my life.

'Have you heard from Evie today?' Dad would ask me each time we spoke.

'Why don't *you* call her?' I asked him on one of the consecutive phone conversations.

'I don't want to keep badgering her. She needs to rest, not have to keep answering the phone to me.'

'I'm sure she'd like to hear from you, Dad.'

'No, no,' he said, decided. 'She'll get in touch if she wants to. It's best if I ask you how she's getting on.'

Afterwards, I would call Evie to ask her to call Dad. I was pondering the slight absurdity of this circle as I hung up on Dad again, when my goSphere lit up with Seb's face.

'Evie's been taken into hospital,' he said. 'She's gone into labour early. I'm going there now. I'll call when there's news.'

And then he was gone, so quickly that I felt as though I had only imagined the phone call. I rang Dad back, who had more questions than I could answer, and then all that was left to do was to wait.

'Please don't let anything be wrong. Please let Evie be well.'

I chanted it. Saying it out loud made it stronger, somehow. She was thirty-six weeks gone. My mind quickly tried to summon my knowledge about this period in the pregnancy from Evie drilling herself about each stage of development. I comforted myself by remembering that by thirty-six weeks, the baby's lungs should have developed enough so they could breathe independently.

I tried to work. I was listening to more of Jonah's conversations with his daughter. I had decided that I wanted to bring even more about their relationship into the life document. Some of the drafts I'd sent off had been approved and so I lost myself in old videos of Jonah with a pint-sized daughter driving along the coast. There was a spot on a tidal island close to where they lived that they returned to frequently. I wrote this place into the new piece and was pleased with how it turned out – it was nostalgic, private but relatable. Somehow the night passed by.

The next morning, we were summoned to Evie's hospital with five short words. *He's here! E well. Come!*

Dad and I went together. It took us a while to find a parking space, which annoyed Dad although he wouldn't say it aloud. He huffed to himself impatiently, little sighs that rippled through the air gently. When he did see a parking space, he gave a shout, 'There's one!' and swerved so violently into it that he came close to brushing the car that was parked next to us.

Evie, Seb and Jakob were cocooned in a circle when we arrived. Their arms wrapped around each other, their fingers interlocked, Jakob in the very centre. They looked up at us, their cheeks glowing, and together, there, in that moment, they were a perfect picture of happiness. I sometimes hold on to that image of them as we found them in their hospital room that day. I remember it, I examine its details.

The way that you could not tell where Evie's arm ended and Seb's began, they were so entwined. The flushing rosiness upon their faces, the brightness of their eyes, their ready smiles. In the wake of what followed, I would remember that simple, blissful scene. It was like a single, lighted candle in the darkness, a lone flower amongst the weeds.

'There's someone we'd like you to meet,' Evie said, grinning broadly. We crowded a little closer to study Jakob's tiny, sleeping face. 'Would you like to hold him, Dad? Grandpa!'

'Oh, give him to Kit,' Dad said, stepping back bashfully, his eyes on Jakob. I saw on his face the same satisfaction that I'd seen when he looked at his beloved allotment, surrounded by a tumble of squash plants and tomato plants that were heavy with the fruit they bore.

'He's beautiful,' I said, running a finger over the perfect, almost translucent skin of his nose. Evie and Seb did not reply but only smiled helplessly at each other, and then back towards their baby son.

'We won't stay long,' Dad said. 'Just wanted to say, you know, well done!'

'Thanks, Luke,' Seb said. 'Stay a while though, take your coat off.'

Evie and I shared a quick grin as Dad pulled his coat around him a little closer. It was an old grey-green thing that he'd had for ever and never seemed to take off.

'No, no. We must leave you to rest. We just wanted to pop in,' Dad replied.

Despite what he said, we found it hard to draw ourselves away from their bedside. Time passed at an unreasonable speed, the visiting hours were coming to an end and bewilderingly Dad and I found ourselves back on hospital corridors, searching for signs back to the car park. Our time with Evie, Seb and Jakob felt like a dream.

Out of their room, the wail of a baby's cry pierced through our trance. We caught glimpses through the round porthole windows on the doors we passed of a few other families, newly created, shrouding their pristine infants, but most of the rooms were empty.

'Not many people getting through induction,' I muttered, more to myself than to Dad.

I wasn't even sure that he had heard me until he said, some moments later, 'I really don't know how they can stand it. What with OSIP lurking at every corner.'

'Not here, Dad,' I said. Just then a nurse passed us on the corridor and I found myself turning back to see if she had noticed what Dad had said. Her heels clicked rhythmically down the walkway and she disappeared round the corner. She hadn't looked back.

'She didn't hear me,' Dad said, a little wearily.

'It's not worth it, though, is it?'

Dad didn't answer me properly until we'd slammed the car doors shut.

'Do you really think anyone cares what an old codger like me is saying?'

'I don't know, Dad. But the point is that they might. This is how it is now. Now that they've had him, they have to avoid extraction.'

'I can't see anyone giving me the time of day.'

'Dad! Promise you'll be careful. For Evie's sake, and for Jakob's. It's like I said, it's just not worth the risk.'

'Fine,' he said, although he was quiet as we drove from the hospital. Only later when I remarked on the amount of hair on Jakob's head, his resemblance to Evie, did he cheer up.

'Same time tomorrow?' I asked him when we said goodbye.

Dad agreed, although I think both of us felt that it was too long until we could reunite with Evie, and delight in our respective nephew and grandson.

Only the next time we went to see them, it was nothing like the first.

The uncomplicated happiness had evaporated. The worry had set in.

When we arrived the next day, Seb quickly came to the door and told us briefly that he and Evie needed to see a specialist with Jakob and could we wait until that was over.

'Nothing to worry about,' Seb said before he disappeared inside. The door swung closed behind him and so I glimpsed for a moment, Evie, sitting forwards, her arms closed around herself, her tear-stained face fixed upon the midwife talking to her. She was pale, her hair heavily black against her ashen cheeks.

'There's nothing to make you worry like someone saying there's nothing to worry about,' Dad said. We sat down, side by side, deflated.

'As long as they're getting the help that they need, I'm sure it will be all right,' I said, unconvincingly. I had seen Evie's face.

We waited out there for so long that I wondered if we would even be able to see them that day, but then the door opened and there was a flash of a white coat as the doctor exited the room. Dad made a move as though he were about to stand but then thought better of it and stayed put. I found myself reaching out a hand for his. We squeezed each other's palms as we waited.

Then Seb was at the door, beckoning, apologising, apologising again.

'What's going on?' I asked as soon as the door closed behind us. Jakob was sleeping peacefully in the cot next to Evie's bed. There was no trace of tubes or monitors around him. Evie sat hunched a little on the bed, her legs drawn up to her chest, hugging them tightly to her. It had been raining heavily since we arrived and so the windows of the hospital room were fogged with condensation, patterned with rivulets made by rainfall.

'You tell them,' Evie said to Seb. 'I'm not sure I can think straight, let alone talk right now.'

'We're having a little trouble with—' He broke off from speaking as Jakob suddenly clenched his fists in his sleep. Jakob turned his head abruptly to one side, contracted his legs a little, and then relaxed again. When he didn't make any more movements, Seb started again. 'We're having a little trouble with breastfeeding,' he said in a low voice. He looked guilty, almost furtive as he said it.

'What he means is that I am having trouble with breast-feeding,' Evie said.

Dad and I both started a chorus of reassurance. It'll get better, we told them, you'll get the help you need now. 'Doesn't he look well?' Dad pointed out, as Jakob rested peacefully amongst us, oblivious to what surrounded him. But there was nothing we could say that would take away the strained expressions from their faces.

'Hopefully it'll get better,' Evie ventured finally, with a brave sort of smile. Dad seemed more assured than me by this admission; he went off in search of some tea for us all, taking Seb with him. I gave Evie a long, hard hug as soon as they left the room. It felt as though she were dissolving in my arms.

She started to cry, in large gulping breaths that shook her body. I kept my arms encircled around her, holding on to her as she shuddered and quaked. It reminded me of the old tales of shape-shifters, where if their captor could hold on to them through their many forms, they would tell them some truth afterwards. Or reappear in their true form. I couldn't remember the exact way the story went.

When she stopped crying, she started to laugh at the tears that still stained her cheeks. 'I've got to pull myself together, Kit, haven't I?'

'Don't forget that you've just given birth, you're knackered, you have a new little person that you'd do anything for. I mean, yes, you do need to pull yourself together. But in the kindest possible way to yourself.'

'I just keep wondering if—'

'You're wondering the worst,' I finished for her. 'And that's perfectly natural. But you have to concentrate on the here and now. Not what might happen.'

'I'm all over the place at the moment,' Evie acknowledged.

'What new mum isn't?'

'I have to be stronger than this. If we want to stand a chance, I have to be more… more than this.'

Evie wringed her hands frantically, as though she desperately wanted to shed the skin that she was in. Her eyes widened, in panic, as she spoke. 'I'm not sure I can do this. I thought I could but what if I can't?'

We had reached another dead end in a maze we were walking, the walls around us daunting, too high to see over, the passage to the centre too well-concealed. The room greyed before me. Without our talking, the shifting sound of the rain against the windows filled my head.

The rain surged, the wind billowed past the glass. I peered out at the downfall but instead of focusing on the torrents of water falling from the sky, I was drawn to our reflections, Evie's and mine. The way our bodies seemed crumpled, Evie's sitting up in bed and mine, standing. And there, between us, the angular outline of Jakob's crib, where he slept on regardless.

'Evie, I believe you can do this. Dad, Seb, too. You need to believe it now. For Jakob. But for yourself, for yourself as well.'

At that moment, Dad and Seb returned, clasping hot paper cups of steaming tea, bottles of apple juice and snacks. I grasped on to a cup, although the room wasn't that cold really. Maybe out of comfort, or the need to hold on to something solid.

'We'd better be going,' Dad said when our cups were empty. They waved us off, steeling themselves for the night ahead.

We joined paths with other visiting relatives who, like us, stumbled through the hospital corridors towards the exit, with the sense of having left part of themselves behind.

NOW

The green exit sign at the end of the corridor flickers. The light shudders on and off before it dies completely.

I knock gently but soon my hands turn into fists and I pummel at the grey lacquer. It rattles the door and I hear people speaking inside, exclaiming surprise.

'Please, please,' I say through the door. 'I'm here for M—'

Before I can say her name, the door is opened. I tumble inside.

I'm in a nice sort of home. Someone has made an effort to make it jolly even though the boxlike room is in itself uninspiring and carries the same claustrophobia as the long corridors of the building. There's a jam jar full of twigs and branches, with gaudy baubles hanging from the wooden fingers. Masses of pictures hang on the wall; each one is vibrantly colourful and, hung together, they resemble a tapestry or quilt.

I take it all in – it's surprising, the colour and the care transforming this narrow room – but I can't see what I've come for. My gaze travels around the room for any sign of my daughter – one of her stripy socks that she peels from her feet at any opportunity, one of the colourful blocks she likes to tap on the hard wood of the floor.

'Mimi,' I manage to say, although all of a sudden it is hard to breathe.

The people before me look like a couple. She has long, dark hair tied in a low ponytail so loose that her hair spills on to her shoulders. The man is thin and neatly dressed. He has a ginger beard that is hard to spot at first because of the lightness of it.

'Kit?' she asks quietly.

I nod, still breathless, still desperate. I whirl around the room, hunting for any trace of my daughter.

'Please,' the man says gently. 'You must be calm. We must not raise suspicion – you know this.'

He speaks so quietly, he speaks as though we have already met, and maybe it is that which stops me from careering through the flat, knocking down everything in my path.

'Where is she?' I ask.

The woman takes a step towards me with her hand out-stretched, almost in a shrug. 'She is sleeping, of course,' she says.

'Can I see her?' I gasp. 'I need to see her.'

The woman takes my hand in hers – it surprises me with how cold it is in mine. She leads me to one of the doors and opens it a crack.

It's dark in there and I can't see anything for a moment. Then I make out a cot and a sleeping body within it, I rush past the woman, twist my hand out of her grasp. I run towards it.

Mimi has her back towards me and the blanket is wrapped

almost over her head. I pull it back gently, internally chiding the couple for letting her cover her head with a blanket – I'd seen only a few days ago on the Spheres a piece about a child smothering themselves with a blanket in the night. Mimi had a sleeping bag at home in which she would never come to any danger.

But when I pull back the blanket, I am stunned. It's not my girl, there's not the fuzz of her wispy blonde hair. I am faced with a dark-haired boy, his hair cut so short that it makes him seem older than a baby.

'She's in that one.' The woman points to the other side of the room.

I had not noticed when I rushed in, there is not just one cot in the room; there appear to be at least three.

I stumble in the direction that she pointed me in.

I pull back the covers

THEN

S he rocked his crib gently, back and forth, back and forth, intuitively. For the first time since Jakob had been born, I saw a shift had occurred within her.

I remembered my struggle to find the right words for her in hospital, the unease I'd felt. *Believe*, I'd told her. Seeing Evie now, it seemed to me that she did believe she was a mother. A good mother, one who was capable, who tried, who loved. And because she thought this of herself, she embodied it.

They were back home now. Their small house was transformed. Every patch of space was covered with Jakob's things; muslin cloths, soft toys, the angular black bouncer that dominated the sitting room. It was akin to the light covering of a first snow; fresh flakes that settled where they fell, one by one, until they covered the entire ground, turning everything to white.

'*Everyone's* different,' she said. 'And so I guess that's why it can be so confusing. And annoying. I can't tell you how many times someone's told me what's worked like a charm for them and which has had just no effect for me at all. They thought it was tongue-tie but when we went for the appointment they said it wasn't that. But, finally, I read about using a formula top-up and now his weight is up. It's up, up, up!' she said with a flourish. 'And you'll never guess who I ran into at the clinic?' She didn't pause for an answer. 'Roger! He asked after you. He said something, now what was it? He said: whatever happened between you, he hopes you're happy...'

I pulled a face to make light of the comment although there was something about it that felt jagged. Roger was the last person I had been in a relationship with, but we had broken up when he had pushed me to start induction.

'I know, I know,' Evie spoke quickly. I only vaguely noticed that she had barely stopped talking since I arrived. 'But he seemed genuine, like he meant it. And then he told me that he'd started working for OSIP, that he was really loving it. I made my excuses to go then. I'm sorry, you probably don't want to hear about him, do you?'

'Not really,' I said. 'Tell me more about Jakey.' Evie launched into the intricacies of the new feeding plan for Jakob; the fluctuations in his weight, the advice from the health visitors and lactation consultants. She spoke feverishly about his sleeping and how that combined with feeding. Through it all she described that though she'd felt the shadow of extraction around her, she could only keep moving steadily forwards to stay out of its reach.

I tried to follow everything she was saying, prickly and bothered by the mention of Roger; the message he'd passed to me, the fact that he was now working for OSIP. Once he'd had the idea that he wanted to have a child, he'd become fixated on us starting induction. I'd broken up with him as quickly as I could when I realised where he was heading.

I remembered the way his eyes had hardened in our last few wretched conversations, how his tone had turned so cold and angry. He blamed me entirely, said that I'd led him on, on purpose.

I drove my mind back to Evie who, not noticing my distraction, continued to list every detail of Jakob's days and nights in relation to the multiples of OSIP standards. It reminded me of the way that she would talk about the legal cases she was working on before she'd had Jakob. There would be an enormous amount of information from all different sources that she would distil down to one single course of action, the irrefutable most logical way of doing things. But by the way her eyes glazed as she spoke I could see this was a practised speech, and I wondered if the person that she had mostly been talking this over with was herself.

'So his weight is where it should be now?' I interrupted her. We'd spoken for so long that Jakob had already woken from his nap, been fed and was now asleep again in Evie's arms.

'Almost. Very nearly. But the important thing is that it's going up. It won't be long. It won't be long,' she repeated. She continued to sway back and forth even though Jakob was sleeping now. As though she could read my mind, she continued, 'He'll wake up if I stop. He loves the motion.'

'Do you want me to take over?' I asked. 'You could take a shower, whatever you need to do. I'm sure I can do a good sway.'

'No, don't worry about that. It's just good to talk, really. I have all these thoughts going round and round in my head. Especially in the nights. Seb listens, of course, but he's almost

as tired as I am. I get the feeling he's not really following me
all of the time.'

So that's how we would spend most of our time together in
those early days, with Evie talking and me listening, nodding.
She gave me updates on Jakob's weight and sleeping, only
breaking off if he began to snuffle or when he was due a feed.
He would lie nestled into Evie and we would gaze at him,
delighted that he was in the world with us. We'd point out
which parts of him were Dad and Mum, which parts Seb,
which parts Evie. She organised the naming ceremony where
I first met Thomas and where I learnt they'd received their
first warning. That shook them both, but in the end Evie
seemed more determined and sure of herself than fretful.

I tried not to notice that Evie never let me hold him after
that first day in the hospital. I had offered and been declined
too many times for me not to realise that she didn't want
anyone else to hold him but her.

It didn't take me long to realise that she couldn't leave
him even for the shortest time.

'You're beautiful, you are,' I told Jakob, bobbing him gently
in his bouncer. He stared up at me, his eyes serious and
contemplative. 'He really is perfect,' I said to Evie.

'He's all right, isn't he,' she said with a grin, reaching to
stroke the down of his springy hair that he'd been born with
and had not yet lost.

'Breastfeeding is still difficult but we're managing some
feeds. It still hurts a lot though. We had to go to hospital
earlier in the week.'

Evie didn't notice my alarm and continued talking at a
rapid pace.

'Nothing to worry about. It was just that there was some blood in his nappy but it turned out just to be from my nipples cracking.'

'Are you OK?'

Evie waved off my concern. 'Nothing to worry about. And you have to keep feeding through it. Still working on the latch. But the formula gives me a break.'

She fell to silence abruptly, as though in a trance.

'Are you sure you don't want to take a nap or anything? I can watch him.'

'No, no,' Evie waved her hands in protest. 'I'm fine, really.'

It wasn't wholly convincing; her face was pale from tiredness and she focused on me vacantly, as though she couldn't quite see me properly.

'Not even just ten minutes?' I asked. 'I'll come and get you if he cries?'

'Honestly, I'm OK,' Evie said and as though to prove it, she picked him up and started to sing nursery rhymes with the baby on her knee.

She couldn't stop Seb from picking him up, and he would give Jakob to me or Dad to hold. She would watch very carefully; at first she'd steal glances from the side but soon enough she'd clearly tired of this charade, and openly, hungrily watched whoever was holding him.

It got worse, to the point that she didn't stop at just watching. It happened one afternoon Dad and I had gone round together. Dad was holding Jakob after Seb had pressed him into his arms while he helped Evie set out some lunch for us. Dad reached over for a glass of water from the table and at the very moment that his hand closed around the glass,

Evie dropped the plates on the table in a clatter and reached out for Jakob.

'I can manage,' Dad said.

'It'll just make it easier for you,' Evie insisted. 'You can use both hands.'

'It's fine, love. I've got him.'

'No, Dad, please, give him to me now. I'll take him.'

She plucked him from Dad's arms and Jakob immediately began to cry at being disturbed. Little bleating cries that he emitted regularly, like an alarm. Evie swayed him desperately from side to side until he stopped. Both she and Dad very carefully and deliberately avoided each other for the rest of the visit.

'She's taking it a bit far,' Dad said as we drove away. But then he sighed as though he'd remembered something.

I nodded vaguely. I didn't want to share with him that something very similar had happened to me the last time I'd been over. That time, Seb and I had been feeding Jakob using the formula milk which Evie had just started him on and the teat had slipped from his mouth without me realising.

'Umm, Kit, the bottle,' Evie had said awkwardly. She appeared embarrassed. For her? For me? 'You need to keep watching him as he feeds. You have to keep an eye on him the whole time.'

'Sorry,' I said.

'Don't worry, it happens all the time,' Seb said.

'It's fine,' Evie chimed in but there was an edge to her voice.

When it slipped out a second time, without saying a word, Evie took Jakob and the bottle. She hooked him in her arm securely in a way I had not managed to replicate and finished the feed.

I left after that, saying I'd just remembered I needed to pick up a parcel, for work. It was easier for us all to believe my lie.

On later visits, I'd decline to hold Jakob, and avoided any awkwardness.

That period was marked with these highs and lows. There was the delight in Jakob, that reflected from us to him and back again and again like a hall of mirrors. Then there were the moments when the only thing to do was to keep your mouth closed to avoid a falling out. There was the day when Seb and Evie had a screaming match because Seb had let Jakob suck his finger for a moment to stop him crying and Evie was worried it would give him wind or that he'd catch a bug because Seb hadn't washed his hands. There were the mornings Evie would hardly speak to me because she was inputting data about Jakob's naps and feedings and they weren't aligning with the guidelines. Her face would be drawn and pinched in the faint glow of her workSphere and I'd quietly let myself out.

I told myself that Evie's overprotectiveness was simply born out of wanting the best for Jakob, and made my peace with those episodes.

But only around a month after Jakob was born, two things happened that changed everything.

It began, and ended, with a phone ringing.

One night, I found myself dialling Dad's number. There was no particular reason for the call; I hadn't heard from him in a while and wanted to try to catch him. His phone rang and rang, only stopping when the message system kicked in.

I wasn't worried. I ran through at least five reasons why he didn't answer and then carried on with my evening. I left a message saying hello and not much else.

I forgot all about calling after that and only the next morning did I remember and think it odd that he hadn't rung back. I tried to call again. Once more, the phone rang out until the automated voice of the answerphone started to play. I left another stilted message asking him to call me.

In the end, when I still had not heard back, I drove round to his flat. Even as I walked up to the stairs to his front door, I didn't really imagine that something was wrong. Years ago there was a problem with his phone and he could not tell if it was ringing or that there were messages. Only that time, it had been Evie who had sounded the alarm as I had been away for a few days with Roger.

My father had become a studied creature of habit since he'd retired. He had openly liked the routine of going to work each day and Evie and I both worried that he would find retirement too aimless, like a winding, empty road stretching out before him, with no features, no landmarks along it. We needn't have worried. He'd revealed his allotment like a card trick, with a sleight of his hand, a hidden ace.

When I found him face-down, unmoving and cold on the sitting-room floor, the television droning on tonelessly, I wished he could have died on his allotment, his lips pressed against the dark, rich soil that he so loved. Surrounded by the squashes and the legumes that he'd tended since they were seeds, when they were only the promise of something more.

That was what I first thought.

There wasn't much of him in this flat. Afterwards, when Evie and I had packed up his belongings, stripped the cupboards, taken the few things off the walls, we were struck by how the flat seemed hardly different to when all of his things had been laid out about the place. It was in a nicer part of the quarter than where I lived and was practical and easy to maintain, but to the point that it was devoid of any character.

He was lying across the beige carpet, a daub of colour amid the drab. At first I could not make sense of it, that it was him lying there.

In the moments that followed, I began to close down; as though there was a darkness travelling through my body, a numbness that disconnected me from what I was seeing. There was silence outside; not the sound of a car driving past, the song of birds, people talking, the hum of the Spheres.

I could just make out a clock ticking, a drum beat that never lost its rhythm. I wanted to call Evie; I should call an ambulance. Before I did either, I ran to his side.

His arms were at angles, his palms to the ground. I wondered if he had tried to get up, if he had realised that he was lying there and that there was no one to help. His body was stiff and heavy to turn over; I was sure that there was nothing that could be done but I made myself roll him over, and faced him eye to eye.

He was so utterly still, he didn't look like himself any more. His face was a hollow mask. He stared past me, the brown of his eyes dull, lightless.

'Dad,' I whispered. 'Dad.' It seemed important to say it aloud.

I had no hope of rousing him. As I knelt there next to him, I was suddenly aware that this would be the last time I spoke to him, the last time I would hear his name on my lips with him before me.

I thought I would cry. I wanted to, but couldn't.

Instead, with one hand I calmly picked up my goSphere to call Evie and with the other, I closed his eyes. It looked like he was only asleep.

NOW

She's fast asleep, curled in a crescent moon, much like how Thomas sleeps.

She's grown in the month I have not seen her. Her cheeks are paler, her hair is longer, almost straggly.

I want to wake her, I want to hear her say my name – the only one I have that matters to me at the moment – but I content myself with picking her up in a close embrace. Her body slumps on to mine; her head cradles into my neck, I slide her legs around my hips.

This is where she is meant to be: she fits.

It feels as though my whole body is wrapping itself around her.

I bury my head into her hair and, ignoring the clinging scent of a strange shampoo, I inhale the very smell of her. That is unchanged and perfect.

The woman's eyebrows are raised as I carry Mimi out of the bedroom with me. The man puts a hand to her arm as if to steady her.

'I'm taking her,' I say simply.

'Your choice,' the man says. 'But please can you wait just

a moment? We need to make sure you are not seen. We have other children in there, as you saw.'

I bow my head in accession. The man goes into another room, I hear him talking on a phone.

Mimi mumbles something, I wonder if she is half waking.

'Hey baby,' I croon. 'It's Mummy, Mummy's here.' Her head lolls backwards, I fail to catch it and swear as her neck jolts downwards. There's a smear of drool across her cheek.

'She won't wake up,' the woman says. It slips out from her.

'What do you mean?'

'Sometimes – sometimes we have to give them something to keep them quiet.'

'You've drugged her?' The woman flinches as my voice rises.

'Please,' she says. 'You know the way it is. It's not easy but we do it to help people like you. We didn't want to but there were enforcers in the building; we have to be careful.'

I want to continue to shout, I want to shriek, but I pacify myself with shaking my head. I clutch Mimi a little tighter, more certain than ever that coming for her was the best thing I could have done.

I should never have let her go.

'You can leave now,' the neatly dressed man said, returning. 'Be quick.'

He's about to open the door for me when the woman speaks again.

'Wait,' she says. 'Are you sure you want to do this? She can't come back now. This is it. Her boat's going in two days. And they will find you if you stay here – you can't keep her hidden for ever.'

Thomas would want me to listen to these words.

'I can't,' I stammer. 'I can't be away from her any longer.'

I wrap Mimi up in my arms, realising as I do that she's barefoot from having just been in bed. 'Do you have her slippers?' I ask. I'd packed a pair for her when they took her, tiny bunny slippers that were soft and downy, but the pair they bring out aren't hers. I pull them on to her anyway. She's so floppy that I have to lie her down to do it.

'This,' I gesture to my drugged and sleeping daughter. 'This is not right, it doesn't feel right.'

'It's difficult, but it's for the best. It's for you all – to be together, to stay together as a family.' She's crying now, the woman. Tears flash down her face and she makes no move to wipe them away.

The man takes her into his arms.

'Go,' he tells me. 'Go now.'

She continues to cry.

THEN

Evie was crying when she answered her goSphere. For a moment, I thought that everything had gone back to front, that she had rung me to deliver the awful news. Her sobbing highlighted what I could not bring myself to do, to weep for the death of the parent who'd raised us, to acknowledge the depth of his absence. Tears rose in my eyes and then I was gasping, overcome by the strength and multitude of them.

'How did you know?' Evie asked me, her voice sounding distant through the goSphere.

'I was going to ask you the same thing. Had you just been round there?'

'No, they came round here. They turned up unannounced yesterday. I haven't stopped crying since.'

'They?'

Her voice fell to a whisper as though she were afraid that we would be overheard. 'OSIP.'

'OSIP?' I asked. 'What's this got to do with them?'

'We were given an IPS, Kit. For using formula milk. We got a bloody IPS because we were giving Jakey formula.'

'Evie, stop. I wasn't calling about that. It's Dad.'

After I told her there was silence on the other end of the line apart from the sound of Evie drawing breath.

'Can you get over here?' I asked. 'I'm at his flat. I'll call the ambulance now but can you come?'

'Of course, I'll be right there.' Then she hesitated. 'Kit? Is it really true?'

'He's gone.' I spoke the two words slowly, gently, and had the uncanny sense that it wasn't Evie I was telling, but myself.

As I waited for Evie to arrive, I couldn't settle. I couldn't sit down on the sofa or tuck my legs under myself on one of the chairs around the dining table. I picked up framed photographs, studied the frozen, smiling faces. I sifted through the pile of post that was by the side of the toaster and placed it back there again. I tried to remember the last time I had been here and found that the only memory which sprang to mind was a dinner a few Easters ago where Dad had cooked lamb for Evie, Seb and me.

Had I really not been here since? It made me regretful but then I thought about the last time I'd seen him: we'd driven over to see Evie and Jakob and afterwards he taken me to his allotment and proudly shown off the tomatoes he was growing in his greenhouse. His fingers had never rested while we were there; he was constantly plucking leaves, rearranging fruit so it hung more easily, and so it seemed that the plants were fecund, blooming, from his touch. On our way out, he'd nodded to everyone we passed. A couple of people stopped him to ask his advice or tell him how the seedling he'd passed on to them was growing. It'd taken us so long to walk out that I'd left him there and gone on ahead because I was meeting friends for dinner.

'Cheerio, love,' he'd said, although his attention was elsewhere. As I'd left, I was aware of the gentle timbre of his voice that softly accompanied my footsteps. I let myself cry once more then, remembering that last time we'd been together, and parted. But they weren't the gaping, widening sobs I'd shared with Evie on the goSphere, the tears came from remembering a happy, contented moment with someone I'd loved, someone who'd loved me.

I didn't cry again that day. I was calm, almost distant, with the paramedics who took away Dad's body. I answered their questions with precise detail. No, I hadn't been aware that there was any heart disease in our family. Yes, I'd turned the body over. No, I hadn't attempted CPR. Why? Because I knew that he was dead.

I didn't break down when they left, wheeling his body off on a stretcher and covering it with blankets so he resembled nothing more than a few lumpy sacks.

I didn't cry when I started leafing through one of our old photo albums that I found stacked upon Dad's bookshelves. I smiled at the two-year-old me on Dad's knee watching Evie twirling in front of us, and flicked through the many pages and pages documenting our life together. I only came close when I opened the fridge and saw the almost empty, organised shelves: three pale courgettes and a handful of French beans in the crisper, a shepherd's pie ready meal for one on the centre shelf.

He'd always told us that after Mum died shepherd's pie was the first thing that he had learnt to cook, and lucky for him that it was, because it was also one of the only things he could make that Evie and I would agree to eat.

When Evie arrived, rushing through the door with Jakob nestled into a car seat on her arm, I wondered why I had insisted that she come round straight away. It seemed absolutely critical at the time, but now, now that Dad's body was taken, now that I realised the world hadn't stopped spinning, all urgency had drained away.

'I came as quickly as I could,' she said, breathlessly, glancing around her with the air of wanting something to do. Moments later, she, too, deflated, walked around the flat much as I had, wandering, searching for something. Picking up odd things and placing them down again.

'The paramedics suspect it was a heart attack but they'll be able to tell us more in a little while. Once he's been examined. But there's not a rush because there's no sign of wrong-doing or anything. It looked like he just collapsed.'

'I checked my goSphere,' Evie said. 'We spoke just after midday – he happened to call just after the enforcers had left and so I ended up blurting it all out to him. But he was so supportive, he kept saying that we would be fine. I hate to think of him lying there. And neither of us knowing,' she ended. I nodded. There had been a moment when I had been busy doing something – having dinner, listening to more of Jonah's phone calls with his daughter; or perhaps I was asleep, listening to music or lying in the bath. There had been a moment when he was alive and a moment later when he was dead and I hadn't known it.

'I hope that he wasn't in much pain,' Evie said. She almost made it to the end of the sentence, but not quite. Her words faltered, her face crumpled.

We clung to one another.

It reminded me of those long nights after Mum had gone when I would creep into Evie's bed and we would hide ourselves, every part of our bodies, under the duvet as though to mask our voices, to protect ourselves from forces unknown. It would become hot under there, our breath making the air stuffy and Evie would use one of her larger books to prop up the covers to make a sort of tent.

On those dark nights, talking side by side, our hands twisting around each other's, it felt like the safest place that we could possibly be. Later, Dad would tell us how he had tried to move me back into my bed but even whilst sleeping, I would protest so much that he would give in and leave us there together, over-spilling, silently, indisputably together.

'I suppose that we should talk about what to do,' Evie said once we released one another. 'With the funeral and… and everything.'

'There's time. Let's not start any of that just yet. Anyway,' I suddenly remembered, 'tell me about the IPS. What happened?'

'Oh, that,' Evie said bitterly. Her face twisted with the recollection. 'She just arrived at the front door. Like, out of nowhere. I had no idea what she wanted. I even offered her tea, for Christ's sake.'

'What did she look like?' I asked sharply, the face of the female OSIP officer at Marie and Leo's door flashing through my mind, her dull brown hair, her hard, scrutinising eyes.

'Um, she was quite young. Pretty. Long, blonde hair. Not like the one we met in the car park. Almost the opposite of her. Skinny, well-dressed. She was very factual about it. She just said that she'd heard that we'd experienced problems regaining birth weight and I told her that we were OK now, his weight was in the correct centile. But then she asked me if we were using anything other than breast milk.'

Evie's voice wavered and for a moment I felt as though I was reliving the conversation before me. Evie would have hesitated, as she was now, as the woman had questioned her. Her eyes darted to Jakob's bag of things, the bottle of formula milk amongst the spare nappies and wipes and dummies.

'I couldn't lie. I knew exactly where she was going with it. But there was no point, it would only have made things worse. She already knew, I could sense it. And so I told her exactly what we were doing. That we did use breast milk but that we also use top-ups of formula to keep his weight up.'

Evie took a breath, almost a gasp, as though by talking so much she had forgotten to inhale. It caught in her throat, the air sounded strangled, but it didn't stop her from continuing her story.

'Then she said... she said that because we'd used formula milk without the proper authorisation that she would have to issue us an IPS immediately.'

'You have to get authorisation for using formula milk?'

'Yes,' Evie said, not quite meeting my eye. 'They're so pro-breastfeeding. You can get an IPS straightaway if you apply to use it. That's why I got it from somewhere else, not through the official channels. I thought that if I could just... well, it doesn't matter any more. She asked us where we'd got the formula from and I had to make something up about being given a bag by a mum at a playgroup who had been authorised but didn't need it any more. She asked me for her name but I said I'd never seen her again. And then she told us that we couldn't contest the IPS because it fell into some kind of grade or something. I stopped listening after that. I was just looking at Jakey. I just stared and stared at his face so hard and so I couldn't see anything other than that. Just his tiny nose. His eyelids. His cheeks. She said something like, "Did I understand?" no, it was "Did I comprehend what I had done?" She filled out the paperwork and then she left. Just left me with this crumpled piece of paper and was gone.'

Evie rummaged in Jakob's bag for a flimsy onion-skin-thin piece of paper. I recognised the navy letters of OSIP at the letterhead, the logo of cartoon-like circles that were placed together to look like a family of three. The rest of the paper was covered in neat handwriting; small, even print that reminded me of a child's.

'How many is it now?' I asked. 'How many would you have to get before—'

'Seven. So we have six left. And we have just over ten months until he's one.' Children were never immune to extraction but statistically it was a lot less likely to happen after a baby reached their first birthday, and they reset with every year. If you could make it through the first twelve months without receiving too many IPSs then it normally meant your child would not be extracted. It had been drilled into us that though families were still monitored, if OSIP standards are upheld in that first, crucial part of a child's life then it was an strong indicator that they would be maintained from there on.

'It's not going to happen, Evie,' I said. 'There's no way. You're doing everything right, you're working so hard.'

'Whatever I'm doing, it's not really working, though, is it? And we'll have to stop giving formula top-ups for now. What if his weight drops? That'll surely bring them knocking again. But more importantly than that, I don't want to go back to him going down percentiles again. It's not healthy, it's not good for him. I'd rather he was taken away from us, happy and healthy, than keeping him with us by making sure that he's not thriving.'

'But it's important that you were prioritising that, surely? I mean over Jakob being malnourished.'

'Not the way they see it,' Evie said miserably. 'She said something about me not giving breastfeeding a chance. We could apply for authorisation to use formula of course but that will mean another IPS straightaway.'

'Where did you get it from? The formula you were using?'

'Oh, someone told me about a place to get it,' Evie said vaguely. She winced as though she didn't want to remember it and so I didn't press her. She hugged her arms around herself. 'Maybe… maybe I haven't been trying hard enough with breastfeeding…'

'That's completely mad.' I'd seen the way that Evie had been struggling. She'd told me that on the first few nights, Jakob had screamed and screamed and every time she'd tried to latch him on to her breast, he'd reared away from her and screamed even harder.

'Kit, you can't say that. And what choice do we have but to follow their rules?'

NOW

Before any of this happened, I would never even have considered breaking a travelling-with-a-child regulation but now I bundle Mimi into the back of the car. I lie her across the seats and tuck my coat around her as best I can and so she's as hidden as she can be. I loop the seatbelt around her and double-check it's correctly latched but it's a poor substitute for a car seat.

I drive away as slowly as I dare without arousing suspicion. I glance at Mimi's lolling, sleeping face in the mirror. She won't wake for a while, it seems; I have a little time to get her out of sight.

There had been an idle thought in my mind that I might try to find the boat myself – that I would insist that they take Mimi and me together – but I don't know where the boat is and I have no way of contacting anyone who would tell me.

I can't go to a hotel. I think of the bag tightly wadded with cash that, in my rush to leave, I left behind. We'll be too easily found if we go to Santa's. I want to get to Thomas but I can't be sure where he is now and I have no way of contacting him.

What I need is money and plenty of it. I need someone to give me money.

There's only one place we can go to – it's not perfect but it's somewhere.

And somewhere will do.

THEN

We were caught in another reality – somewhere that felt far from life before, somewhere we could not escape. I took a break from work and spent most of my time at Evie and Seb's. My days were filled helping Evie with Jakob or sorting out Dad's effects. In the evenings we gathered together, us three. For Seb and me, meals were little more than a few mouthfuls of toast or picking at a takeaway bought days before, but Evie was trying to boost her milk supply. We kept making up plates of food within reach of the one hand that wasn't supporting Jakob's head, refilling water bottles which she seemed to drain when we were looking the other way. She started using a breast pump when she wasn't feeding, she'd heard that it could help increase milk production. She'd sit hooked up to a double pump, trying to eat, trying to drink, trying to take calming breaths and at the end of it all, she'd hold up the bottle that would hold only a centimetre or two of milk.

Her face would drop when she saw the meagre amount but she wouldn't complain about the fact that after an hour, this was all there was. Jake would start to cry with hunger again and, without saying a word, she'd put the pump away and pull him towards her.

It felt at that time that we were only just surviving. We operated under a cyclical mixture of grief, anger and desperation.

Our conversations on those nights together inevitably circled around Dad. There seemed too much to organise: the funeral, the flat, the unpicking of his life from the small things like cancelling his subscriptions, to the question of what we should do with his allotment. But beneath it all lurked the IPSs and our worries about Jakob and what OSIP would do next.

We rattled each other easily. One morning, just a few days after Dad's death, I went to his flat for no reason other than just being drawn there. I wanted to feel close to him, to find some old photographs, search for any instances of his handwriting. But when I arrived there, I heard the sound of movement behind the door.

'Evie?' I called out.

'What are you doing here?' she said. She rushed out to meet me, a little red-faced. I couldn't tell if she had been crying or whether it was something else.

'No reason,' I said. 'I just wanted to be here.'

'I'm going through Dad's stuff,' she said.

'I'll help,' I offered.

'No,' she said. 'I mean – it's sort of my responsibility. As the oldest. I want to do it.'

'Are you sure?'

'Yes – but it's all over the place. Do you mind coming back later? So I can concentrate? Jakey's asleep but I've only got so long before he wakes up.'

'Well – I suppose so. Listen, are you sure I can't help? You being older than me doesn't mean that you should do all the work.'

'I don't mind, honestly,' Evie said. 'I want to do it.' There was something steely in her voice that stopped me asking again.

When I did return to Dad's place later on, Evie had taken all of Dad's paperwork with her – letters, photographs, documents, the lot.

I rang her immediately on my goSphere.

When she answered her face was turned away from the screen; she was speaking to Seb.

'By watch him, I mean *watch him*. Watch him, or I'll swear to God I'll… *Thank you*,' she said, her voice lined with sarcasm, before she turned to face me. 'Kit? I haven't got long. What's up?'

'I went round to Dad's. You took almost everything.'

'What? Some of his paperwork.'

'All of it. All of his paperwork.'

'I'm just going through everything for the solicitor. It makes more sense to do it here.'

'Well, let me come and help.'

Evie raked a hand through her hair as though she were trying to pull out the strands and then her gaze wandered back towards Jakob.

'Can we talk about this later? I'm sorry, Kit, this isn't a good time,' she said. 'I can't…' But she never finished the sentence. 'I'll call you soon.'

She swiped the screen closed before I could answer.

I told myself it was because she was tired, it was all just

down to her being under so much strain, but I couldn't stop the lump in my throat building, the sudden sense of loneliness that swept around my shoulders in a whisper.

I resolved that I would try to help her as best I could; although she never did call me back about Dad's documents or indeed mention them to me again, she willingly accepted my help preparing the house for any unexpected OSIP visits. We started with the formula milk; I could see that Evie didn't want to throw it away and so I said that I could store what they had left and after that we set about cleaning, starting in the kitchen, as though we could exorcise its presence from our lives. Evie breastfed with a stubborn, grim determination but, as though he could taste the surliness in her milk, Jakob would break off from feeding often and start to wail. Nothing soothed him. Not more milk, not the usual rocking on a shoulder.

'I think he's hungry still,' Evie would say beseechingly. She didn't have to say another word; I understood what that meant.

After we'd used up the last of the milk that I'd been keeping for them, Evie asked me if I might be able to get hold of some more. It was not possible to find it in a shop, it was only prescribed through official channels, but Evie had found a means of getting it. There'd been no mum at a playgroup; it was all done through a library.

'A library?' I questioned dubiously. 'Where did you hear that from?'

'That was from another mum. When I was out one day. I was trying – failing – to breastfeed and she came over to me.'

'What did she say exactly?'

'She just asked if I was OK and then said had I tried the library in the South East quarter if I needed any extra help.'

'So she didn't mention formula at all?'

'Well – not in words as such… When I first went, I wasn't even sure what would happen.' Evie looked a little lost. 'Would you go? I would do it myself but I can't go back there again, just in case…'

Evie told me where to go. The library in the South East quarter was located in a room in a local hospital. Since books had been uploaded on to the Sphere network, libraries no longer took up whole buildings. They had been shuffled into small rooms, tucked into corners of public buildings and were often run by volunteers, as this one was.

When I arrived, the place struck me as strange in a way I couldn't quite identify.

The young woman behind the desk seemed at first to have been expecting someone else, but then her features quickly rearranged and she shot me a small, tight smile. Her hair was cut so close to her skull that I could see the exact shape of her head, every bump and every line. She wore an oversized dress and ankle boots. There were still some books on a shelf. And lots of OSIP pamphlets, they took up a whole wall. It would not have taken me more than a minute to walk around the entire room. There was an older man sitting at one of the tables, hunched over something. For a moment, perhaps because I was nervous about being there, I tried to give the impression that I was just browsing, just popping in. I walked over to the books, yellow, faded paperbacks with pages that curled at their corners. I shot a glance and saw that the man was doing a jigsaw; the outer frame of it was almost fully completed.

I glanced back over at the woman. She was biting her fingers, her eyes on the door. In that moment, in the way she gnawed at her knuckle, she appeared even younger than she had before. Then she sensed my gaze. Her hand dropped from her mouth and she met my eye.

'Are you OK there?' she said.

'Umm, someone asked me to come for them,' I said. I kept my voice low even though, in the quiet of the room, the man sitting at the jigsaw would have been able to hear me. Then it struck me why the room was so odd: there were no Spheres ticking over. It was still, quiet and peaceful without them.

'She said I should show you this card.' I handed over a library card. It had nothing on it that identified Evie, just a long number and the emblem for the library.

The woman examined it, made a note of the number, and then passed it back to me.

'Come back tomorrow. We don't have any today. It won't be me here but we'll have what you need. Don't forget a bag. Bring the card again. And we only take cash.'

'How much?' I asked, although Evie had already given me money to cover it. She'd told me that they just accepted what people could afford but I wanted to check in case things had changed.

'It's a pay-what-you-can kind of thing.'

The next day I returned and, as she had told me, the young woman was not there; it was a much older woman. She wore bangles that chimed every time she moved her wrists. She was sitting with the man who was still silently contemplating the jigsaw puzzle.

'Can I help you?' she asked me.

'I think so. I came here yesterday—'

'Have you got your card?' she asked.

I handed it over and she glanced at the number and then handed it back to me.

'How much do you need? You can have a maximum of eight hundred grams today.'

'I guess eight hundred, then, and we'll see how we go.'

'Give me your bag and I'll put it in.' I handed over the shabby rucksack I'd brought along and she disappeared through a door into what looked like a large storage cupboard. When she reappeared, the rucksack was reassuringly bulky. I handed over the money, which she took without counting.

'Thank you,' she said with a brisk smile and a ring to her tone that seemed to mask what had just happened.

Only when I got home did I inspect the contents of the rucksack. Inside was an unlabelled glass jar of creamily white powder. It could have been a type of flour, perhaps. There was nothing to distinguish it from something completely innocent.

I kept it in a work bag I would carry around with me always and so if there came a day when Jakob was hungry and distressed we could make up a bottle from this stash as well as his breast milk feeds.

'Do you know any more about what happens with the people at the library?' I asked Evie.

'No,' she replied. 'And I don't want to.'

Evie asked me not to tell Seb about this arrangement.

He was more rattled by the IPS than he'd admit. He'd joke about OSIP when we were together at their house and then he would laugh loudly, the sound of his booming chuckle ringing out conspicuously so you felt its vibrations. He would hold his hands out expansively as though he were giving a speech, and grab you by the elbow or shoulder to labour a punchline. But his joking did not reach his eyes, which were permanently glazed with worry.

'How do you think she's doing?' he asked me in a low tone one evening when Evie had gone to tend to Jakob's cries.

'Evie? As well as can be expected. How are you doing?'

'Me? Well, you know, I feel completely powerless and I hate it. That's how I am. But I wanted to ask you about it because I just worry that Evie feels more responsible about all this than me. What with the breastfeeding being hard and then because she thought that formula milk was the only way forwards.'

I bristled. 'The formula milk helped him gain weight. It was the only thing you could do.'

'Well.' Seb shrugged and leant back from me slightly. 'It wasn't authorised.'

'You're beginning to sound like you're on their side,' I remarked.

'Of course not,' Seb retorted. 'I'm just trying to understand why it happened to us and I'm worried that Evie might feel more responsible for it all.'

'Do you think she is? More responsible?'

'Well, of course not. But if we used formula milk without authorisation we were going to end up in trouble, weren't we? Evie didn't tell me it wasn't authorised.'

'What was the right thing to do, then?'

Seb began to bluster but he was saved by Evie reappearing. 'Everything okay?' she asked.

'Yes, fine.' Seb smiled up at her. Evie shrugged her shoulders, aware we had been speaking about her. She sat back down next to us but she watched Seb through narrowed eyes and, I noticed, sat just far enough away from him on the sofa so that no part of their bodies touched.

I started to look at Seb a little differently after that night, too.

The next morning, Evie opened the door to me, Jakob slung over her shoulder, with the violet shadows on her face, her eyes red-rimmed and bloodshot.

'What happened?' I asked immediately.

'Just another argument – where we couldn't properly argue in case anyone heard us,' she said.

'What do you mean?'

'OSIP are all about positive family relationships. Fighting with your partner is a big red flag to them. If the neighbours reported it or an enforcer happened to be passing, then…'

'But surely they wouldn't have heard?'

'We can't be too careful. Even though it's maddening. I could just scream right now but…'

She took a deep breath and closed her eyes, as though she was trying to contain a wild energy.

'I almost stormed out. I've never been so mad,' she continued. 'But then I thought that I couldn't leave Jakey and I stopped myself. Seb found the formula milk.'

'What did he say?'

'He just keeps pushing for us to ask for authorisation for it. I'm just… furious with him. He can't understand why we can't do it. It will draw more attention to us; it'll be like inviting OSIP in. He blames me for what happened although he won't admit it. I'm not sure what annoyed me more – that he's pushing us to try to get authorisation, that he thinks it's my fault or that he won't be honest about it and tell me how he really feels. What we need to do is get through these next few weeks. I know I can do it.' She gritted her teeth as she spoke and I could see the tension running through her whole body.

'I'm sorry, Evie. Is there anything I can do?'

She took another deep breath. 'You mustn't say anything about the formula that you keep for us, OK? I didn't tell him about you being involved.'

'How is Jake's weight now?'

Evie frowned. 'He's not gaining enough really. He's gone down a couple of centiles.'

She peered over at Jakob who stared unblinkingly back at her, his eyes large and fixed upon her, as though they were in a silent dialogue.

'We'll get better at breastfeeding, hey buddy? Then we'll be rid of those enforcers for good,' she said. She reached out a finger towards him. He grasped it tightly in his fist.

A handshake, of sorts.

The lead-up to Dad's funeral passed us by as though it were happening some distance away. We managed to stumble through the organisation of it all. Because of what was happening with Jakob, I told Evie I would plan everything and then run it past her to make sure she approved. Her mouth fell open to object when I first suggested it, but then she wearily agreed as Jake started to cry and she had to see to him.

Though we were spending more time together than we had in years, there was an expanse growing between Evie and me. Sometimes I would catch her staring into the distance, her face glazed over with a mix of emotions that I couldn't quite unpick: sadness, disbelief, anger, a great weariness. But when I reached out to her, she'd pull away a little. She'd look at me like there was something that she wanted to say but her mouth remained set, her eyes troubled and she'd say it was nothing. 'Just tired,' she'd say, turning away.

I went back to the library a few times for more formula. Each time, it was the same back-and-forth. I saw the older woman a couple of times but never again the young woman from my first visit. Evie continued to breastfeed despite blocked ducts and mastitis. She swallowed down her pain, though it was written all over her face. But she persevered and one day she said I didn't need to go back for any more.

There were more and more decisions to be made. They loomed above me, these towering choices, until I would snap and decide everything based on the very first thing that popped into my head. Granite headstone. Oak casket. A poem. If I tried to unpick these decisions or think about what Dad would like best, I was lost in a maze of uncertainty.

Through it all, I visited his allotment daily. I would pick up the pots that he'd left out for more tomato seedlings, sieve through the bundle of brown envelopes of seeds and begin to plant, as he'd taught me.

At first, I found the silence unnerving, I was so used to the constant noise of the Spheres filling my ears, my mind. But in no time at all, I looked forward to it and began to crave the quiet. I could hear the sounds of what I was doing there, the slicing of the earth with a trowel, the squelch of my boot in the mud, the clear, pure song of a blackbird overhead.

It rained a lot and I would stand in the greenhouse or the small, overcrowded shed until it stopped. And I listened then in a way I never had before. I listened to the rainfall and found myself falling in love with it, the sound of it hitting the ground and pattering upon the roof.

I'm not one who believes in ghosts or the afterlife, but I took particular pleasure in imagining Dad's hands guiding my own as I gardened. Boring a hole in the black, clinging compost and dropping in the seed that looked like little more than a fleck of dust. It really felt like he was there with me. Sometimes I realised I was listening for something else amid the quiet: the sound of his voice. It was during one of these times that I thought I had the most brilliant idea for the funeral, one that finally seemed worthy of my father, and called Evie immediately to tell her.

'I've finally worked out what we should do for flowers,' I told her. 'We won't have any.'

'What, and have a donation for a heart charity?'

'Well, we could do that but what I meant was that instead of having flowers on the casket we would decorate it with allotment-grown vegetables. Don't you think Dad would like that?'

'Kit,' she said, hesitating a little before deciding that brutality was called for. 'That's a terrible idea.'

They were carnations in the end. Floating pink and white puffballs that waved gaily on their silver stalks. They were too trivial, too bouncy, but what did it really matter? He couldn't see them.

Evie and Seb received a second IPS the day before the funeral. This one arrived in the post in a nondescript white envelope with a typed address. It looked very different to the first, handwritten form they'd been handed, and as we inspected it, we wondered if it had been spat out from a computer and never been touched by a human hand.

In stark capitals, it listed Jakob's weight as a cause for concern and, unlike the first, stated that the IPS could be contested within twenty-four hours if parents believed a weight increase had occurred and the child would be removed from their register of concern.

Evie rang to tell me while I was cooking food for the wake. In one of my fits of decision-making, I'd decided that I'd make quiches, but it was an idea that I was already regretting. The pastry was crumbling in my hands and I'd had to start again from scratch. The concept of finishing them seemed so impossible, so far away, that I almost missed Evie's call, thinking better of my rebuttal of shop-bought food.

I was at the door, keys in hand, when her face flashed up on my workSphere, peering out of it desperately, as though she might be able to step through it into my sitting room if she tried hard enough.

'I don't know what to do. I don't know what more I can do,' Evie told me that morning.

'But has his weight gone up?' I asked. 'Enough...'

'I think so. We tried to weigh him here. He's more than they say he is on the letter but they're not the proper type of scales. Seb's gone out to buy some OSIP-approved ones. We're going to film weighing him live to OSIP when he gets back, and then tomorrow we have to take him to a clinic for a weigh-in. That's the only way we can contest.'

'But the funer—'

'I know, I know. We'll be there. We'll come straight after the weigh-in. But you understand that we have to do this too.'

And so, at our father's funeral, I stood grieving for him alone.

NOW

I'm not alone any more. Mimi is with me.

She's stirring. She does not know where she is and she begins to cry immediately. It seems as though she woke up already crying.

'It's Mummy, my darling,' I coo to her from the front of the car but then her shuffles quieten to nothing.

'Mimi? Mimi?' I can't see any movement, I don't hear any sound. I chide myself for not asking the couple when she last ate, when she last had milk, how long it had been since they'd changed her. I can't be sure if she's skirting on the edges of hunger or if it's just tiredness or something else.

'Stay there,' I tell her. 'Just hold on.' I draw up to a run-down restaurant that squats at the side of the road. Never have I been so glad to see one.

I run round to the back door as soon as I stop the car and open up my arms to her.

'Mimi,' I cry. Her eyes flicker open for just a moment but then they close again.

A weight lifts within me as I circle my arms around her and cradle her body into mine. She is solid; she is here. I bury my face in the top of her head, my tears make wet patches on her thin hair, and I swipe them away: I want to see her clearly.

I simultaneously want to hold her as close to me as I can and gaze into her face.

It's hard to let go but when I do, I clasp both hands around her cheeks and kiss the velvet mushroom top of her nose. But still she sleeps.

There's not the smile of recognition, that look of delight which would take over her whole face each time she'd lock eyes with me after waking. Here, now, her face is heavy with slumber, her eyelids stay closed. I refuse to believe it. I imagine her eyes scrunching up into a giggle and my face responding to hers – my tears turning to laughter, to delight. It's as though I am trying to will her to wakefulness. I pull my mouth into a silly shape, I balloon my cheeks and touch her nose with my own, which would have made her chuckle even louder – if she were awake.

When I cannot wake her, I hold her face in my hands and trace the curve and chub of her cheeks, her tiny rosebud lips, the downy lobe of her ear. Every detail of her is miraculous; I can't get enough of just gazing at her face.

She sleeps on.

But in the next moment her face screws up and she cries out, her eyes still closed.

'What is it, darling?' I croon. I check her all over and find her nappy is full and stinking. She's still not awake. It was what Thomas and I used to call 'a sleep squeak' but I talk to her anyway as though she is listening to my every word. 'Let's go get you changed, there'll be toilets in here,' I tell her, although I don't know what with. I'm completely unprepared.

There's the too-strong smell of disinfectant in the air as I open the doors of the restaurant. A young girl wearing a uniform made up entirely of different shades of brown is mopping the floor in broad, bored strokes. The mop is too wet. Its head is grey from use, and hangs heavily, leaving a trail of splatters as she flings it with force from the bucket across the floor.

'Excuse me, I need to use the toilets. Where are they?' I ask.

The girl doesn't stop mopping but she shrugs her head to the left and I spot the door.

I delight in all the mundane details of changing Mimi, although I have to improvise with toilet paper and towels. Every moment feels wildly precious. I chat to her nonsensically throughout, washing her thoroughly and carefully, hoping that changing her might pull her from her slumber.

When we come out, Mimi slumped over my shoulder, it is quiet but for the drone of the air conditioning, the rhythm of the mop drenching the floor and the Spheres that hang from the ceiling, suspended above me. I can't stop myself from glancing towards them.

A report from OSIP drones on, a list of figures and statistics, one after the other, that all sound the same. A repetitive chain of information, each one indistinguishable from the next.

The figures flash across the screen, in a blue, softly edged font that I suppose has been chosen to look unaggressive. Then the screen flashes to a piece about XC babies.

I go to leave, but a movement through the window catches my eye. At first, I think there is nothing to see. It's a patch of grass, a grey, dusty bush, next to the grey of a near empty car park. I can see the edge of my car in the corner, but there seems little to define the view.

Then, a flutter of wings and I see two eyes, shiny black balls, inquisitive and hungry, peering up at me. It's a robin. His red breast is faded, almost orange, as though he is a little aged and there is something else about the straggly shape of his body that suggests he's not in his prime.

He tilts his head to his side, in that way that birds do when they have spotted something, but this time it is as though it is me that he has spotted, that he has recognised me.

There was a robin that lived at Dad's allotment who used to visit us for worms, so Dad would say. He lived in a hawthorn not far from Dad's plot and over the years did not venture far from it.

The robin jumps forwards a few steps in quick, darting movements, a little closer to the window. He is very still, only moving in the smallest of twitches. He looks inanimate. Then, without warning, he flies off. My eyes cannot follow his path and I lose him.

But moments later he is back, by that grey little bush. He flies into the bush, once again, out of view. All I have to do is wait patiently for him to fly out again. This is his home and he will not go far from it.

Sure enough, moments later, I see him once more. I sense, though it's impossible, that this little dance he's doing, this forwards and backwards, his sharp darts and the speedy flurry of his wings, is a show, just for me.

I watch him until the waitress asks if I want a table. I shake my head and turn to leave.

Seeing that robin disappear one last time into his dusty bush, in that stale-smelling restaurant, makes me consider an alarming thought: where was home to me now?

And would I be able to find a way back to it?

THEN

I wanted to go home but Evie and Seb had still not arrived. The wake had gone on for a couple of hours already and almost all the food had been eaten. My throat was dry and sore from talking too much.

I swayed on the spot, then the sound of a baby bleating made me stiffen.

'I'm sorry,' Evie mouthed over the heads of Dad's allotment friends, who'd opened a bottle of whisky and had started making toasts in his name.

'How did it go?' I asked her when we reached each other.

'I was just about to ask you the same thing.'

'Did they throw the IPS out?'

Evie smiled at me sadly and her eyes filled with tears. She sniffed loudly. 'Yes,' she said, at last, as though she could not believe it to speak it.

'Oh, Evie.' We collapsed into one another.

'How was it here?' Evie asked, her voice muffled in my hair.

'Oh, fine. Awful. I didn't make the food in the end. I bought every last morsel. I don't know what I was thinking.'

'Good. That's good.' She laughed but wiped a tear from

her cheek. 'I'm just so glad it's over. Not the funeral, I mean. You know what I mean.' She touched a strand of my hair as though it were out of place. 'I'm sorry we weren't here. I can't believe the timing.'

'Don't worry. It's what Dad would have wanted.'

'Still… I'm sorry. Do you want to take off? We can clear up. You look done in. This might go on for a while.' Evie eyed the whisky glasses.

The evening was cool after the heat of the small hall that we'd hired for the wake. Rain had started to fall lightly on the streets but I headed past the Tube station. I liked the feeling of it dampening my face, a gentle caress after the hardness, the steepness of the day. I tried to concentrate on the sound it made falling on to the streets, but the Spheres buzzed overhead with story after story, drowning it out.

I was tired from talking, from standing in groups, from wearing the black clothes that weighed heavy upon me, but I wasn't ready to return home yet. I stepped into one of the pubs that was full, turning to the side to squeeze myself through the heaving bodies towards the bar.

With Evie not at the funeral, I had unwittingly become its centre-point and now I enjoyed passing unnoticed through the crowds. No one stopped me, no one wanted to offer their condolences or ask how I was. There was nobody who talked about how much Dad meant to them, nobody here who even knew that he had died.

There was a terrible part of me that felt it was all a charade. I was tired of saying the same thing over and over, weary of putting my grief into words; each time that I did, it became a little more tired, a little more dreary, a little less real.

Just then, someone touched my shoulder. Their hand glanced upon the edge of my top and rested for a moment on the bare skin of my neck. It was the lightest of touches but in that crowded bar, it was so intimate, so tender. I took a breath and exhaled raggedly; something within me stirred.

'Kit?' His voice was soft but I heard it nonetheless through the din as though it pierced me. He said my name thoughtfully, as though it were something important, something to consider.

I turned towards the voice and there he was, this man I felt I both knew and did not know at all, as if we were meant to be meeting, at this exact time, in this very place, as if it was always meant to be. He was smiling at me in such a kind way that a lump rose in my throat, the sadness that I had contained all day amplified at the sight of his gentle face.

Without thinking of what I was doing, I let myself sink into his arms. He didn't say anything as I reached towards him, my head come to rest upon his chest. His arms closed around me. I felt the warm strength of them. And I had the overwhelming sense that here I was safe; here I could rest; here I could be.

The beat of his heart sounded louder then than anything else that surrounded us. Louder than the frenetic, drunken talk in the bar, stronger than the grating voices of the Spheres that morphed from piece to piece in an unending loop.

And then, as though I were waking from a dream, I realised what I was doing and straightened, released him. His arms tightened around me for just a moment longer as he felt me shift. Then he let me go.

'Thomas,' I said. He looked at me in the same way as when we'd met at Jakob's naming ceremony, as though he were committing my face to memory. I leant into him to talk, my face close to his. If I turned to the side I could have grazed my lips on the stubble on his cheek. 'I'm sorry, I'm not in the habit of greeting people like that, I promise. Especially people I have only met once.'

'That's good,' he said back. 'That means that you only do it for me.'

'I... I...'

'It's OK,' he said gently. 'You don't have to explain. I don't, umm, do that either. Maybe it's just that—'

But then before he could finish his sentence I surprised us both, leaning in towards his face and lingering there for a moment and so our eyes were just centimetres apart. I saw his eyes widen, his pupils dilate to a molten brown.

We kissed softly at first, our lips only lightly brushing, but then his hands were in my hair, cupping my wet cheeks, and we held each other with a sort of desperation. A longing that until that moment I wasn't aware I possessed.

'I'm sorry,' I said again when we pulled apart.

'Don't be. Do you want to go somewhere a little quieter?' He'd had to shout 'quieter' as the group next to us started to yell something. It made us both laugh. I nodded.

When we reached the street, Thomas put his hand out to catch the raindrops on his fingertips. And then he rubbed his fingers together, pondering it.

'Shall we walk? Do you mind the rain?'

'No, I like it.'

We fell into step together and walked easily along the pavements. Our hands swung next to one another, almost touching.

The streets were dark but lit up by the Spheres' ghostly glow. We crossed the road and headed down a residential street. The houses were old, tall and narrow and were decorated with different types of cornicing, and semi-circles of stained glass above the front doors that depicted their house numbers. Most of the windows were lit up and so we could see into sitting rooms, bedrooms and hallways. There was the further glow of workSpheres which dominated many rooms, and sometimes we saw people sitting around one, loading different channels across the whole of its globe.

'You never feel properly alone, do you?' Thomas said, gesturing to the Spheres at the bus shelter, which droned out monotone words.

'No,' I agreed.

'Do you know anywhere that doesn't have them?'

'One place,' I said. 'My dad's old allotment. I've been there a lot since he died.'

'I'm sorry. Seb did tell me. We don't have to talk about it if you don't want to.'

'It's fine, it's just... I've been talking about it all day. It was his funeral today. That's why I'm wearing this.' I pulled at my black clothes uneasily. 'I don't usually look quite this maudlin.'

Thomas reached for my hand and I held on to him gratefully. We didn't speak for a while, which I liked about him. There was a quiet between us but it didn't matter, the way he touched me was more comforting than words.

We walked and walked that night. At each turning, we just chose a left or a right. At each junction, we patiently waited to cross the road. At times I would sneak a look at him but he would always notice and meet my glance with a smile.

I shivered, even through my black coat. The rain sank insidiously through the layers and chilled me.

'This is no good,' Thomas said. 'I would happily walk around with you until the sun comes up. But I'm rather worried you might get hypothermia.'

'I've had a good time. On a night where I didn't think that was remotely possible. But I'd better go home.'

'I'll walk you.' We laughed together again and then as naturally as if we'd been united for years, we fell into each other. He kissed me on my forehead and then down in a line, in between my eyebrows, on the tip of my nose, on the ridge above my lips.

And suddenly I didn't feel as cold.

NOW

I'm almost out of the door of the restaurant. If I'd not stopped to look at the robin, I would have missed it.

The Spheres flash with a familiar image – it's a building, grey, squat and large. I recognise it immediately and just seeing it makes my lungs crush, all the breath in my body is expelled so quickly I feel it as pain. It's the building I have just come from. The building where Mimi was hidden.

I don't need to read the headlines, or hear the disembodied voice to know the story. I catch a glimpse of the dark, short-haired boy I saw asleep in bed carried out by an enforcer. He looks very small in his arms. I notice that he is still asleep.

More OSIP raids found hidden babies. It appears they have been heavily drugged.

I catch sight of a figure in the crowd for just a second before the camera pans away. It's the way he is standing, it's the shape of his face. I only see him for a second but it's him, I'm sure.

He is outside the building in the crowd watching the children being brought out.

Thomas.

*

I'd gone back to the library in the South East quarter.

When we had received our first few IPSs it struck me that that was where I should go. I felt myself pulled there, magnetised towards it. I arranged with Thomas that he should take Mimi for part of the morning, then I set off towards the hospital, in a winding route.

When I walked in, the first time that I had been back there since I'd got the formula milk for Evie, there was no one there. A different puzzle was on the table. It was not quite finished, missing just a handful of pieces in a patch near one of the corners.

'Hello,' I called out. 'Anyone here?'

A woman with short, untidy bobbed hair appeared from the storage cupboard.

'Hi there, can I help you?' she said. It took me a moment to realise that it was the same young woman that I'd seen on my first visit. Her hair had grown out in that time. She looked like she hadn't slept properly in days, her skin pale, almost translucent. But it was definitely her.

'I hope so.'

What I never liked about the plan was that it all depended upon on us being split up from each other.

'But you have to go separately,' Iris said shortly. 'Travelling as a family is too conspicuous.' That was her name, Iris, the young woman at the library. She reminded me of the flower, her thin body resembling its spear-like stalk, surging from the ground.

'Mimi would go first. She'd be taken to a safe place –

somewhere you have no affiliation to, somewhere no one would begin to consider looking. And then you'd leave too, staying in safe houses, moving from quarter to quarter. Always moving.'

'And Mimi—'

'She'd be looked after,' Iris cut in. 'We are connected to a network of helpers through the libraries. Some people think libraries are obsolete now but in a way that's helped our movement. They underestimate the power of this space to unite us.' Iris's eyes glowed as she spoke.

'When do we see Mimi again?'

'After that, you and… what's your partner's name?'

'Thomas.'

'You separate too. We'll get you both onto different boats, take you across the Channel. Then you'll all meet up.'

'In France,' I said dully. My mind swarmed with the little I knew of our neighbouring country. The democratic government over there had been overthrown years ago and I'd heard stories of child-trafficking. I wished that I felt something like relief or conviction but though Iris was offering me the kind of lifeline that I hadn't dared to dream of, I was numb with doubt. 'It just doesn't seem possible that we can do this.'

Iris didn't linger on my reservations. 'And from there, Germany. They are still receiving immigrants. You'll get support there.'

'In Germany,' I tried to sound convinced although the enormity of what Iris was telling me was too much to imagine.

'It's the only way,' Iris said shortly. 'Or you stay here. You know what will happen if you do that. Think it over. Talk to…'

'Thomas,' I said again.

'But don't leave it too long if you want to do it. There'll be someone else who will take the space.' She turned away from me and picked up a small stack of books that were on the desk in front of her. I could tell my hesitance was irritating to her.

'Has it worked? For other people?' I blurted out.

'Yes.' She paused. 'For some of them, yes.'

Telling Thomas changed everything.

He went back to the library the next day to speak to Iris or whoever was there. It was as though he couldn't believe that we might have this chance until he heard it from someone else. When he arrived back, he could barely contain his enthusiasm for the plan. He'd already set up a meeting the next day for us both to speak to Iris about what to do next. He'd asked questions, found out more about the operation than I'd thought of.

'The library network is part of a larger underground resistance movement,' he told me. 'There's someone involved who works for OSIP who removes the wristbands apparently. He's the brother of someone, of someone. He's risking everything. He thinks the wristbands are not only receptors for the IPS data but they are trackers too and so they'll take them off as soon as they take Mimi.'

I noticed he was speaking about it as though we had already decided it was going to happen, we had already agreed that we would do it. I swallowed hard, trying again to visualise the plan unfolding; imagining, unsuccessfully, us travelling across Europe to safety together.

'Apparently,' Thomas continued, 'though OSIP will be looking for us, they won't publicise it. They don't want it out on the Spheres that people are on the run from them. So it's possible to avoid them if we follow all the instructions and keep a low profile.'

'Are we really going to do this?' I said, but Thomas wasn't listening to me. He had swept Mimi up, high into the air, and so she gave a gleeful chuckle and then dangled her from side to side. But then he wrapped her close into a hug and looked right at me.

'We have to.'

The following day Iris said she would arrange for us to meet with the person who would oversee us and told us not return to the library unless we had to.

'We need a meeting place that is private. Away from Spheres,' she said. 'It's better if it's somewhere that's linked to you but if you can't think of anywhere, we can come up with one.'

'I know a place,' I volunteered. 'The allotments in the west quarter.' Thomas squeezed my hand. I'd taken Mimi there a few times but it was too difficult to keep things going when she was little and I hadn't been at all since we'd started receiving IPSs.

'That will work,' Iris said. I told her in detail which was our plot, drawing it out as a simple map.

'Be there at ten o'clock on Wednesday morning. Just one of you. Don't bring Mimi. If no one comes then we won't have been able to go ahead for some reason.'

'Why might that be?' Thomas asked quickly.

Iris frowned. 'I don't know, sometimes it's just not possible.'

She eyed our panic-stricken faces. I hadn't felt sure of the plan, but now the thought that it might not be a possible felt like a vice griping my heart.

'Just see what happens on Wednesday,' she said. I had the strongest sense that she couldn't be any more reassuring.

On the day of the meet, I packed a bag with a flask of tea, the key to the small shed, my gardening gloves, as though I really were going to spend time at the allotment like I used to. It steadied me to do it. We'd agreed that it would be better that it was me that went to avoid raising suspicion. I had felt utterly torn between the distinct desires of needing to be the one to do it and wanting to relinquish the job wholly over to Thomas.

I'd marched over to the allotments with a briskness that I didn't feel. After what Iris had said, I felt sure that no one would be there but until that moment came, there was still the hope that there was the chance of not losing Mimi.

I thought I saw a figure standing by the entrance as I approached but as I got closer I saw it was just some loose tarpaulin caught on the hedge. I hurried forwards anyway but when I reached the gate I made myself not look around. Thomas and I had talked endlessly about how we must try not to look conspicuous, that perhaps the person we were meeting was watching us to judge if we were capable of undertaking such a dangerous operation. And so I didn't linger. I headed towards dad's old patch with a certainty I didn't feel and though no one was there, I opened up the shed door, busied myself with finding a fork and started attacking one of the beds, pulling up the weeds that were choking it.

I could feel tears building, a lump in my throat growing;

part of me wanted to sink down into the damp earth and howl, but something stopped me. I carried on sorting and working as methodically as dad would have done. I didn't even notice the man until he was at my side.

'This is a good place to meet,' he said, eyes roving over my dad's neglected beds.

I carried on working, thrusting the fork firmly into the ground, pulling at roots and removing stones as though he wasn't even there.

'I wasn't sure you were going to come,' I said. I glanced in his direction. He was bald, maybe in his fifties. He wore a grey-green overcoat even though the sun was warm, but I noticed he didn't look out of place standing talking at the allotments on a Wednesday morning.

As though I hadn't spoken, he carried on: 'I understand that you have been taken through what would happen and you want go ahead.'

'Yes.'

'I can send someone for your daughter on Sunday afternoon. You'll have to leave immediately afterwards. You need to take as much cash with you as you can but don't withdraw it too soon so as not to draw attention. I'll give you a list of safe houses to go to.'

'That's it?'

'Yes, more or less. I'm going to give you a map. On it are the roads that you need to avoid and the safe houses that you can travel to. I was told you have your own car. You'll swap vehicles a few times. It's all marked on the map but I'll take you through it now so you can get familiar with it. Use the next few days to prepare.'

I nodded although my mind was whirring.

'Will it really work? Just by avoiding roads and moving around, we won't get caught?'

'Nothing's definite but yes, unless you're unlucky, it should work. Your route takes you through areas with lower resources so there's less chance you'll be found.'

'OK,' I said, although I still felt unsure. 'And it's got to happen so soon?'

'If you leave it any longer, it might be too late.' He bent down towards the vegetable bed and cleared a few weeds by hand. When I looked again, I saw that an artichoke seedling that was sprouting there now had space to grow.

'What about all the stories on the Spheres about kidnappings in Europe?' I said in a rush. I had all kinds of questions like this and I had the sense that this man might disappear at any moment and my chance would be gone.

'It happens but it's not as bad as they say,' the bald man said simply.

'And where will Mimi be taken to on Sunday?'

'It's best that you don't know.'

'I have to know,' I said. 'I don't think I can go through with this if I don't.'

He shook his head, but he must have seen something in my face as after a few moments he relented.

'OK, I'll tell you a postcode and a number – the number will be the flat where she'll be kept. Don't go there, though. I can't stress that enough. You will endanger not only your daughter but everyone involved in this operation.'

'I won't,' I replied quickly.

He gave me some more details, taking me methodically

through the map I held in unsteady hands. When he was finally gone, I had the uncanny feeling that I might have just imagined the whole conversation. When I related it back to Thomas he kept asking questions that I wished I'd thought of.

'OK then,' he said when he realised I couldn't tell him anymore. 'Sunday.'

'Yes. We are sure about this, aren't we?'

'Yes. I mean it's far too great an opportunity to turn down.'

'It's just all happening so quickly.'

'It has to though,' Thomas said gently. 'Remember... it's our only chance.'

Thomas tried to make me view it how he did – like it was a miraculous discovery. If I hadn't helped Evie with the formula milk, I would never have known about the library. If there hadn't been a space, they might not have been able to help us. Though I agreed that it was the right thing to do, I couldn't shake my discomfort; it all just felt too unreal to come true. I thought a lot about Evie, wondering if, as she and Seb approached the mounting number of IPS for Jakob, she would have considered doing this. I even wondered if she had gone to the library when Jakob was taken after all, despite her emphatic dismissal of the place.

Like a weight hanging around my neck, a part of me questioned what we were doing. Was Mimi really better off with us? If we'd received this many IPSs, would a compound offer her a better chance? I tried to ignore it and listen instead to that fierce, burning instinct that told me she should be with us, that no one could love her more. And wasn't that better than what a compound would provide her with? I couldn't voice it to Thomas, though I wondered if he ever thought it too.

But last night, at the charging station, I had seen the Spheres.

Raids were being led by OSIP on houses where they found children who had been hoarded. That was the word that they had used: *hoarded*, as though they were little more than cargo.

The children were kept under floorboards. They were malnourished, in ill health; they needed urgent medical attention. There was a video clip of them being carried out by enforcers, one after the other. Each child looked more waif-like than the next; their eyes were large and haunted. One, glimpsed covered in a blanket on a stretcher, had not survived.

Despite what Iris and the bald man – we never knew his name – had told us about OSIP not wanting to publicise that people tried to escape them, things were changing. It was out in public, it would only be a matter of time before our faces would be broadcast over the Spheres.

The news piece felt like a message too, directly from OSIP to us. It said: *You handed your children over to strangers and look what happened. You didn't keep them safe. You didn't protect them.*

That was when I decided that I had to come for Mimi, that I would leave the very next morning. I would not wait to debate it with Thomas, who would try to convince me not to believe the OSIP propaganda, who would waste precious time talking over what the best thing was to do. I had to get to Mimi, I had to go to her.

What if they were going to keep her under floorboards? What if she ended up being carried out on a stretcher? I couldn't let that happen. I wouldn't.

THEN

Thomas showed me his paintings.

He painted in the hours when he was not at work, either early in the morning or late into the night.

Faces, never turned towards the painter, caught in a moment. It felt almost voyeuristic looking at them, as though I was spying on someone. I stopped in front of one, just the profile of a face, tilted downwards in thought. There was something about the sweep of the hair, how it framed the face in a line, the shape of the cheek.

'That's me,' I exclaimed.

Thomas nodded. 'It was after we first met. First ever met. At Evie and Seb's.'

'Really? You painted this after that?'

'That very night. Smelling of burnt sausages.'

It was like the final piercing of the arrow, the killing shot.

'I love you,' I told him. It was too early to say the words, even though it was how I felt. I remembered coldly how they'd lost their lustre with Roger, and how I didn't want to say them aloud to Thomas and not mean it, fully, completely and utterly. I didn't want them to become haggard with time, shapeless with familiarity.

'I bloody hope so,' Thomas said back. 'I mean… I love you too. But I think you knew that. Without me having to say.' He kissed me lightly on the lips and then left me in front of the portrait he had made of me.

I couldn't stop examining it. I ran my fingers over the ridges the paint made. I traced the line of my face that Thomas had captured, my eyes never leaving the shape of the profile, as though she might disappear if I turned away.

NOW

I try to feed Mimi. My breasts have filled again. I wonder if it might wake her but she doesn't latch, her eyelids remain glued shut, her mouth sealed. I try again but her chin just bumps gently off my body, missing the vital connection. I want to keep trying although part of me realises that it's pointless, and as I place her in the back of the car, the frustration stays with me. I keep missing the seatbelt fastening. It takes me several tries before it clicks.

I tuck my coat around Mimi's sleeping body once more and as I do my mind fills with all of the violations I'm committing. As if they are real, the IPSs I'd be given flash before me.

I realise that I am trying not to think about Thomas. Not when I finally held our daughter to me, not as I drive away with her lying behind me like a secret. I don't want to think about him being at the building – I don't want to think about him being close by.

I find that it's difficult to piece his face together. The longer I drive, the more he seems like a character from a dream that I have difficulty remembering. I can see his shades of light and dark, but cannot pin him down into hard lines; clear, defined shapes.

My husband.

I look at him so little now.

I don't see him properly, face to face. Eye to eye. Not since Mimi went, or maybe even before that.

It's not because he looks like Mimi. It's not that he reminds me of her too much. There are, of course, gestures they share, the way they rub their eyes when tired, the very specific shape that their mouth makes when they yawn, the curled position when they sleep, that only I, a studier, a lover, a mother could know about. That mundane, sacred knowledge of which I am the only expert.

It's because I worry that if we search each other's faces for too long, we will find nothing left of the love we once had. We will be forced to accept that it has fled.

I think Thomas feels the same.

He doesn't demand it either, he ducks away from my eyeline too. I believe that we are both just waiting, keeping our heads down, and so perhaps a seed of our love will grow again, coiling new roots around the carcass of what we once were. And perhaps that waiting, that refusal to leave until something changes, something grows, perhaps that is love to us now.

THEN

It was the day after one of our first dates, where we seemed to spend the whole dinner marvelling at each other rather than actually eating food. I had been working or putting up a good pretence of working at a life document for one of my newer clients. I'd rewatched some videos so many times that, watching them again, I knew exactly what was going to happen, just before it did. It felt like some sort of forecasting, made from the very safest of positions.

Then I turned to some old files of Jonah's that I wanted to revisit. There was the phone call that I'd listened to, all that time ago, on the day that Evie and Seb were beginning induction, saved into his daughter's file. They had been speaking but Jonah had ended the call out of the blue. There had been noise interference and so I hadn't been able to understand what Genevieve was telling him.

I listened to it a few times in a row without trying to clear it up at all. I tried to zone into that other sound that just covered their words. The dog's paws clacking, the static whir of a workSphere, disjointed words, the hasty goodbye. What was I missing?

It was an audio call, which wasn't unusual for Jonah, although video calls were generally more common for most of my clients. Sometimes it helped to see their faces during phone conversations – particularly with family members and close friends. It all helped 'to paint a picture', as I was repeatedly told during my training all those years ago.

I spotted a tiny face icon in the corner of the file as it played. I touched it and the visuals opened up from the jagged peaks and troughs of the audiograph to the faces of both Jonah and Genevieve filling the screen. As they spoke I could see that neither of them were looking at the screen.

The audio-graph footage had recorded the visuals even though it had not been a video call. I was catching them both unaware as they were speaking. Very few clients turned their cameras on like this, although it was an option. I'd never known Jonah to do it before.

Genevieve was reading a manual about dog training in her kitchen. She was cooking something on the hob – I could see it steaming in the background. That could have been the sound on her end that was muffling the audio. And then, just at the point when I could tell from the rise in her tone that she wanted to tell Jonah something, a small blue light appeared in the background above one of her angular-looking taps and the slow rumble of water coming to a boil. I quickly removed the kitchen sounds and swiped to replay the call.

'Dad? There's something I want to tell you,' Genevieve was saying. She peered up towards the camera. 'We haven't told anyone yet…'

Jonah was studying his goSphere as he listened to Genevieve. He was flicking through item after item at such a speed that I couldn't keep up with what it was he was reading. They were articles upon articles but I couldn't see their content. The only discernible feature was that a few of them were marked with the same OSIP logo – perhaps not all, although I couldn't properly tell – but there were certainly a number that were. He stopped swiping as Genevieve said that, leaving a document bearing an OSIP logo open on his goSphere.

'Are you all right?' he said, turning towards the workSphere.

'Yes, I'm fine. It's good…' she mumbled. 'It's good news.'

'What is it, Gen?'

'Josh and I – we want to start a family,' she said quietly. She smiled. It spread across her whole face and so I could see the wide gap between her front teeth.

Jonah sat up straight suddenly from his hunched over position. The OSIP document on his goSphere continued to blink. I was able to read a couple of words that were written in stark capitals; it said something about 'the XC children', although I couldn't be certain. 'Hold on,' Jonah said, standing now. 'Don't go anywhere – I'll be right with you.'

'Dad? You don't have to—'

'Bye, love.'

And he'd closed down the call.

I pondered it. It was valuable for his life document but what really struck me were the documents I'd seen flash through his goSphere.

Jonah had no association with OSIP that I knew of. I'd never seen him reading anything about them before in any other context, nor had I heard him talk about them.

I could understand why he would rush over to Genevieve

on hearing her news; they were close and she didn't live terribly far away. I'd known him to take off to see her at a moment's notice before. But since this call they hadn't spoken about it again, unless I'd missed it. As far as I was aware, Genevieve hadn't started induction or begun the process of creating an XC baby.

I turned this over in my mind, trying to piece it together, when there was a knock on the door.

It was Thomas, brandishing a bag of foil containers.

'Dinner!' he exclaimed.

I pulled him and the steaming bag of food towards me and forgot everything else.

NOW

Mimi's a heap in the back of the car.

I can't stop looking in the mirror to try to glimpse her face. I'm looking backwards more than I look forwards. But then I catch the red haze of the recharge light.

I remember as a child being in Dad's old car with Evie, him telling us to lean forwards to help the car up the hill. We'd fold ourselves over so our heads hung downwards; it really felt as though it did make a difference.

My body tenses into something like that position now. I hunch over the wheel, willing the car onwards with my thoughts and my body. We only need to get close enough so we are able to walk the rest of the way.

When I'd looked up the postcode that the bald man had given us for where Mimi would be taken, it seemed almost cruel that it was close to the area where Evie now lives. We have never been to their house. I haven't even seen pictures of it, but I had her address and couldn't stop myself from working out the distance between the two places. Before Mimi even left us, I half hoped that if something went wrong perhaps we could collect her and go to Evie's before we made our next move. Despite everything, I wondered if my sister might help us. It wasn't a real plan, though, and as I press down on the accelerator, I realise I never believed that I would actually have to do it.

We haven't masked the distance that's grown between us with birthday cards or Christmas presents. It feels more honest to call our fracture what it is: a splintering, the breaking of us.

I can't bear to speak to my sister.

I can't bear her but, right now, she is the only one I can turn to. It's simple geography that leads me to her – that where she moved to is not far from where Mimi was hidden – and a matter of chemistry: I only have so much charge that will only get me only so far.

I have no desire to see her and part of me is terrified that going to her will be a mistake. I'm not certain that I will find the refuge that Mimi and I so desperately need. I hope that she will help me without ever knowing of it, that they won't be there so I can take from her the things we need and leave.

The likelihood is low; it's early afternoon on a Saturday and I imagine she'll have gone out in the morning but will have returned to relax for the rest of the day as used to be her rhythm. I feel my shoulders grind thinking that we might see her, that we will have to talk.

But I've run out of options.

And I won't give up.

THEN

It didn't feel so much a choice as a necessity when we moved in together after a few weeks.

It was so quick that even Evie raised her eyebrows. She asked if perhaps the relationship was moving too fast.

All I could answer was yes, it was, but it still absolutely felt like something I had to do. I moved into his flat, which was far bigger than mine; I would never have been able to afford a place like it on my own with my capped salary and housing credits.

'Kit's in love,' Seb said, almost petulantly, walking past with Jakob in his arms. 'Remember that?'

Evie ignored the jibe, dismissing him wearily with a wave of her hand.

I didn't want to ask how things were between them. I had the sense that there was something they weren't telling me. They'd begun sniping at each other more and more. Seb was usually the one to start the exchanges. It was often so quick and underhand, I was reminded of those old movies where two adversaries are talking calmly, then suddenly they draw daggers on each other and begin to fight.

I spent less and less time with them. Partly because of Thomas, partly because of the tension between them and the small but unshakeable feeling that Evie and I were not quite connecting, somehow. Each time I saw Jakob he'd grown so much more that he almost seemed to be different baby to that first, tiny sleep-filled face I'd held in the hospital.

His cheeks ballooned, somewhat comically, like a caricature. His forehead deepened, widened, and he developed a slightly worried expression that would cross his face each time he encountered something new. I'd cry out in surprise watching him grasp at the toys set in a wooden bar across his bouncer. The last time I'd seen him he hadn't known that the toys were there but now he reached for them, studied them, explored the texture of them in his palm.

'Yes, he's starting doing that now,' Evie would say busily, as though she didn't see it as the miracle that I did. She was distracted, expressing milk into bottles or putting on another wash of baby-grows that had once been too large for Jakob and were now too snug. Evie, too, was changing. Sometimes when I remembered how she used to be, in her life before Jakob, working into the night, talking through her cases, she didn't seem like the same person in front of me now who was so singularly wedded to home-making.

I'd grow silent and in those moments would often imagine how Dad would have loved to have watched Jakob change, every phase. He would have studied each detail as though he were watching a seedling unfurling and his watchfulness could somehow coach its growth along.

'I wish Dad—' I'd start to say but I'd stop myself when I'd see the look that cast over Evie's face. Every other emotion had quite fallen away; all that was left was a sinkhole of pain and loss. I felt it too then, within myself.

Getting together with Thomas so soon after Dad's death troubled me sometimes. I wondered if the many aspects of grief – the shock, the disbelief and then the ache, the persistent ache that he was gone – had poured themselves into the ferocity of my love for Thomas.

But other times, especially when I was with Evie and Jakob, the grief would open inside me. It was as though I touched something in a certain place and it would overwhelm me: an ever-extending, multiplying expanse, infinitely growing, infinitely painful. Then I would be certain that my grief for our father was on its own, it lived and breathed quite separately to any other emotion, and it would rear up in a single beat if I let it.

We were selling his flat – although Evie had in fact done everything. She'd taken her responsibility as the eldest seriously; she insisted on handling the finances and the division of his estate. She said it was the least she could do after she had missed the funeral.

Jakob's weight wasn't a problem now. His belly grew distended and globe-like, his neck fell in soft folds, his legs were reassuringly squashy and chubby. Sometimes Evie showed me the graph that the health visitors would fill in that showed his weight rising in a line that swooped upwards, angular, like the wing of a swallow.

There had been no more IPSs since they'd contested his weight gain on the day of Dad's funeral.

At least, there had been none that Evie had spoken to me about.

NOW

During one of the last times that we spoke, Evie had told me one detail about the house they were moving to.

It was a stilted, uncomfortable conversation through our workSpheres, built out of silence, repetition and interruptions. It was as though we couldn't bear to hear the other speak and so our words tumbled on top of one another's, struggling to be heard.

'It's just off the canal,' she'd said. 'Our only neighbour is the boatyard that's a ten-minute walk away.' The house was out of the quarters. Now she was part of OSIP, doing work that I didn't ask her about, she was ranked much higher in housing credits, high enough that she could live beyond the quarters' boundaries now if she chose to, although not in the elite areas where the XC children were raised.

I'd taken her tone to be boastful and hadn't been able to resist saying in reply, 'I suppose when you can't get on with other people then having no neighbours is a benefit.'

Evie was stunned into silence for a moment before she bit back: 'I was trying to help you, Kit. If you can't see that then you're going to have a nasty awakening. I was helping you.'

'You think you were,' I snapped. 'That's a pretty convenient way of seeing the damage you do, if you ask me.'

'You can't resist giving your opinion on everything, can you? The world according to Kit.'

'Evie,' I said. I had tried to take a breath. 'Evie.'

But she had already hung up.

The car makes it to just a short distance from the boatyard.

'Time to walk now, Meems,' I say. She's still sleepy, the drug they gave her still in effect, and so I bundle her up to me. She stirs a little, utters a mumbling sound that makes me ache for her. There's the sharp, needling sensation of my milk letting down in response to her being close to me.

I need to feed her, and myself. I'd thought that the ravenous hunger I'd had in spikes during pregnancy would pass once I had her, I didn't realise how much fuel I'd need for breastfeeding. In the early days, I was eating with an intensity I'd not encountered before, desperately trying to replace the calories that I was passing on to her.

The makeshift nappy I made for her has already soaked through. I hold her even more closely and start to walk along the canal path. It's pretty and unreal, like something out of a brochure or an advertisement on the Spheres.

A soft light bounces along the towpath. As Evie told me, there is no one else there – no other houses, and we don't pass any walkers either. I'm glad, as I'm exposed out here on the path. I'm very aware that Mimi's not wearing enough. I try to wrap my coat around her and though she doesn't seem cold pressed up close to me, my eyes wander guiltily from side to side.

If we meet an enforcer now, everything will be over.

I won't be able to explain why neither of us is wearing our bands. There's no doubt that we would be stopped because of what Mimi is wearing, and indeed what I look like. I'm still wearing my pyjamas underneath my coat; I haven't showered or brushed my hair or teeth. I don't want to know what I look like.

I can't be sure if we turned the right way down the canal. If we don't come to a house soon then we will have to turn back in the opposite direction. I examine Mimi to see how she is faring from being outside. Her cheeks are blossoming pink, her eyelids still sunk closed. I'm guessing that she has not been out at all from the flat that I took her from – did she wonder what had happened? Did she think we had deserted her?

I ask her now: 'Meems, what did you do in the flat? The one with the other children, with the man and the woman?'

I stroke a finger on a cheek.

'It looks like you were given enough to eat. Did they take care of you? Were you all right?'

Mimi's face crumples for a moment in her sleep.

'You know that you were only there with them, we were only apart so we could all be together again – you, me... and Daddy.'

'Think of the bigger picture,' I hear Thomas's voice ringing out in my head. 'It's painful now, but it means that we can have a future. We can be together.'

He must have almost driven himself hoarse repeating those words to me. Because I never wanted to be parted from her, not for a single second.

THEN

Evie said that she had to see me. Alone. Right away.

'I'll come to you,' she said on the goSphere.

'Are you bringing Jakob?' I asked.

'No,' she said shortly, and gave no other explanation.

We met at a coffee shop that was round the corner from our flat.

She was late arriving. I'd already drunk one of the strong coffees that came in a glass and the caffeine was teeming through my mind, reverberating against my skull. I couldn't stop myself from doing a double-take when I saw her pulling open the door of the café. She was thinner than I'd ever seen her. She looked almost swamped in the clothes that she'd pulled on and her hair hung in dull, heavy ropes around her face. For a moment, I hadn't recognised her.

'What's going on? It sounded like an emergency.'

'I haven't been completely honest with you,' Evie said. 'There's something you need to know. We decided not to tell anyone until we got to this point, I'm not sure why but we did. Anyway, we're there now, we're at the point where we have to tell people.'

'What is it? You're talking in riddles.'

'OSIP,' she said, dropping her voice. 'We've had another four IPSs.' She poured her coffee down her throat as though it were a strong whisky that could numb her.

'So you have five,' I said.

'So we have five. And if we get two more then, then...' She tilted the glass as far it would go until it was quite empty.

She let the words settle, permeate.

'You need to come and spend some time with Jakob. Just in case.'

I couldn't speak. The coffee I'd drunk hung in my stomach, all of a sudden it made me feel nauseous. My mind was a blur. I imagined Jakob going, what it would to do to Evie. I briefly wondered if this was the reason why I had felt a little disconnected from Evie recently. She'd been keeping this all in, perhaps even to shield me from it.

'I don't want to sound melodramatic, but it's a real possibility now,' Evie said. She was speaking quickly but then she stopped, as though she'd run out of words, the wind gone from her. She didn't need to say it; Jakob was only five months old, a huge distance before he'd reach his first birthday and the system would reset.

'Of course,' I said. 'How are you?'

Evie tried to smile but her mouth wouldn't make the right shape, it twisted awkwardly, falsely. 'I'm... terrible, actually.'

'Do you want to talk about it?'

'What good would it do?' But then she launched into a string of dialogue. She spoke fast, as though the words were running out from her, escaping a captor. 'I can't sleep any more. I just don't sleep. And then all day I feel half asleep,

I keep making mistakes, I can't hold on to my mood. My hair's falling out, handfuls of it come away when I wash it. I can't look at Jakob any more without crying. I cry when I get him up in the morning, I cry when I play peekaboo with him, I cry when I feed him. I didn't know that I had this much water inside me. And all of that, it doesn't matter. How I feel is... irrelevant. It's nothing. I've failed Jakob, Kit. I've failed our family.'

'No,' I said. 'No, Evie. Of course you haven't. It's just...' But I didn't have the words to make things better and I had the sharp sense that this was how she felt. Powerless, the world so far from her control, as though she might as well give up.

'Seb and I are barely speaking to each other, although we have to pretend that we are. One of the IPSs was for a "tense family atmosphere" and so we have to play happy families whenever we go out. It's just all such...'

She trailed off.

'Maybe—' I started to say.

'Please don't say that it might not happen,' Evie continued. 'All five of them might not have happened, but they did. We'll have been red-flagged now, I'm sure of it. Just like your friends – Marie and Leo – in your building. It's only a matter of time now. The important thing is making sure that we enjoy every moment that we have left with Jakob. Although that also feels impossible.'

'OK,' I said. 'OK. There's nothing I can say that will make this any better but I'm here. I'm here for you. For Seb and Jakob. I'm on your side, all right? You're not alone.'

'Thank you, Kit,' Evie said, her voice sounded tired and

weary. 'You're... you're... but the problem isn't with us, it's with, it's with...' Evie looked lost.

'OSIP,' I finished for her. 'The problem is with OSIP.'

'Come on, let's walk,' Evie stood quickly.

'Now?'

'Now.' She reached down for her bag and turned to leave the bustling café. I had to rush to keep up with her.

'Did you see them?' she asked when we reached an empty street. 'That couple. They looked like they were listening to us.'

I tried to picture them but found I couldn't.

'No,' I admitted.

Evie moved quickly through the streets, turning down alleyways, crossing roads, in what I imagined she hoped was an unpredictable way. Only when we were away from the café did she tell me what she'd seen.

'They were sitting a few tables down from us. They'd been there since I arrived. I wouldn't have noticed them except there was a moment when the woman reached out for the teapot and began to pour it but there was no tea left in it. And then they just continued to sit there. Not moving, not talking. The man made some kind of gesture with his head when you mentioned OSIP. Then the woman turned to look towards us. That's when I dragged you out of there.'

I didn't answer but ran through the scene in my head. It seemed unlikely that we were being spied upon, but Evie's fear was very real; I saw it her eyes, in the way she walked stiffly as though she were carrying a great weight.

'You thought that they were listening to us?' I asked.

'I should have been more careful.'

'But nothing you said was bad.'

'It was bad enough,' she said. 'I'd better get home. But come over soon, will you? Come and spend some time with Jakey. Just... well, you know.'

I nodded, not wanting to speak the words either. It was unthinkable, unimaginable.

'Also, I know we haven't heard anything about Dad's estate for a while but I am chasing things up with the solicitor tomorrow—'

'Don't worry about it,' I told her. 'There's no rush. It must be the last thing that you want to think about right now.'

'I just want you to know I'm on it.'

I waved my hands; I didn't want to talk about it.

We agreed to meet the next day and kissed each other on the cheek.

I watched her walk down the street until she disappeared from view and then I set off in the direction of home.

Though I wasn't sure that I believed that the couple in the café were listening to us, I found myself glancing over my shoulder the whole way home.

NOW

I turn around sharply at a rustling sound behind us. Footsteps, I imagine, but the quiver in the grass and the flash of a tail tells me otherwise.

'It's just a rat,' I say aloud. I can't stop myself from speaking to Mimi now she's with me, even though she's asleep, even though she can't understand me.

I see the outline of a building ahead of us. It's huge, imposing. Black timber and the sheen of thick glass; it doesn't look like a home, more like modern art. It couldn't be more different to the small, red-bricked house Evie left behind.

I exhale in one long breath as we approach it; it sounds like defeat. My plan to come here dissolves before my eyes. The sharp lines of the building, the gleaming glass, seem indicative of what Evie is like now. She has a hardness, a coldness that I had not imagined she could possess.

I hold on to Mimi tightly as I walk closer still, curl her small body around mine. We are shielded by shrubs that grow densely along the side of the towpath and as we approach the side of the building, I lose sight of it thanks to this foliage screen. It's only when we emerge on the other side that I see a gap in the hedge leads to a footpath through a field, towards the house.

'Let's go this way,' I say, heading towards the gap.

Mimi's head lolls to one side. A line of clear drool shines across on her face. She's completely out. I try to adjust her and so her head can rest on my shoulder. She slumps forwards with a heaviness that makes me tense. Something feels wrong; she's too unresponsive. I rebuke myself silently for not finding out what drug they'd given her.

'Let's go see this building, then, shall we?' I say. I force some jollity into my voice, making it sound like I am about to start singing a song.

THEN

We could hear raised voices through their door as soon as we arrived.

Thomas's hand hesitated in the space before the doorbell. 'Are you sure this is a good idea?'

'No,' I said. 'It's a terrible idea. But Evie said that they had to continue like normal. Otherwise everything would fall apart.'

'Maybe we should have said we couldn't come,' Thomas suggested, blurting it out in a rush. 'We could make up an excuse. It can be my fault.'

I raised my eyebrows at him sceptically. 'I want to see Evie,' I said.

They had received their sixth IPS that morning. Ironically, it had been in the very same car park that they had received that first warning, on the day of the naming ceremony, the first time Thomas and I had met.

'And they've seen us now,' I added as Evie's face appeared at the window.

She'd blow-dried her hair and wore make-up as though she were going to work. She looked professional, groomed, but she couldn't quite conceal the dark shadows under her eyes. Her blusher was a little too garish, oddly bright on the white of her cheeks.

'Thomas, hi!' She pulled him in and kissed him on the cheek. Her voice was a little too loud, just a shade too high-pitched. When she turned to me, we did not speak but a look passed between us. Evie's face fell from her delighted, welcoming smile to grim weariness.

'You didn't have to have us round, you know,' I told her, as we embraced.

'I wanted to see you,' she said in a whisper. 'I needed to.'

She squeezed my palm to hers and we walked into their kitchen like that, hand in hand. I wondered how it was that we could swing from feeling so far away from each other to as close as we'd ever been. It reminded me of the little spats we'd had as children when we could turn on each other as quickly as the wind changed direction and just as quickly come back together.

'Hi, Kit,' Seb said, raising his hand in a wave. There was a very small moment when he might have come over to greet me, kiss me on the cheek as he usually would, but he noticed that Evie and I were holding hands and that seemed to stop him. A silence descended upon us all.

'Jakob's sleeping well,' Thomas remarked, his voice filling the emptiness. He gestured towards Seb's workSphere, which showed a link up to Jakob's room. He was turned to his side, his face towards the camera so close up that I could see the flutter of his eyelids as he dreamed.

'It's a great angle,' he continued as neither Evie, Seb nor I spoke up.

'We have so many different cameras set up in there, we just change to the one that shows him best,' Seb said. He made a couple of sweeping movements on the Spheres and so we toured around Jakob's sleeping body from almost every angle.

He landed back on to the close-up of Jakob's face. Once more, a silence descended upon us. His face was ghostly grey through the night-vision camera. Now and again, he would frown as though he were able to sense that we were all there watching him, and worrying.

'Right,' Evie said, in a 'let's get started' sort of way. 'Seb, can you sort out drinks. Kit, come with me and have a look at that patch in the garden we spoke about. Then we'll eat.'

Everyone nodded mutely but no one moved until Evie pulled at my hand, directing me through the glass doors that led out on to their narrow garden. We'd spoken a few weeks ago about me helping her set up a veggie patch out there, since I'd taken over Dad's allotment, but I hadn't expected that she would want to talk about it now.

'It's this part here,' Evie said, tugging me towards the end of the garden. 'But I'm not sure if it gets enough sun. What do you reckon?'

'Are we really doing this?' I asked, gesturing to the forgotten patch of grass.

'I made a huge deal with Seb about having to have you over to talk about the vegetable patch. We just need to be out here for a bit.'

'Why'd you—' But then I thought better of finishing my question.

'He was saying that he wanted to cancel, after this morning, and I... I so wanted to see you that I just started going on about the vegetable patch. I said if OSIP found out about the vegetable patch it might stand in our favour.'

'Evie... I'm sorry, I shouldn't laugh.' It erupted out of me and then Evie was laughing alongside me. The sound of it bounced through the garden, but we both clasped our hands to our mouths as though the act of laughing was forbidden.

'I know, I know, it's ridiculous. We've just stopped speaking to each other properly. I can't just tell him that I need to see my sister any more. I have to link it back to OSIP.' Whenever she said their name, she dropped her voice, as though she were burying it under her breath. 'If I didn't laugh, I'd cry. I'd rather laugh. Although Seb, I'm sure, thinks I'm losing it. It's just that I'd rather Jakob hear this sound. If it's the last thing he hears while he's still with us, I'd rather it be laughter.'

'Do you want to talk about what happened this morning? We don't have to go through it again if you'd rather not,' I added quickly.

'You know how it goes now. It's like I can't even remember what it was this time. I mean, I can, of course. But they've all just merged into one another. The breastfeeding and the weight and then the sun hat and remember that time when I was showing him the pigeons flying in the park? And then it just comes down to putting him into a car seat.'

Evie had been by herself and was strapping Jakob into his car seat. She'd been running late in the supermarket and he was starting to get tired. The queue was longer than she'd expected. She'd forgotten to get nappies, which was the reason that she'd made the trip in the first place.

'I could see that he was beginning to change. You know

what it can be like. It's like the sky suddenly darkening over. It's beautifully sunny one moment and then the next, it looks like it's going to storm. He just needed to go to sleep, he just needed his nap. That's what it was. I almost ran towards the car to get him into it. I could see what was going to happen. His eyes started to close then, just from the motion. Once we got in the car and I started driving he would fall asleep straightaway.

'As soon as I lifted him out of the pram, he started screaming. But like I said, he was going to be all right as soon as we'd got going. That was what I thought. And I'll tell you this, Kit, although I won't admit this to anyone else, not even to Seb, I knew what I was doing was wrong. Because I looked all around me just before I lifted him out. I checked to see if anyone was watching me, to see if there were any enforcers there. I'm always paranoid in that car park after we received that warning there.'

I could see Evie then, so clearly, ducking her head this way and that, her dark eyes flashing from side to side, to see if there were any spectators. It was the same look I had seen as a child, as I would follow her into some light mischief. Stealing a biscuit before dinnertime, coating Dad's bed with itching powder she'd bought from a joke shop.

'And there was no one there?'

'Not a soul. If anything, it was too quiet. When I imagine what they must have thought when they saw me there, looking around me for witnesses.' Evie shook her head as though she could expel the idea from her with the movement.

Evie had piled the shopping bags into the car as quickly as she could and then picked up Jakob.

He began screaming straightaway.

'I'm sure I said, "There, there," I'm sure I did. I'm sure I patted his back and jogged him on my shoulder a bit. You know, in the way that he likes. But I just wanted to get him into the car seat and drive away. It says, on the IPS, that I made no attempt to comfort him. No attempt. But I'm sure I did, I'm almost positive of it.'

'Can you contest again?'

'No. I thought that too. But they said that they had filmed me. They even showed it to me. You couldn't see I wasn't doing anything to calm him from the film.'

'But still—'

'It's my word against theirs,' Evie said. 'I haven't got a chance.'

She'd been wrestling a screaming Jakob into his car seat while he twisted and squirmed, when she'd heard the footsteps. She'd known right away what was happening.

'I tried to be calm. I started blowing raspberries. I was manically blowing raspberries, singing songs. Anything that would distract him, stop him from crying. Making crazy faces. Sometimes that works. But his face was so screwed up by then, he was screaming so loudly, I don't think he could see me, let alone hear me. Anyway, by then it was game over.

'You know in a way, it wasn't that bit that was the worst. It was all over so quickly. They gave me their piece of paper and then went back into a car that was parked nearby that had tinted windows. I couldn't have seen that they were sitting in there—'

'What, they were just there, lying in wait in the car park?'

'Who knows?' Evie shrugged despondently. She kicked at

a piece of mud on the ground and a smear of the black dirt clung to the toe of her shoe. 'It doesn't matter, does it? Whether they were already there or whether they just happened to be there?'

'I just mean does everyone know that they are everywhere like that? Hiding out behind tinted glass, spying on you? It's like that couple we saw in the café.'

Evie shook her head. 'It just doesn't matter. I thought about that a bit afterwards too. Even if I had realised that that was what they were like, I'm not sure I could have changed anything. You can't live your life like that, always imagining that someone is watching you.'

'But do we have to do that now, though? Maybe we do?'

Evie sighed, and as she did, it was as though some force within her, the force that drove her forwards, the force that wrote out the tiny, intricate coloured notes to pass the induction, the force that had made her a mother, was finally expelled from her. The sun cast pink lines that ribboned across the sky, as its light fell away from where we were and the earth revolved us into darkness.

'The worst thing was telling Seb,' Evie said in a murmur. 'I don't think he will ever forgive me.'

'No, I'm sure that's not true.'

'He looks at me differently now. Watch him tonight. He looks at me like... like he doesn't want to see me.'

We fell silent as Thomas wandered down towards us holding two oversized glasses a little precariously. One was filled with the mellow amber of white wine and the other, something clear and fizzy. Thomas handed the wine to me and the other glass to Evie, who took it from him with a frown.

'Did you want something else? Seb said—'

'No, it's fine.' Evie took a sip as though to prove it. 'Thanks.'

'Seb said we'd eat in about ten minutes.'

'Sure,' Evie said. 'Can you tell him we'll be back in for then?'

Thomas and I locked eyes for just a short moment. A flurry of unspoken messages passed between us.

As soon as Thomas had disappeared back up the garden, Evie took me by my elbow.

'Seb blames me,' she said again. 'It's written all over his face. Even if we get through the next few months without another IPS, I don't see how we are going to get past this... this distance between us. You can see it on his face.'

We lingered outside for longer than we should have until Seb called out to us that dinner was on the table. It reminded me, not for the first time that night, of our childhood. Of stretching out seconds into minutes more of playtime. The games we played together that only we understood. Only this time, Seb's voice replaced that of Dad's beckoning us in. Only now, we weren't playing games any longer.

Evie edged towards the kitchen, pausing in each shadow, picking her way through the strip of grass reluctantly, as though her home was the very last place that she wanted to be.

Seb had overcooked the salmon and so it was discoloured on the edges. It broke away in dry flakes on my fork.

After a few false starts at making conversation, Evie sat back in her chair, pushed the salmon around her plate in a desultory manner before placing her fork on the full plate, and set it away from her with a sense of finality. She was drawn to the workSphere showing Jakob's face. It was set behind her at an angle and so she had to keep turning her head to catch a glimpse of it.

In the face of Evie's prickly quiet, Seb talked, over loud. His laugh ricocheted around the room powerfully, as though it were a hand that was slapping you on the back, asking for your agreement.

Once Evie had pushed her plate away, she stood up and very slowly, deliberately, took the glass of sparkling water with her. When she returned, it was full of white wine, a comical amount, due to the huge swell of the glass.

Seb raised his eyebrows at her and then he shook his head, staring hard at the coil of silver salmon skin that he'd left in one neat pile on the side of his plate.

Evie raised her glass to Seb, in the smallest of movements, before taking a large mouthful. I watched her swallow, the ripple upon her throat. Then she took another and another. She drank with a force, with effort, as though it were medicine. Seb started to pile up our plates, hastily throwing them on top of each other. The china clashed together with dull, hard chimes.

Thomas and I looked all around us, at anywhere but the dinner table, the wine, the plates. There was the briefest of moments after that when Thomas and I were left alone. Evie had gone to check on Jakob and Seb went to retrieve the dessert that they'd left in the car by accident.

'Please say we can leave soon?' Thomas whispered. I nodded back at him in agreement before Seb came bustling back in, dumping a packaged box of profiteroles on the centre of table.

'I'm not sure if they'll be any good,' Seb said. For that moment he appeared so vulnerable and worried that I wondered if he might begin to cry, but then Thomas and I both started in a lively chorus.

'They look great.' 'Delicious,' we chimed. Seb straightened, righted himself, and lost the ragged expression from his face.

Evie slipped back into the room, almost unnoticed, and wrapped her fingers around the glass of wine that was now almost empty.

When the first knock came, we almost missed hearing it. Seb had involved Thomas in recounting some work story to me. He'd given up trying to communicate with Evie, who had drawn her legs up, hugging her knees to her chest, her shoes balancing ostentatiously on the edge of the chair.

'Did you hear that?' Seb said.

The knock came again. A little louder this time.

'Who can that be? At this time of night?' Seb's voice became a little higher.

'It's them,' Evie said. 'They've come for him.' With every word she spoke, there seemed to be just a little less of her.

'No,' Seb said, standing. 'It can't be.'

He threw a worried glance at Jakob's face that slept on, filling the workSphere with his dreamlike presence.

Suddenly, Seb gripped Evie's wrist and he pulled her to standing. She almost fell because of the way she had been sitting. 'If this is it,' Seb said to her, 'if that is them, then I want to spend these last minutes with Jakob.'

Urgency turned over in his voice.

They saw each other then, understood one another. Evie nodded and they both fled from the room, leaving Thomas and me alone at the dinner table, the sound of another insistent knock on the front door. It almost sounded gentle, unassuming. I wanted to believe that it was just a neighbour asking to borrow something, someone asking for directions, something entirely innocent. I was transported back to being in Marie and Leo's flat, the knock at the door, the desperate hope it was anyone but OSIP.

'Should we answer it?' Thomas asked me.

'Let's see if they go away.'

'Maybe they're wrong about it being OSIP,' Thomas said hopefully.

Evie and Seb were with Jakob now. They'd lifted him from his cot and so there was now a blank space in place of where he had been resting on the workSphere. I imagined him slumbering on in his parents' arms as they encircled him; there was no safer place that he could be.

But now the knocking had turned to banging. I imagined a huge fist hammering upon the door. Thomas and I sat before the half-eaten bowls of profiteroles, unspeaking. Then there were voices. 'Open up. Evie Moss? Sebastian Maybury? We know you're in there. If you do not open this door in the next minute, we will use reasonable force to do so.'

Thomas and I both moved then; we rose from our seats as if pulled by strings from above. Thomas was there before me.

'Sebastian Maybury?' A plump man in spectacles peered over a goSphere. He was wearing a shabby green jumper which had patches sewn on to its elbows.

'No, I—'

But before Thomas could finish, the man had pushed past him. Two more men followed him in. I can't remember what they looked like, they merged together, grim lines of expression that were interchangeable and hard. They barged past each other as though they were competing in a race.

'Evie Moss?' the man with the goSphere said to me.

'She's my sister, I'm—'

He was already gone. Into the dining room, littered with our discarded bowls and glasses, the disassembled tower of profiteroles slumping at its centre. He paused, as though he might look under the table to see if they were crouching there, then moved onwards, through the kitchen, into the softly lit sitting room. Then came the gentle sound of Jakob beginning to cry and he ran up the stairs, taking them two at a time.

I went to follow him but one of the men who'd followed him in stood across the bottom of the stairs, a barrier.

'You can sit down there,' he said pointing us back to the dinner table.

I opened my mouth to object but Thomas was at my side. 'There's nothing more we can do,' he said gently, and so we sat down again, helplessly. And we waited.

For a long time nothing happened. We heard voices from upstairs but not the words they were saying.

Now and again there was the bleat of Jakob's cry but as quickly as it started, it would disappear as if were not really there at all. Then for a second, Jakob's face suddenly appeared on the workSphere.

He'd been put down in his cot again and for just a few seconds he writhed towards the camera, his face wrinkled, his eyes searching.

Then, he was picked up again and disappeared from view.

NOW

I see myself in the reflection of the glass door. It looks like the type that's mirrored from the outside but from the inside is transparent.

My hair is greasy, lying flat across my forehead and hanging over my shoulder, tangled, heavy and matted. I try to put my fingers through it but they get too caught up in its knots. Then I remember the glass and wonder if anyone is watching me. I quickly extract my fingers.

Is anyone there?

There's no warming light shining from any of the windows, only the grey rays coming from the pale circle in the sky. I can't hear the sounds of music or conversation or a workSphere's prattle.

'Shall we knock on the door?' I say to Mimi as I look round the front door for anything that resembles a doorbell; I find none. 'Shall we see if there's anyone home?'

I make a big show to Mimi of knocking but she slumbers on. She shivers and that makes me knock harder. The glass is thick, my rapping muffled.

No one answers.

We walk around the whole building. Each window is dull, each door closed. It's an impenetrable fortress.

I tell myself that there is no one here.

I tell myself that no one can see me.

Then I start to search for something heavy, something hard.

I find a pile of bricks stacked by a wall. I pick one up and then another and another. It's difficult to do, holding Mimi at the same time, but I don't want to put her down for a moment longer than necessary. I move them all in front of one of the large walls of glass.

When I think I have enough, I take off my coat and place Mimi wrapped up in its folds a safe distance away, around the corner, nestled in the grass. She doesn't stir. It takes me a moment to be able to walk away from her and back to the window, back to my pile of bricks.

I throw the brick as hard I can into the glass.

It splinters, but it does not break.

My ears ache to hear if Mimi has woken up, if she makes a sound. But there's none.

I throw another brick at the glass. It bends, it ripples but it does not smash.

I throw another. And another.

My reflection is broken into a multitude of fragments, I can no longer see my face.

Finally, I hear it.

A crack.

It only takes a few more and then we're in.

I wait for the sound of an alarm.

I wait for someone to come rushing towards the splinter of a hole and demand what is happening.

I run back to where Mimi lies, my gaze fixed on the gaping cavity of glass that I created.

We wait and we wait.

When no one comes, when no alarm pierces, I lift Mimi up to me. She's heavier than she was; I can feel a strain in my back from carrying her.

I kick through the shards around the hole and bent over, making myself small, we enter the house.

THEN

What was left after Jakob was gone from the house? There was nothing, there was everything.

There was the space where Jakob had lain while we'd talked and ate and drank and simmered. The indent on his blanket, on the sheet.

There was all the stuff, the things that had been so important to his survival back then. The baby bottles, the car seat, the especially expensive pram. Everything had come at great cost now that manufacturing was so affected by the population drop. There were the things he loved in that short time he had been with us. The wooden toy with two eyes at its centre, shaped like a sunflower. The black and white patterned muslin cloth he was always drawn to.

There was an emptiness that filled the house, that was leaden in our bodies. It weighed down our hearts, ached in our heads.

There was a relationship, once so full of hope and expectation that now hung together with the thinnest of threads. At any time, it seemed close to breaking.

There was blame that hung around unashamedly, like a

dog that smelt with age and disease. It tripped us up. It didn't give up.

And then there were the memories. The memories that were hardened to the physical, the photographs, the videos. Evie watched them over and over, and I was by her side. Seb and Thomas did not want to see them and I wondered if perhaps they relived Jakob in the way that I preferred: the feeling of the memory. A bounce of joy in my heart. The rush of expectation as I rounded the corner to their house each time I came to see him. The way my heart danced when he smiled.

In those days, it seemed that if you knocked Evie and Seb together, they would sound hollow. There was less of them.

Evie became harsher, more likely to lash out and sting, whilst Seb lost his edges. He would start a sentence but be unable to finish it. He would dither over the smallest of decisions.

I clung to Thomas in the days after. Sometimes we'd be walking side by side and I would suddenly feel as though I might fall, that my feet would fold in on themselves beneath me. I'd clutch on to Thomas for support, and though I thought it often, I did not fall, I stayed upright.

There were dreams. There were nightmares. But none were as real or as painful as the realisation on waking of what had come to pass, that Jakob was no longer with us and we might never see him again.

It was impossible to concentrate on anything other than the pain that rubbed inside us. I tried to work but listening to Jonah and his daughter made me only more bereft. Evie would never have these conversations with Jakob.

The Spheres sounded louder in those days. Their volumes ramped up. Was it because everything inside of us was quieter, stiller, emptier?

A week after Jakob's extraction, late into the night, Evie rang. The sound of the call echoed through the empty flat and woke me.

She had already started speaking before I'd picked up. As soon as I swiped the workSphere to answer her, her face was filled the dome, close up to it, and her voice rang out into the room mid-sentence.

'—where he is right now,' she said. 'I can't stop thinking about it, Kit. And will he remember us? Will we pass each other on a street one day? Will he know me? Will he remember?'

She didn't need me to answer.

'Of course he won't remember me,' she continued. 'I'll never know who he'll turn into, who he'll become, what will happen in his life. Sometimes I think, sometimes I wish... that I had been the one to die. Instead of Dad. I would never have known this. I wish I could have ended knowing that he was alive, that he was loved, and that was it. None of what has happened since.'

'It's so—' I started to say but Evie carried on talking regardless.

'I used to think that it just mattered that we tried. That we tried so fucking hard. But now I know that's all bollocks. It didn't matter one bit. He's gone. My baby's gone and I... I...' Her words broke down into sobs and then cries and then a heavy silence of harsh, ragged breaths.

'Evie, darling—' Before I could say any more words, Evie turned quickly to a sound from behind her.

'He's coming,' she said. 'He doesn't want me to talk about it. I've got to go.' Her thin face disappeared and a news story about a new mushroom farm initiative appeared on the Sphere.

Rows upon rows of mushrooms filled the screen like a private army standing to attention. I imagined Evie now, hiding away from Seb who wouldn't or couldn't speak about what had happened. There was no right way to behave but it seemed a cruel joke that Evie and Seb had reacted in such opposite ways. What one did aggravated the other; they could not help but be at odds. When Evie was loud, abrasive almost, Seb retreated. But when Evie was quiet, and Seb tried to find a way to her, she turned fierce in protection of her privacy, craving space alone as she had never done before.

I swept the images of the mushroom farms away. The workSphere closed down to a silent black orb. I was about to get back into bed when I found myself swiping the screen back to life. I started to dig through my work files until I brought up that phone call I had flagged between Jonah and Genevieve where she told him that she had decided to start a family. I wanted to see again the files that Jonah had been looking at – the OSIP ones that he'd been flicking through.

But when I found the audio-graph of the call, I couldn't see the face icon. I tried again and again, I even closed the file down and reopened it, but however much I searched I could not find a way to see the camera feed as I had before.

I was trying for the third time to reset the Sphere when an OSIP film took over the screen. Images of parents and children danced across the monitor as though they were on some sort of carousel. I gave up then and walked back to the bedroom.

'How is she?' Thomas asked, sitting up in bed.

'As terrible as you'd imagine,' I said. I stooped to climb under the covers, a tide of exhaustion overtaking me. 'Let's never have kids.'

'Never,' Thomas agreed and we tried to sleep through the muted sound of children's laughter ringing out from my workSphere.

NOW

A workSphere whirs from its dormancy; I hear children's voices.

I pause. I'm paralysed, although I can see it's just an OSIP film starting up.

I grip hold of Mimi and linger there, just on the other side of the hole in the glass.

I catch the scent of Evie. The particular perfume she wears, the smell of her deodorant mingled with the brand of her shampoo. She has passed by this spot not long before us. She brushed against the bulbous coats that stick out on the rack, she slammed the door shut behind her, sure of its solidity and permanence.

But the smell of her dissipates and when I search for it, it's no longer there.

I feel a twinge of longing for a time gone, of being with her, of her home being as familiar as my own. The days we spent together that were so innocuous that now I see as something precious.

I miss my sister. I miss being with her, the very essence of her, but I can only recognise this fact as being more important than anything else that came between us, here, alone in her home. In a place where Evie should be, and being without her.

I take a step forwards as the film continues to play. I cradle Mimi to me, and walk through the wide-open spaces of the rooms.

There is something revealing about seeing the pieces of someone's life through their home. Their true home. Not one that has been tidied for guests, with piles of old post forced into drawers and plates stacked away neatly into the dishwasher.

What do you leave behind when you believe that no one will see it? What pieces of yourself do you leave bare, exposed?

There's the crumpled skin of a banana left on the counter, brown and sweetly rotting. Three cups that still have lumpen teabags at their bottom and the dark brown remainder of over-brewed tea. There's a small saucepan left on the hob with what looks like cheese stuck to its side. I imagine Evie eating her dinner straight from the pan, standing in the kitchen, a fork in her hand. Every small trace stands out against the industrial chic of the kitchen.

The living room is untouched and tidy, so much so that I wonder if she's spent any time in this room recently. The sofa cushions are plumped and straight, the tables clear of detritus, toys piled carefully in storage boxes. Everything is tucked away, set neatly in lines and right angles.

Mimi feels quieter still in this immaculate place. I check her breathing and yearn for her sounds to break the silence but she is still sunk in sleep.

'Why don't you get comfy on here?' I prattle to her. I pat the sofa cushion, which is more firm than squidgy. I nestle her there, placing cushions and blankets around her, and pull my coat back over me; the house is cold. 'Now I just need to find something for a nappy.'

Jakob will be too old for nappies now but I should be able to make something better for her than the paper towels from the restaurant toilets.

There's a jumper of Jakob's hung over the sofa that will keep her warm. I grab it. I take tea towels from the kitchen and quickly fashion a make-shift nappy.

'I'm going to be right back,' I tell her when I've finished. 'Just a moment. I'm going to find something for you to wear. I'll be right back, OK?'

She buries her head into Jakob's jumper a little. How long before the drugs they gave her leave her system? I try to calculate how long she has slept already. After a few moments of stroking the silk of her hair, I reluctantly leave her.

Along one side of the room is a wall of books. From the dust lining the bookshelves I can see that Evie has not touched the books for a long time. I ease one out carefully – *Of Mice and Men* – it looks like the same copy that Evie stuffed into her school bag years ago.

I hold my breath but inside the front cover I find two twenty-pound notes, flattened sharply like daisies preserved in a press.

She always used to do this. Hide money in her books. She started when she was a teenager and carried on through her twenties, but I'd started to doubt in this sterile place whether she would be the same person. This little habit makes me again yearn for Evie. It makes me think: I do know her after all.

The next book holds no money. But in *Pride and Prejudice* I find eighty pounds and soon I am able to guess the books that Evie has chosen to stash the notes in. She prefers to use the classics, although I find thirty in between the pages of a poetry anthology by a name I do not recognise.

I stuff some notes into the pocket of my pyjamas and then, following Evie's lead, I start to place more notes in between the pages of a trashy crime novel that was poked into one of the bottom shelves, stuffed into the space at the top of the books, almost like an afterthought.

I glance back at Mimi. She is still asleep, her breathing deep and even.

I quickly reroute to the kitchen. I place the book into a sturdy bag with fabric handles and then I start to hunt for food.

I take a tall glass water jug that sits by the side of the sink, fill it from the tap and then drain it. I fill it again, drink some more and then carry it with me to the fridge.

There are leftovers of something in a bowl – some kind of lentil stew. I don't heat it but devour it in seconds, in just a few spoonfuls. Then I cram a piece of bread into my mouth, I have to tell myself to chew before swallowing, as Thomas would remind me in those first days of breastfeeding when I couldn't eat enough, fast enough; I have the same thirst and hunger now. I find a pack of biscuits in one of the cupboards and take one after another, washing them down with mouthfuls of cold milk. Only minutes have passed since I began eating but the food is already restoring me.

Now I can plan ahead.

I take the contents of the fruit bowl – glossy apples and thick-skinned oranges, tins of baked beans, the remains of the loaf of bread, a block of cheese from the fridge.

I take some cutlery and a few more of her tea towels from the drawer. I pluck a couple of water bottles from the draining board and fill them from the tap.

Then I check back on Mimi. As I whip around the kitchen I have the sudden dread that when I return to the sofa, I will find an empty space in place of her: an indentation on the pillow instead of the solid squishiness of her body.

I breathe again when I see her still curled up there. I shouldn't have left her, I tell myself, and this time I scoop her up, nestle my head into her shoulder and climb the stairs carefully.

Clothes next.

Evie's bedroom is the first room that I try. I settle Mimi on the bed. She flops down, still lost in a soundless sleep. I worry again that she's still not woken, what drugs she was given that have made her this way. Though I say her name, stroke her cheek, squeeze her feet, she will not be roused. Reluctantly, I leave her on the bed.

It's there, in the bedroom, skimming through Evie's clothes and opening drawers to search for what is tucked at the back that I have a sensation of guilt. I detach from what I'm doing and see it from another side and not my desperate, skewered lens. I find tops that I remember Evie wearing years ago but which I have not seen her wear since. An old black jumper that she bought when we were out shopping together and she wore until moths took a liking to it. She has kept it still. I can't help but take off my coat and pull it on over my milk-stained top. I tug at its sleeves so it covers my wrists. I begin to feel a little warmer, wrapped up in its softness.

I can smell her again here; vestiges of her perfume linger in the folds of wool and cotton. I wonder briefly what she will think when she discovers the broken window, when she follows the trail of my looting. She will work out it was me. Will it fill her with anger or drown her in sadness? I'd rather not find out.

I put my guilt aside and delve into the drawers with renewed energy. There are many new things, recently folded and tucked in with the old. They look like they've never been worn. Evie's been shopping recently. They are softer, cleaner and glossier than anything else.

A light grey jumper with a diagonal neckline and blocky three-quarter sleeves. A white T-shirt that will never look this clean again. I resist the temptation to take them, though they lure me with their newness; I want these things that are fresh and untouched. A new skin.

Grudgingly, almost, I find some loose trousers that have been squashed into a ball at the back of a drawer and a T-shirt that is somewhere in between blue and grey. A thin, ivory jumper that is a bit too small and will cling to me, but will have to do. There're some white vests that Evie has multiple versions of and so I pack a few of them, and some outstretched underwear that looks forgotten and unloved.

I steal a lip salve from one of the bathroom boxes, a small tube of handcream, a half-empty deodorant. My luxury goods, I tell myself.

The bag feels reassuringly full now and the edge of the book that I filled with money knocks against my side.

That's when I hear a sound from the bed – an unmistakable sound. I rush towards Mimi and as I do, I drop the spoils. They tumble from the bag, decorating the floor with my thievery.

THEN

'Have it,' Evie said, pushing the bag into my hand. 'I don't want them. If you don't want them, just give them away.'

I peered into the bag to see a few of the velvety soft toys that Jakob used to favour; a white bear that doubled as a rattle, a felt owl with wide-spaced round eyes.

Jakob had been gone for three weeks.

I'd met up with Evie and we walked together round and round the small park that was near her house.

Sometimes our footsteps would slow until we almost came to a standstill but still we walked quietly around the circular path, past flowerbeds that had become so drenched with water that they were muddy trenches where nothing could grow.

Now and again, a child on a scooter would come past us so close that they almost knocked into us. They'd be kitted out, wearing a helmet, clad in arm and leg protectors in case they fell.

One child we saw was allowed to ride her scooter only if she let her mother keep a hand on the handlebar at all times.

They wheeled slowly along, like a version of the three-legged race. Other parents ran after their scooting children with no chance of catching them up. They shouted out warnings, they tried to predict the future to create one where no tears were shed, where no one was hurt.

Each time, I heard Evie's sharp intake of breath as they glided effortlessly past us. At first I thought she was worried that they might fall but then, from the way her eyes followed them, I wondered if she was imagining Jakob, grown, solid and speeding past us.

'I've found this woman in Bristol who's written a programme that will take all your input of your child from your workSphere and goSphere and use it to make pictures and videos of what they might look like when they're older. It can go right up to them being eighty, if you want to. I think I'm going to do it.'

Evie spoke in waves. She was either babbling, full of ideas, or silent, as though vocalising anything was far too great an effort.

Her face was white without its usual blush, her lips, flaky and dry. I tried to push the idea from my mind that she was almost unrecognisable; at the very same time as wanting to meet her gaze, I found it difficult to look at her.

We walked past the large oak tree that sat in the middle of the park and, as we had four times already, circled it before taking one of the paths that led away from it and would eventually bring us back again.

'Have you gone back to the library?' I asked. 'Maybe someone there could help?'

Evie shook her head emphatically.

'What does Seb say about everything?'

Evie laughed loudly, a hyena shriek, but as quickly as she started, she lapsed into silence.

'Seb,' she said slowly. He was an afterthought. Then she cackled again, harshly, sharply. 'Seb wants us to try again.'

'Well, maybe in time—'

'Kit, no. Not you too. It's not the same for him. It just doesn't compare.'

Evie had not often let her guard slip before she'd had Jakob about how different the induction process was for her than for Seb.

'He has no idea what it was really like. Going through it so many times. I was convinced at one point that my body was shutting down, that I was not going to recover, let alone have a baby. But that wasn't the worst part. He didn't have to give up every single part of himself. He didn't have to carry it.'

'What do you mean... Jakob?'

'No, of course not. I mean that's just another thing. No, I mean he didn't carry the weight of the responsibility. It always came back to me. It always felt like I was the one who had to make it right. I was the one being judged. Even that first warning we had, do you remember? It was the way Seb was holding him but I hadn't picked up on it. It was my fault.'

Her pace sped up a little as she spoke fast, without stopping, and so at the end of her sentence, she inhaled noisily, as though she had only just remembered that she needed to breathe.

'Did you really feel that?'

'Yes, absolutely. The responsibility always comes back to

the mother in the end. You've always understood that or you wouldn't have decided to be an Out, right?'

I grappled to reply. Had I truly realised that, I wondered. Or was I as conditioned as everyone else to accept that the mother had to take on the full weight of accountability?

'You know how ridiculous this all is,' she continued. 'And you made the right decision. I wish that I could have decided that too.'

'No, you don't. You don't. Or you would never have had Jakob.'

Evie bit her lip hard so the colour bleached from it. She muttered, repeating my own words back at me. 'I would never have had Jakob, I would never have had Jakob.'

When Evie spoke again, it was as though she was talking through a filter. Like her voice was not her own but just a sound piece.

'We got sent this letter about trying again. Maybe Seb wouldn't have brought it up if we hadn't received it. It's all about how first extractions are common but that they lay the path for avoiding extractions in the future. If we try again in the next two months, they'll award us more housing credits.'

I shook my head a little.

We'd walked to the end of a path, it forked in front of us.

'Have you...' I hardly dared think the words, let alone say them. But I persisted. 'Have you found out if there's any way of getting Jakob back? When Tia was extracted, I explored it a bit but I couldn't find anything – have you looked?'

I didn't tell Evie that I had been trawling through everything that I had on Jonah to see if I could find any other link between him and OSIP. I still returned to the phone call that had shown me the video of him flicking through the documents stamped with the OSIP logo, but I could never access the footage again.

I had nothing to prove it but I felt sure that he was somehow connected with OSIP. It brought OSIP just one step closer. I would do anything to help Evie and Seb. If there was anything I could do to get Jakob back, I would do it.

Genevieve's XC baby, Jonah's first grandchild, was in gestation. I hadn't heard anything about it for a period since that first phone call, but suddenly it was announced. I got lost in the films and phone calls that leaked down to me now about how it was progressing, and all the details of the development of the foetus. After almost six months of gene therapy, their embryo was made. I worked these into Jonah's life document and at the end of these sessions, I would find my face wet with tears.

'I need to be alone right now,' Evie said to me. Her face, her voice shutting down, blankness shifted across her features.

'Do you want to go home?' I asked her.

'No,' she answered quickly. 'I'm going to stay here for a while longer.'

'Evie, I didn't mean to upset you.'

She laughed again.

'I'm sorry, Kit. I'm past upsetting now. It's not you. I just want to be… by myself.'

'OK,' I said. I buried my hands in my pockets and began to walk away, but then I heard Evie's voice ring out once more. It stopped me.

'You know, just after he was born, I found it really hard. I couldn't tell anyone. Not Seb. Not even you. Not after everything that we had gone through to get him. It seemed absurd. To find yourself not wanting something that you've wanted for so many years, that you've worked so hard to get. Where is the sense in that?

'Jakey needed me so much. It scared me, I suppose. Feeling that. Feeling that life would never be the same again, that I wouldn't be alone, not really, ever again. Because he'd always need me, or he might need me, at any time. I started thinking about what it was like before, before he was here. And I wanted it. There was a little bit of time when I thought that I wanted that freedom again. Without Jakob, without Seb even. To be just me, with no one else to worry about.

'That makes me sound so selfish, doesn't it? You're wondering how could I possibly want that, but I did, Kit. There were moments when I wished I could undo things I'd done. Of course I was so happy that I'd had Jakey, I was, but there was darkness too. I wondered if I'd done the right thing, if I was going to be able to cope. I yearned for that freedom I had before, freedom I didn't even realise I had until then.

'And now, look at me… No Jakob. Soon, there'll probably be no Seb. And it will be just me. Just like I wished for.'

NOW

I run to Mimi, I can't be with her quickly enough.

Her body convulses with every heave. There's vomit splashed across the white carpet in a comically large splatter.

'Oh my darling, my darling,' I sing to her, reaching to rub her back. I'm struck by how useless my words are, how violently her body shudders with each expelling.

Her eyes flicker open for a moment and she looks at me, astonished.

What happened? her eyes seem to ask me.

I rock her and she melds into me. She's floppy, perhaps a little hot. I hold her head in my hands and try to examine her face, place my palm on her forehead, but she sinks into me, unable to hold her body upright. It's like when she was a newborn again, her limbs beyond her control.

I survey the vomit over her shoulder; it's creamily orange – spongy lumps scattered like an abstract pattern across the white of the floor.

Then Mimi jerks against me and before I can move her, she retches again. Her sick goes through the layers of my coat,

Evie's jumper, my pyjamas. It's surprisingly warm; its stench makes me catch my breath.

'Oh baby,' I say again, pointlessly. I can't help a shaving of dismay sliding into my voice and I try to conceal it. 'It's okay, it's okay,' I tell her. 'What's making you sick, my darling?'

I think again of the medication that she was given. In my haste to leave I hadn't found out its name, if it had any side effects. Or has she caught something from one of the other children that she was with? Perhaps one of them had just been ill.

Mimi shudders and heaves again.

THEN

A lashing feeling, not unlike nausea, filled me as I
approached Evie and Seb's house.

I hadn't been back there since the night that Jakob was
taken. Unbelievably, that was now almost two months ago.

I only realised it as I walked up to their jolly red front
door, my hands clasping themselves into stiff fists, my breath
turning shallow.

I wasn't sure that I would be able to contain the
sickness. I swallowed hard, aware of every little detail of
my body; the way that sweat collected above my upper lip,
a nagging sensation in my shoulders, a viscous lurch in my
stomach.

Evie and I usually met up in the park or we spoke on our
workSpheres or she'd come over to us. But when I hadn't heard
from her for a few days, when messages were continuing to
go unanswered, I'd set off to her house, trying to dismiss the
last time that I'd journeyed to Dad's flat when he had stopped
answering his phone.

I'd spent the morning processing more material for Jonah's
life document. Genevieve's XC baby was in its final weeks of

gestation. The gestation times for XCs worked very differently to babies in utero. They were longer than forty-two weeks as there was no birth or placenta degradation to consider and so the XC babies were born with greater organ maturity. The gestational periods were responsive to individual foetal development; her baby was now at forty-five weeks. The more I'd written about the new, upcoming arrival, the more I'd thought of Evie.

As I reached the front door, I put a hand out to steady me and then as soon as I touched the bright red paint, I wrenched my hand away as though it had been burnt, suddenly flashing back to the way the enforcers had knocked and hammered upon it.

I waited there while I calmed down. I could see into the living room from when I stood; Evie had left the blinds up. I could make out the shapes of Jakob's things that still filled the floor of the sitting room; his bouncer, his toys, a playmat that was in the centre of the carpet. Everything was in its place, still and waiting, a museum without visitors, a library without readers. The only thing that was missing was the child it was all there for.

I knocked lightly on the door and then when no one came, again with more force. When still there was no answer, I bent down and called through the letterbox. It looked like the house was empty; there was a stillness in the air, almost a greyness to the things that had been left. It appeared as though it had not been disturbed for some time.

But then I heard a shuffle from upstairs. I called again, louder this time. It seemed as though my voice might knock things over.

Finally, a shadow appeared through the mottled glass semi-circle of the door and it opened.

Evie looked like she'd either never been to bed or hadn't got up yet. She wore a mixture of layers that were at odds with each other. A camisole top, a blazer she used to wear to work, a draping scarf, threadbare pyjama bottoms that floated baggily around her thin legs.

She didn't speak but headed into the kitchen. Walking seemed an effort. She sighed heavily from time to time as though she were remembering something, over and over.

'What's going on?' I asked her. 'Where's Seb?'

'Gone,' she said as she filled the kettle with water. It took a couple of attempts to place it back on its base and as though the effort of that was enough, she did not switch it on but stood, her back leaning against the kitchen side, pulling the thin sleeves of her blazer over her wrists, up to her knuckles.

'Gone – gone?' I asked.

'Gone, gone,' Evie said. 'Like left me, gone.' She reached for her head suddenly, grimacing, as though she was reaching for a pain, or remembering one.

'Do you have a headache?' I asked.

'No,' she said in a snap.

I took hold of her, enclosed her in my arms. She remained stiff and did not return my embrace.

'I'm sorry,' I muttered into her hair. She smelt stale and yeast-like. 'I wish I could... do something.'

'Don't say sorry.' Evie struggled away. 'You've got nothing to say sorry about. You shouldn't keep apologising for something that has nothing to do with you.'

'You're cold,' I said, trying to ignore the dagger-sharp anger in her voice. 'Let's have some tea to warm you up. I'll put the heating on.'

'Just leave it,' Evie said sharply. 'I'll make tea if you want it. It's my house.'

She clicked down the button on the kettle then and let it boil. It vibrated on its base, steam poured from its spout. She made no move to find cups, pull teabags out of cupboards and I, a mirror of her, leant against the kitchen counter too. We stood silently, together.

'If you ever want to talk—' I started to say and just that, my saying those words, lit a fuse within Evie. She pushed herself away, broke our symmetry, and rushed from the room up the stairs.

I stayed there a moment longer, wondering if I should follow her or if I should leave, but before I could decide, she'd come back and was swiping at her workSphere. She brought up a few documents, dismissed an advert, opened up a payment transfer screen.

'The money from Dad has come through,' she said. 'I'll transfer your amount now.'

Her business-like impersonality jarred. I hesitated, tried to speak and could not. How could she not have told me that she'd sold his place, that things had been wrapped up and so that now, at the end of it, there was just a figure? Evie was trembling, her face pale. It was as though there was something that was stirring inside her, bubbling up and over.

'I can't stop thinking about Mum and Dad…' she blurted out, but then she stopped herself abruptly.

'What about them?' I asked gently.

'Nothing… just, what it must have been like for Dad – after Maia and Mum died,' she said vaguely.

'I can't imagine. Losing one after the other.'

Evie mumbled something.

'What did you say?'

She turned her face towards me. 'I've decided I'm going to go away for a few days. By myself. I need some time alone.'

'Where will you go?'

She sent through the money in a swipe of the screen. 'Not sure yet,' she said. 'I just need to get away from here for a while. Just another quarter. Just for a bit. Work some stuff out. I've got to go – get ready to leave.'

'Well, get in touch when you're back. Or while you're away – if you need to talk… about anything.'

I turned to leave. I almost stopped before I got back to the door, I almost turned back but there was larger part of me that was glad she had provided me with the opportunity to escape.

NOW

There'll be no quick escape now if Evie arrives home.
I carry Mimi into the bathroom next door to Evie's
bedroom and place her, stained clothes and all, in the bath.
I peel off her top and see how far the sick has spread. It's on
her pyjama bottoms, her slippers, everything.

I try to make light of it. 'Time for a little wash,' I say to
Mimi encouragingly, as if it's no big deal, not a problem.

It takes me a few tries of turning the blank, silver boxes on
the wall to make anything happen and then the water that
spurts out is too forceful, too cold then too hot. Mimi cries
out in unison with the water blasting against the pristine
white enamel.

She lets me wash her although I can see she is tiring
quickly. When I turn the water off she has already started
crying. She has always hated the end of a bath, the feeling of
the cold air against her wet skin.

I pluck a thick towel from a rail with one hand and wrap
her in it. It's so large that it engulfs her and for that moment
I'm so grateful that Evie had left a towel. So stupidly happy

she bought an expensive one that's so big and soft that is comforting my daughter as she cries.

'That's better, isn't it?' I say, towelling her hair, hugging her to me.

It was inevitable, I suppose, that the moment I think that we've come through the worst of it, Mimi heaves again. The sick dribbles again over my shoulder and down my back.

'Oh dear, oh dear,' I parrot. 'Mummy better have a wash too.'

I catch in the mirror how her vomit clings to my coat. There's so much of it, it's surprising seeing as she has been sick three times already. It's a greenish bile.

'All gone,' I tell her. 'You're all better now.'

I try to convince myself.

THEN

Santa insisted on throwing confetti; it fell upon us, skittering, like leaves in autumn.

Thomas and I married in a small ceremony with only a handful of guests. Part of me wondered if we should have delayed or not told anyone at all. It didn't seem the right time for those we loved most.

Not for Evie, who said she was coming but then left a message to say that she couldn't make it on account of some kind of emergency she didn't go into detail about.

Not for Santa, Thomas's mother, who had just had a knee operation and had only recently come out of hospital. She walked with a limp for the day although she did not let this dampen her spirits.

We'd started having conversations that began with, 'If we did get married then...' and slowly, almost without our noticing, plans crept around us until they lay in front of us, fully formed and detailed. The idea of not being married didn't bother me, but the idea of not being married to Thomas somehow did. If the convention had been climbing to the top of the highest building and screaming it out to the passersby below us, then that's what we would have done. But instead, we made do with a wedding ceremony, two rings and a piece of paper.

I woke up on the morning of our wedding, already smiling. We'd dispensed with all the traditions and I immediately rolled over to wake Thomas who was still asleep beside me. I folded my body around his and held him until he woke.

'We're getting married today,' I said out loud. It was as though I was testing it out. 'You and me. Married.'

Thomas mumbled something into his pillow that I could not decipher but then he lifted his head with a jolt and turned over.

'We are,' he said. 'We are getting married today. Are you having second thoughts?' he asked, his eyebrows raised.

'I want to do it,' I said carefully, considering each word as I said it.

If we hadn't got a phone call from Santa saying that she was on her way and did we want to meet her there earlier, we might have stayed like that until the very last minute when we had to get up.

We showered and dressed, as though it were any other day. I wore the same dress I had worn to Jakob's naming ceremony on the day we had first met, Thomas wore his favourite shirt, and we were ready.

Santa was dressed in a beautiful gold and orange dress with a violent turquoise scarf like the breast of peacock flung over her shoulder. She was sitting in the café in an art gallery that was near to the town hall.

'Hello, my darling,' she said to Thomas, kissing him close and then holding him by the shoulders before her, as though to check it was really him. 'And, hello, my darling.' She turned and embraced me. The smell of her magnolia perfume was sweetly addictive and as I breathed her, I realised that beneath the perfume, under the fragrance of freshly washed hair, I could smell something of Thomas too, the same base tones of him.

'Ready to get married?' she asked us, with a mischievous grin.

We nodded, grinned back.

We drank cups of coffee while we waited for our time slot, and then Santa insisted we drink something stronger and we decided on three tangy orange Bellinis that matched Santa's dress in hue.

'It's a good thing, if I spill no one will notice,' she said merrily, holding the glass to her. 'I'm so... so co-ordinated.'

The first time I met Santa we'd gone to see her for lunch over a weekend. She lived in the same quarter as Thomas, in one of the larger blocks close to the river.

I'd felt oddly nervous. I was overly worried that we were running late even though Thomas assured me it wouldn't be a problem.

'Darling!' I'd heard Santa's voice call out once we knocked. The door flew open in a flurry with Santa, small but large, reaching out for Thomas.

'Kit!' she'd called. She'd smiled at me warmly. 'It's such a pleasure to meet you.'

We'd dined for hours around a low table that was placed in the middle of the sitting room. Santa's paintings were stacked all around us, leaning against walls, placed in a line against a cabinet, there was just a small path of floor space so you could get around the room.

'It's just something I'm trying,' she'd said with a wave of her hand at the canvases that were filled with the same intense colours that Thomas favoured, only there were no faces, but shapes, abstract shapes, feelings.

Santa had served us endless little dishes of food. Hummus sprinkled with toasted pine nuts, pastry parcels of feta and spinach that were flamboyantly edged in curving waves. Tiny wedges of baklava, dark red cherries glossy in their bowl.

When we'd left, I'd been dazed by everything I'd consumed. Not just the food, or the place, but Santa herself.

'She has that effect on people,' Thomas had said as we walked away, and I'd tried to put it into words.

'She's wonderful.'

'She is a special person. When I left home, I realised that people have a capacity for joy. And Mum, despite everything that has happened to her, protects hers fiercely. She enjoys her life. She makes it her business. It's not a bad way to be.'

'You mean your dad leaving?' I'd asked gently.

'Yes, that. Dad going how he did hit her hard. And her sister, Cecelia, died when she was in her early twenties. They were very close. She had cancer. It was sudden.' Thomas had taken a deep breath as though he were going to say something else but it just turned into a sigh.

'Did your mum always paint?'

'She's painted for as long as I can remember. She started young but then she stopped for a period, maybe when Cecelia died. And then well, the rest is history.'

Santa gave us a painting for our wedding, of course. It looked like a brother or sister to one of the pieces that she'd had sitting in a line against the cabinet that day. It made me feel something like union, something like love.

Our short wedding ceremony was over as quickly as it began. Afterwards felt like the real part. We booked a table in a tapas restaurant for lunch and the three of us sat and ate and drank until it was dark outside and the day was over.

I did think of Dad and of Evie, of course. I hadn't thought this day would come but I would never have imagined that if it had, they wouldn't have been there. Though I wished Evie had been able to come, part of me remembered how she'd acted when I'd last seen her – how her words stung, how she'd treated me coldly, indifferently. A ridiculous and selfish part of me called out for my sister; the sister I'd had before.

'I'm not going to give a speech,' Santa said to me, when Thomas was ordering more food. Her cheeks were flushed slightly from the wine, and I could smell it, just lightly, on her breath. 'But I do want to say to you: you and Thomas, you are happy together, and you are happy apart. And that's good, very good to see. With his father, if we weren't together, it was the end of the world. It was too much. It could only have ended badly. It shouldn't be like that. It makes you so you're not happy by yourself. But I look at my son and I look at you and you can do both. It's very good.'

She squeezed my cheeks as though her words could not express enough and then she turned to Thomas, delighted, and asked if he had ordered some sherry.

When we each had a small thimble of chilled sherry in front of us, Santa said again, 'I'm not going to make a speech. But to Kit and to Thomas, who love each other.'

And at that moment, we told ourselves the lie that so many

before us have told, not that it makes it any less real or true or comforting.

That nothing could dent our happiness, that we were the masters of our little world.

Thomas met my eyes and we drank.

NOW

I try to give Mimi some water but she won't take a sip. She's
slumped drowsily over my shoulder and won't lift her head.

'Baby, wake up. Please try to have a little drink,' I say.
There's desperation in my voice but it does nothing to revive
her.

'Mimi? Mimi?'

I hear the sound of gravel crunching on the drive.

THEN

Not long after we were married, Evie invited us to her house.

It felt like a summoning of sorts, maybe an apology, perhaps a clearing of what lay between us. We had not spoken face to face since the day she'd paid in the money from Dad's estate. I'd written to her about our sudden and unexpected wedding; the messages she'd left about coming and then not being able to had been curt and brief.

Though there was a lot that I wanted to talk to her about, the day that we visited her opened another gully between us. It felt odd that she had not been there for our wedding, but it was again, understandable and not of any consequence other than that I wished we could have shared the day together.

I saw the shape of Evie approaching through the warped glass. She was wearing something brightly green – emerald, almost.

When she opened the door, her smile was red and gleeful – she looked like another being to the person who'd last opened the very same door to me.

'Come in, come in,' she said.

'I'm sorry we're late—'

She batted my apology away as though she were swatting a fly. 'Doesn't matter. It's just brilliant that you're both here. There's someone who really wants to see you.'

She smiled again, straightened her dress, it hugged her waist and flowed out into a wide skirt.

We followed her into the kitchen.

'Look who's here!' Evie exclaimed.

Then the bang of plastic on plastic.

A murmur and a gurgle.

Jakob, sitting in a highchair, as though he had never left.

NOW

I look through the window and make out the shape of a child sitting in the back of the car.

For one moment, I freeze. I have the urge to hide, to run, but with Mimi still draped over me I walk towards the front door.

The engine turns off. A part of me is thumping, yelling. *Get out. Disappear. There's still time.*

The car door opens and closes almost silently. Then another door. There's the same sound: the shush and thud of open and close. I can hear the tread of footsteps across the driveway. I can hear a young voice prattle – I can't make out words, just the up and down of his timbre. Then I hear Evie, in answer to him. I hear her laugh.

Then the footsteps stop. Where they should have carried on and the door should have opened, there is silence.

She's seen the broken glass. She thinks there might be someone in the house. I run through quickly what she will do: she will call for help, she will return to the car, I will not see her. It's what I wanted, to not be seen by her but now, with Mimi sick, I need her. I need help.

I rush to the front door and try to open it but it is of course locked. I dart as fast as I can, carrying a groaning Mimi, to the hole in the glass that I made and I shout out to her.

'It's me. Evie, it's me, it's me.'

It's harder clambering out of the hole than I remember climbing through it. I pick my way past the shards of the glass; I'm looking down at where I'm stepping when I can sense that they are in front of me, that they have seen me.

Evie's mouth has dropped open, her goSphere is in her hand by her side and in her other, she holds the hand of my nephew.

THEN

'Jakey!' I called out before I knew what I was saying.

He did not look up at my appeal and instead chased the rice cake around the white plastic of his high chair.

I glanced at Thomas, who wore a stunned expression, one I imagined I was mirroring. He walked up to Jakob and picked up the rice cake so the child could reach out and grab it. He took it with one, chubby starfish hand and thoughtfully sucked on its corner.

Thomas and I regarded his every movement as though it were a miracle.

Evie laughed, delighted, at her son, at our gormless expressions.

'Surprise!' she said. The shade of her lipstick was a little too bright; it cracked at the bud of her mouth. 'Can you believe it?'

She leant into the top of his head and took a long inhale.

'It's really him,' I said. He was larger, lengthier and had a stability that he'd not possessed before, but he was the same Jakob.

I reached out towards him, and Jakob following the movement of my hand, put out his fingers to meet mine. It was as he stretched forwards that I saw the short sleeve of his babygrow rise and, beneath it, the OSIP band around his wrist.

Evie, spotted me noticing and smiled at me rigidly; her tight expression stopped me from asking her more.

'When did he come back?' I asked instead.

'The day before yesterday,' she said. She ran her fingers delicately through his hair.

On her wrist, she wore a matching OSIP band. She turned it round and round and then drove it further up her arm as though she were worried it would slip off.

'What happened?' Thomas asked in the end, after we had wordlessly looked from baby to each other to baby to Evie and then back to Jakob.

'Well,' Evie said, as she started to tear lettuce into a bowl. 'Remember what you said about trying to find out procedures about getting Jake back? I didn't want to listen to you, but you were right. There are classes that you can take. I did a course, had to take some tests and, well – I passed.'

Thomas caught my eye, his expression painfully disbelieving, as Evie snapped off the yellow heart of the lettuce and scattered its thin petals into the bowl.

'That sounds—' he began to say.

I cut into his sentence before he could finish it.

'Wonderful,' I exclaimed. 'That sounds wonderful.'

I had been worried that he was going to say it sounded easy. Because it did, it sounded far too easy. After everything that Evie and Seb had gone through to have Jakob and the trauma of how he was taken – was it really so simple to get him back?

'And Seb?' I asked quickly.

'He hasn't seen him yet.' Evie sliced a red pepper into thin strips. She sped up as she reached the last remaining chunk. 'But he will, of course. He's still Jakey's father, whatever has happened between us.' She tossed the peppers into the salad and slammed it on to the table so that its contents jumped a little out of the bowl.

'It's the best news ever,' I said. I reached for my sister and she let me hold her for a moment before Jakob babbled something and she knelt beside him, checking over his face.

'Is it back to normal with OSIP now?' Thomas asked. 'Do you get to start over?'

'Thomas,' I said warningly, shaking my head. I didn't want any more talk of OSIP.

'They'll keep doing regular checks,' Evie said. 'But the course I took and passed counts for a lot.' She looked unconcerned.

'What was it called?' Thomas asked.

'It had some kind of abbreviation,' Evie said. 'I can't remember it exactly.'

'Well, it's just terrific. I can't believe it. We should be drinking champagne!' I said. My eyes met Thomas's, willing him not to ask any more.

'Yes!' Evie said. She opened the fridge door and brought out a green bottle. 'We should. And we must celebrate your wedding, too. I'm sorry I couldn't come. It was the course – I'm sure you can understand why I had to miss it.'

'Don't even think about it,' I said. 'What matters is that Jakey is back.'

I bent down to kiss his head. Like Evie, I was drawn to the

smell at the very top of his head. I took a lungful and for a moment I didn't want to expel it, I wanted to keep it inside of me.

All dinner, we were all drawn to every movement that Jakob made, every utterance. We returned to him after every mouthful, with each word. By the end of the meal, he was quite exhausted from all of the attention.

'Did they tell you much about the compound that Jakob was at?' Thomas asked over dinner.

Evie frowned. 'No, they don't tell you that kind of thing.'

'When did you find out?' he continued to ask. 'How long did you have to wait after the course finishing to know you were getting him back?'

'Not very long,' Evie said vaguely. She kept her gaze fixed on Jakob as she spoke.

'It's just brilliant that that course exists,' Thomas went on. 'I've never heard of it before. I wonder if your friends whose baby was extracted found out about it?' he asked me.

'Marie and Leo? I hope so,' I said.

'Well,' Evie said. 'Part of it was that you were selected to go on it. The course. It wasn't open to everyone. They don't tell you how they decided – maybe it was something to do with what kind of IPSs you had or how you behaved or something.'

'Did you meet anyone else on it?' Thomas asked.

'No, it was done in an isolation booth,' Evie said. 'I didn't meet any other parents.'

I was afraid Thomas would go on questioning all night and so when, moments later, Evie left to go to the toilet, I hissed into his ear, 'What's with the twenty questions?'

'What? It's just amazing that it's happened, don't you think?'

'Don't ask any more about it – can't you see how uncomfortable it's making her?'

On the way home, though, with no Evie there, he wanted to talk about it more.

'What is this course?' he said. 'Had you ever heard about it?'

'Stop questioning everything,' I told him. 'Just be glad that Jakob's with us again. It's like a miracle.'

'It *is* a miracle,' he said back.

NOW

Jakob stares, not scared but astounded by the sight of us. He is the one who speaks first.

'Who is this, Mummy?' he asks, his eyes large.

I always thought that if we had given them the chance to know one another that Jakob and Mimi would have loved and doted on each other. I imagine that we would never have been able to leave them in the same room because he would always want to pick her up.

But they are strangers. Jakob does not know who I am. The gulf between Evie and me has extended to our children.

'Hello, Jakob,' I manage to say without my voice wavering too much. 'It's good to see you.'

'What happened to our house?' he asks. 'Did you see who made the hole? Is that baby okay?'

He's curious and articulate, kind and caring; he's everything that Evie hoped for.

'She's sick,' I say.

Evie's head snaps up as I say it, as I knew it would. Through it all, there is still a part of her that cares.

'What's wrong with her?' Jakob asks. He takes a step

towards us but Evie keeps hold of his hand and pulls him back.

'What do you want?' she says. 'Thomas called a couple of hours ago. He sounded upset. He wouldn't tell me what it was about but when he realised that you weren't here, he hung up.'

'We need your help,' I say.

'I can't do anything, you know that.'

'Please,' I say. 'She's not very well. She was drugged, I'm not sure what with, to make her sleep, and I think she's having a reaction to it.'

There must still be a way to reach my sister.

'Who drugged her?'

'Some people who were trying to help,' I say in the end.

'You're on a watch list, aren't you? You and Thomas, you've been... evasive, haven't you?'

'What does evasive mean?' Jakob asks. He almost stumbles over the word.

'It means someone is avoiding something that isn't going to go away.'

'Word gets round quickly.'

'You can't keep running,' she says.

'If only you'd helped us,' I say. Again, it's been said before. It didn't work then.

Evie shakes her head, a violent quiver.

'Come on, Jakob,' Evie says. 'Back in the car.'

'But—' he protests.

'Back in the car.'

They both turn, their footsteps grind against the gravel.

'Why didn't you?' I say to their retreating backs. 'Why didn't you help us?'

Evie stops. Jakob looks up at her. He is a beautiful boy; he is the most beautiful boy. His eyes are wide and wondering. Evie stares back at him. The gaze between them seems visible in the air, like a trace of a spider's web, a dew drop catching the light and making a rainbow.

'Get back in the car, darling,' she tells him. 'Wait for me.'

When she turns back towards us, she is empty-handed.

She seems like she is about to speak. She is hesitating over which words she should use.

'I couldn't help you – or I would lose him again.'

THEN

'Do you want to have children, Kit?' Santa asked over brunch. She'd made another spread of bowls for the meal; sunny chunks of mango, golden-brown granola, yoghurt sprinkled with seeds and steaming walls of toast that were shaped in thin ovals because of the profile of the loaf. We'd stopped by to see her the morning of Thomas's birthday because we were going out together, just the two of us, that evening.

'Mum,' Thomas said in warning, a little sternly, a little whingey. I had a sudden flash of him as a teenager.

'No, it's fine,' I said. I gave Santa my formulated answer, which by now I recited as though it were poem at school, more concerned that no words were missed out than what the meaning of them was. I told her that I didn't think that I could do it, that I'd been an out for years.

'And now?' Santa asked. 'You still feel the same?'

'Well, I suppose I hadn't planned on getting married,' I said. 'I never thought I would have children and now...' I stopped myself abruptly.

Thomas studied my expression. 'Mum, this is something that we need to talk about, alone.'

'Of course, of course,' Santa said. She lifted her hands up as if to say that she meant no offence.

Thomas went out to get more milk and I found that I couldn't move. I sat immobile on the chair as if I were glued to it.

'I suppose,' I said to Santa, 'there's everything that's happened with Jakob too. That has clouded everything.'

'How are Evie and Jakob doing?' Santa asked.

'They're both well – I believe,' I said, remembering guiltily that I had not seen them for a little while.

'It will take time. For everyone.'

I didn't want to admit that there was still a gulf between Evie and me. Though we hadn't openly spoken about it, I could tell Thomas thought that there was something suspect about the course she had told us about, despite the fact that some stories turned up on the Spheres about similar circumstances in the following weeks.

Santa started clearing up her little ceramic bowls carefully; she had a story about the origins of every one. 'It's one of the hardest things,' she said. 'Having a child extracted. I used to believe that it was worse than if they had died. That sounds awful, doesn't it? But I used to think that all the time when they took Sean away.'

'Sean?'

'Has Thomas not—?' She stopped herself. After a moment, she started to speak again, slowly, carefully. 'Has Thomas not told you about his little brother? Sometimes I wonder if it's too painful to him. Or if it's just that he's forgotten, he was so young.'

I tensed. I saw the things on the table in front of me, the

spoon, the crumpled heap of a napkin; they appeared larger all of a sudden as though I had been able to magnify them. I couldn't stop the same thought thundering through my mind: that I knew everything about Thomas, that we didn't keep secrets.

I remembered with sharp clarity our first visit to Santa when Thomas told me about Cecelia, the sister whom Santa had lost. He'd paused for the briefest moment after he'd told me. In that space, in that breath, lived the memory of his brother who was taken.

'It's probably that he wants to forget because it hurts too much,' Santa spoke very quietly. 'Sean was extracted when Thomas was seven. I'm not sure how clear his memories are of him. Not like mine, of course. I remember Thomas rubbing his cheek on my bump, talking away to his brother in a secret language of his own making. He loved him – well before he was born.'

'And you didn't get any IPSs when Thomas was little?'

'Things were a bit different then. I received one or two. You're the same kind of age as Thomas, aren't you?'

'A few years younger.'

'Well OSIP operated in a different way then. It really was seen to be for the good of the child. I mean, of course it still is. The threat of extraction was there but I don't remember them happening like they do now. It seems much more militant than it was.'

Santa puts the small bowls that she was holding back on to the table. 'That said, there was still the threat of them hanging in the air. But OSIP agents were more understanding. You didn't have to be superhuman. I do feel for your sister, and all of you, in your generation. It's so much harder now than it was.'

She traced a finger around the rim of one of the bowls as though it were wet clay and she would be able to mould it into a different shape. There was the very slight sound of the china ringing in the air. But then Santa brought her hand to her face as if she were about to wipe away a tear, although her eyes were quite dry, her voice steady.

'But by the time Sean came along, things were beginning to change. The number of IPSs decreased a little and there were many more reasons why you could get one. There were more and more reports on child development and the higher standards needed to help babies to progress. The effects of the infertility were really starting to hit us. Every child that was born was so precious. That's still true.'

Santa pursed her lips as though to stop something else from spilling out. Her lipstick was an orange red that day; it looked even brighter with her lips clamped together.

Thomas walked back in then, fresh-smelling from the outside.

'What?' he said when he saw our faces. 'What have you been talking about?' He looked over at Santa, his eyebrows raised.

'It's nothing,' I told him and then when the crease that had grown in his forehead did not leave his face, I reassured him further still.

'Nothing we need to worry about.'

NOW

S he lowers her eyes, away from my stare.

'Just tell me the truth,' I say. I have to shift Mimi on to my other shoulder. I hug her closely to me. I am cold in my vomit-sodden coat and worry that Mimi must be too in the towel she's in. Mimi complains from the movement, gives a tiny whimper that tells me she's in pain. 'Please – just tell me. I knew there was something that you were keeping from me. I thought it was easier to ignore it but then you changed, you turned into someone else, you weren't there…'

'I never meant to hurt you.' There's a flash of my sister. 'When Dad died – I mean it happened so suddenly – do you remember it was the very same day that we received our first IPS?'

'Of course I remember.'

'Looking back… if he hadn't had the heart attack then, there would have been no chance that I could have done what I did.' Evie swallowed hard. 'I learnt something… from Dad's papers. Something he would never have told us to our faces.'

'What? What did you learn?' I try to be clear, to sound strong, but my voice wavers; tears threaten to strangle me.

'I can't tell you. I promised I would never tell anyone. Or they'll take him again. They'll take him.'

Through the glass of the car door, Jakob is watching our faces. His eyes run from one to the other, back and forth. It's strange to see him grown up – he's both so familiar and strange to me. There's a touch of the baby's face that was so familiar and dear to me but it's transformed into something entirely new. It reminds me of watching one of Thomas's portraits grow from a few single lines, the suggestion of a curve, to a canvas full of brush strokes that make up a face.

I try not to lose myself reflecting on all that I have missed. I have lost a nephew, a child who I loved and tended as a baby, who now looks at me with no recognition.

I tighten my grip on Mimi. 'All this time you've been pretending about all the good that OSIP do.'

There's the sound of knocking. Jakob's pressed his face to the window of the car and is staring out at us. He is worried, concerned. He doesn't like that I'm crying. Evie tells him to wait with exaggerated lips so he can understand through the thick glass, that everything's okay.

'Did Seb know – what it was you learnt?' I continue. She turns back to me.

'No one knows.'

My head swims. Mimi moves against me, in the tell-tale way that means that she will be sick again. I lower her down and run my hand over her back.

'This is pointless. You're not going to tell me, are you? Not going to say what this big secret is...' But before I can go on, Mimi vomits and buries herself into me again. Her face has grown pale; her head lolls to one side as though she can no longer support it. 'I've got to go. I've got to get her to a hospital. Give me your car,' I say. It isn't a question.

Evie flinches only a little but she doesn't argue. She delves into her pocket for the key and holds it out to me.

'Go,' she says. 'Before she gets worse.' She opens the car door and reaches out for Jakob. He smiles at her when he sees her; I notice how he studies her face as she takes his hand. He is trying to please her, trying to cheer her.

'This lady is going now,' Evie tells him.

'Sorry, Jakob. I would have liked to stay and get to know you again,' I say. 'But my daughter's not well – we have to go to the hospital.'

'Hospital,' he repeats. He reaches one of his hands out towards Mimi. I bury my head into Mimi's and so he won't see my eyes fill with tears.

'Here, take my coat,' Evie says. She pulls it from her and hands it over. I wrap Mimi as best I can in the back of the car.

She seems to have grown paler in the time it's taken to move over to the car.

'I'm sorry,' Evie says from behind me.

THEN

'The thing is,' Evie said, pushing her sleeves up over her elbows. She was passing Jakob some foam balls that he was posting into his playpen with a concentrated diligence. 'OSIP *is* effective. It does work.'

'You don't really mean that,' I said. 'You do remember what it was like before, don't you?'

'But Kit, I did deserve those IPSs. Seb and I both did. What I've learnt through the extraction process has made me a much more effective mother.'

'Are you kidding?'

Evie bristled. 'Of course I'm not. I've never been more serious. That's another thing, I don't think I was serious before.'

'That's not true – you took everything seriously. Remember how much you studied for the induction and how much you tried with Jakob when his weight gain was slow?'

'But I should never have used formula before I'd been approved to – there are so many studies that show that if a mother persists with breastfeeding—'

'Evie,' I said, 'I can't believe I'm hearing you say these things. It's like you've turned into a different person.'

She was silent for a moment. 'Maybe I am a different person,' she said. She paused. 'There's something I have to tell you. It will come as a bit of surprise but I've started training to see whether I could be an enforcer.'

'An enforcer?' I almost spat out the tea I was taking a sip from.

'I want to help other people – people like me.'

'But enforcers don't help people – they act as though they're programmed or something. You know that better than most.'

'I was very emotional when Jakob was extracted.' she said the last three words under her breath. 'Roger said—'

'Roger? Roger Parris? Roger, my ex-boyfriend?'

'Yes, he's training us. Small world, huh? I mentioned before, didn't I, that I ran into him and he's working for them?'

'He's training enforcers now,' I said, shaking my head.

'Anyway, Roger said I didn't see it as help at the time, but now I do.'

'That's because you got Jakob back,' I said. 'You didn't think that when he was taken.'

'But I got him back because I deserved to get him back.'

'Of course you did – but he should never have been taken from you in the first place. You loved him, he was happy, flourishing. It was OSIP who created a problem.'

'You know you can't talk like that,' Evie said sharply. There was a silence between us. 'Maybe we should talk about something else. Agree to disagree.'

At that point, Jakob pulled himself up to standing on a wooden baby walker full of bricks. He took a few steps before it struck against an armchair, causing Jakob to tumble. I glanced towards Evie, who watched him fall.

'Oops-a-daisy,' she said, jumping up and freeing the walker so he could use it again. It was as though I could see the shadow of another Evie, the one from the past who would be on high alert, her anxiety heightening with every move Jakob made. Now Jakob navigated the sitting room for a few turns, Evie following casually in his wake, laughing easily and ready to correct the walker if it became stuck.

'Do you think you would like children?' she asked all of a sudden.

'No, no. Thomas and I are agreed,' I said. The party line. A quick dismissal with no encouragement to talk any further.

But that wasn't quite true any more.

I couldn't put into words how sometimes it now felt that we were living with a ghost. Sometimes, when Thomas sat next to me in the evening, I could see our baby resting on him. It would be curled up on its front, its cheek sunk into the solid warmth of his chest. I could see its face, perfect, closed eyelids, an almost translucent nose, a soft down.

I could make out its outline, the arch of its back that shimmered as it nestled into Thomas, to sleep only deeper still. I knew its face. A trace of Thomas, a trace of me and the part that was just itself, where we had united to make someone new, someone unique.

Then Thomas would reach forwards, for his glass perhaps, and that peculiar wondering about the baby would dissolve away. There was nothing but air – the empty space that only in my mind had been inhabited.

I had barely admitted this to myself, let alone Thomas

or anyone else, and somehow I preferred it that way. It was something that was wholly private, a fantasy that I didn't want to be diminished by reality.

Sometimes, in that space in between waking and dreaming, I thought that my belly was ripe and domed, bursting with life. I believed I could feel a movement inside me, a dialogue that was only between mother and child, and my hand would fly to my stomach. There was nothing there, of course, and I'd rub the skin there, for reassurance, perhaps. Or was it for comfort?

Then I would remember what happened to Jakob and my fingers would grasp the empty air as though the baby that was never there had been taken from us.

NOW

I rub Mimi's back gently before I close the car door and climb into the front seat. It's a huge car. I feel high up sitting in the driver's seat.

Evie leans over me and swipes at the goSphere sitting on the dashboard.

'This is the nearest hospital,' she tells me. The directions emerge from the screen, arrows blinking and pointing across the front window. 'And I've programmed in another address. Go there afterwards – if you can. They might be able to explain to you the stuff that I can't. I'm sorry that—'

'It's too late for that now,' I cut her off. I manage to keep my voice from collapsing as I tell her, 'You'd better say goodbye to Mimi – it'll be the last time that you see her.'

Evie bites her lip and glances down, but then turns back to us.

'Take care,' she says meaningfully. 'I'm sorry, I'm really sorry. I know it doesn't make it better—'

Anger floods through me, white-hot and blazing. 'Don't you get it? It's too late.'

'Did you ever stop to think,' Evie says, 'that I acted like I did for your sake, to try to protect you from—' But I slam the door shut on her words.

I start up the engine and it roars into action. I stare at the road ahead but I can't help catching the figures of Evie and Jakob in the mirror. Jakob is jumping up and down and waving with both hands, Evie stands stiffly, her arms crossed.

It's too late. I feel the certainty of those words sink under my skin.

I glance back towards Mimi, her eyes still latched close. She looks so small with Evie's coat around her.

This is the beginning of the end: this time in the car will be the last that I have with her.

THEN

We started speaking about having a baby in the car coming home from a weekend away and we ended up talking all through the night.

We propped up pillows around us, sitting upright in the nest of our bed, and went over and over the decision that we made, what led us to it.

We remembered what happened to Jakob.

We remembered how impossible it seemed that Evie and Seb were given IPS after IPS and yet it happened.

I told Thomas again about Marie, Leo and Tia.

Finally Thomas told me about Sean. He said he hadn't spoken about him for so long he almost felt guilty and the longer it went on, the harder it became. His memories of his brother were patchy; what stayed with him more sharply was the period after Sean was extracted. He said it felt like what it was: a hole, a gap, a permanent sensation of missing someone.

'I've imagined us having baby, too,' Thomas admitted at three o'clock in the morning. The night had gone on so long, we'd been awake for so many hours, the darkness was a companion to us too. It filled the windows and so all we could see through it was our reflections.

As quickly as he said it, he added: 'But it's an absolute biological imperative. If I hadn't thought about it, it would be strange. That's what OSIP is counting on. That and all the financial pressure to do it.' We knew if we stayed together and didn't start induction, eventually we'd be forced out of our nice flat, and I'd be back in that damp, dingy part of the quarter where I had lived when I first met Thomas.

'Some families keep their children, though,' I said. 'There was that person you and Seb worked with. And remember Jacqui, the woman from Jakob's naming ceremony... her sister. She still has her son.' And then: 'It could be us.'

'If you get through induction,' Thomas reminded me. 'You would have to make the decision that you can put yourself through it. I don't... I can't imagine...'

'What?'

'Losing you. I can't imagine losing you.'

'You won't,' I said straightaway, although even to my ears my tone sounded falsely reassuring. We didn't know the exact numbers of women who didn't survive induction but it happened to enough people that the risk was very real.

'It worked for Evie,' I said instead.

'In the end. That's another thing they're counting on. That blind, unshakeable hope that it'll be different, OK, for you.'

'It could be, though,' I insisted. 'Couldn't it?'

'Kit,' Thomas said in a way that reminded me of a feather falling to the ground. Though it seemed to hurt him to say it, he asked, 'Do you really want this?'

'I... I do. But I want you to want it too. It can't be just me.'

Thomas didn't answer.

A silence.

There was the smallest stain on the floor that I kept my gaze upon. I'd noticed it as we had been speaking. Though I knew it was impossible, in the dim glow of the bedside lamp, sometimes it seemed to have moved, changed positions, grown larger, each time I looked back at it.

I moved my foot over it so I was covering it entirely and you could not see the wavy edges where it began.

Thomas started to speak; I had to concentrate on pulling my focus back to him.

'There's no rush anyway, is there?' he was saying. 'Why don't we just mull it over? See how things are in a month? I feel like I'm playing catch up if I'm honest. I just never expected us to have children. I wouldn't let myself contemplate that we might. And now, just truly imagining it… well, it's… it's probably, it's probably the best thing that I can imagine.' His face dissolved into a smile and for just that moment, the worry that he was carrying with him dissipated. 'But I don't want to let myself get carried away. There're so many reasons why we decided we wouldn't do it. We can't forget that.'

We never did.

We looked for families everywhere. Walking along the street. In supermarkets and parks. Through the glazing of car windows. There weren't many.

One day I tried to see if I could find any information on the Spheres about changes in IPS limits, but there was nothing. All that was left was anecdotal and I couldn't ask anyone that I didn't trust completely, a circle no bigger than Thomas now.

And then, as though there was someone watching our every move, who had heard our conversations, delved into the fabric of my daily thoughts, the IPS level was raised to ten.

You now would have to receive ten IPSs for a child to be extracted. Three more chances.

Thomas noted the news on the Spheres, raising his eyebrows at me. Almost hopefully.

That's when I knew that our tiny family was going to grow, that we were going to try to have a child.

NOW

M*y XC baby*. Evie's goSphere blares out. The film interrupts the directions to the hospital.

I swing past other cars in the road.

A woman's toothy grin fills the Sphere.

I talk to Mimi over the voices. I recognise that I do it to comfort myself, rather than her.

'You're going to be all right, my darling,' I say. 'We're going to find a way to make you better.'

I continue to chatter to her and, as I drive, I try again to remember any detail from the flat about the drugs that they gave her, but I only draw blanks.

We are approaching the hospital. The green arrows are back now that the film has finished and project across the windscreen, urging me onwards. I turn into the hospital, drive the car right up to the entrance at an oblique angle and throw open the doors to reach for Mimi.

'She's been drugged,' I tell the medical team that swarm around Mimi. 'Something to keep her asleep, but she has been vomiting for the last hour or so. She's becoming unresponsive.'

They have question after question for me: what was the name of the drug? How much had she taken? Has she reacted like this before?

With each uncertain answer I give, I'm failing her over and over.

I am in the room with her but she is almost out of sight as the doctors crowd around her, the monitors are attached, her skin is pricked for blood and a drip.

She is pale and limp, my daughter who can roar. I watch the heart monitors keenly but I cannot understand what they mean. All I have are the scraps of talk that I pick over like carrion.

'Her heart rate's slowing.'

'More fluids.'

'Have we got a line in yet?'

There is a slight pressure on my arm. At first I swipe it away but then it intensifies; I realise it's someone holding on to me.

'Can you come with me, please? We have some questions for you.'

I turn to see a man with a receding hairline, the letters of OSIP dangling round his neck. His eyes are creased with tiredness; he has the grey hue of exhaustion.

I take one last glimpse of Mimi, pricked with needles, encircled by tubes.

'I love you,' I mouth to her.

I imagine the words drifting over to her like balloons, landing gently, kissing the soft curve of her forehead.

Then I take a deep breath and with all the strength that I have left, I push past the enforcer, I take off down the corridor.

I run and I run and though I am quite aware that I will get stopped, I run anyway.

When I reach the car, I stall for a second. I can't believe that I've made it this far, I was sure that I would be caught. But I banish the thought; I think of something new.

I swerve from the hospital, from Mimi.

THEN

A mouth screaming.
Fists pumping.
Screaming.
Screaming.
Screaming.

I wake from a dream like this almost every night since we started induction.

It was Jakob alone.

It was Tia.

It was every baby.

It was our baby.

It was me.

All rolled into one.

We decided not to tell anyone about starting induction unless I became pregnant.

Thomas used to say, after we first got together, that we protect the ones we love most in the only way we know how. He had been working on a series of portraits he'd started on families, at the time, a parent with a child.

A father holding his daughter's hand crossing a road. That

portrait translated into a close-up of their fingers, clasped together tightly. They made such a knot, those fingers, that they became a new shape. Abstract and conjoined.

A mother nursing her baby. A light emitted from within them, somehow, bathing their foreheads, the mother's arms in a circular embrace.

The baby we'd dreamed of, the baby we wanted to meet so badly, could we protect it? Could we honestly say we could? We were inching towards it, and we had to reach out to it.

Didn't we?

Shouldn't we?

I started the cycle of drugs. Injections twice a day, to begin with.

In one of our first group sessions, we had a discussion about whether you had an ethical right to have children. At first, everyone was reluctant to speak under the gaze of the enforcers. We twisted our fingers, only looking up to see if someone else would speak first. One of the enforcers, a man called Reynard, began to get impatient with us.

'Tell me your thoughts, people,' he urged.

There was a couple, Susannah and Maeve. They both had sandy, floppy hair, and large, spaniel eyes that fixed in the distance on an unknowable horizon as they talked.

'One of the reasons that OSIP is so laudable is because it not only takes you through the fertility treatment but it helps you to be the best parent you can be,' Susannah said. She entwined her fingers with Maeve's tightly. 'Only through extraction can children be provided for best.'

She sought out agreement with a softly painted-on smile.

I stared down at my lap as though I were thinking hard

about her contribution, trying not to let my face reveal how I truly felt, as I could hear Reynard respond.

Thomas and I had a pact to try not to make eye contact in these sessions, which I swiftly broke as I heard Reynard praising Susannah for 'that insightful comment'. Though a woman called Pamela was speaking now, Reynard saw my side glance to Thomas and interrupted her.

'Kit, would you like to share something?'

I had the urge to say 'no' but no one can dodge a direct question from an enforcer.

'I suppose I wonder…' I started to piece together a sentence that would try to convey at least a fraction of what I felt. 'I wonder if there might be ways other than extraction that would…'

I could feel Thomas tense besides me.

Susannah's voice rang out straightaway. 'A way other than extraction?'

'Maybe extractions can put parents off,' a very timid woman called Patrice suggested. She spoke as I imagined a mouse would, a tiny squeaking voice that I strained to hear.

As if she had not spoken, Susannah continued, 'The parenting standards are here for a reason. They should be honoured and upheld and, if they put people off, then that's no bad thing.'

'Do you not think that it could be a little intimidating, though?' I asked.

'Surely induction is the bigger concern,' Susannah quipped back. 'Whether your body responds to the drugs or how it responds to them. What the effects might be.'

'Now that's an interesting point,' Reynard said. 'And

one which, of course, you've all confronted. The process of induction does not come without risk. But despite the scare-mongering out there, we're going to examine some actual figures that show it's far safer than most people realise.'

From then, we were lost in a blaze of statistics about induction that made my head swim.

After a training day, Thomas and I would come home, and not talk to each other for a few hours. I was afraid that if we did start to speak then we would slowly unpick everything that we had built up so far, undo the distance that we had already come.

We never spoke about quitting, although there was a couple who did after only the first few weeks. The rest of us all noticed their absence. Susannah made a point of asking where they were and so one of the enforcers told us that they had withdrawn.

'I've heard that if you withdraw that you can never try again,' Susannah said.

'No, that's not true,' another enforcer said, an older woman called Sally, frowning a little. 'And there are some studies that indicate that when couples come back after withdrawing they are more successful in meeting standards than first-time couples.'

'It hardly shows commitment, though, does it?' Susannah said, bristling.

'She wants to be an enforcer, herself, don't you think?' a tiny voice whispered into my ear. It was Patrice, who barely spoke. Her eyes danced a little as we giggled as loudly as we dared but she quickly looked away from me as we felt Susannah's eyes upon us.

'Do you have an opinion on this, Kit? Patrice?' Susannah asked us.

'It's interesting to hear the findings of the new studies,' I said back quickly. 'We wondered if there are plans to do more, in the long-term?'

Sally started to talk about the studies in what felt like an endless way. I nodded and made noises at the right times but I wasn't listening. Patrice had disappeared to the other side of the room, as far as she could possibly be from me. And Susannah fixed me with a sort of look that reminded me of a cat stalking its prey, a stare that didn't waver, but glowed with anticipation.

There was a huge amount we were given to learn, as Evie had once told me, but nothing could distract me from what was happening to my body.

I could sense the medication inside me, like lead weights that I was always carrying. Not only physically, in my ovaries, which were being stimulated, hyper-stimulated, and growing larger by the day, but in the way my mind was ragged, torn almost.

I was splitting into pieces. There's no other way of describing it. It was the oddest but most visceral sensation, as though I was somehow leaving parts of my brain scattered outside of myself as I went about my day. Each night, there seemed to be less of what made me 'me'.

I would swing into a mood before I realised what was happening. I simply could not keep track of my emotions. And in much the same way, my body would flush with heat and be taken over by the sensation.

I had daily scans to check the progress of my ovaries. I could see them, picture them, being inflated like two balloons, larger and larger they grew, tighter and tighter it felt. But I wasn't responding 'in the right way', I needed a higher dose, and then another. The nausea that never left me was the easiest part.

I tried to lose myself in the learning, although my brain was sluggish and foggy. I'd left life documenting now. I wondered if I would miss it but I couldn't imagine being able to write and the induction learning took all of my energy. We'd convinced ourselves that it would shield us from extraction if I ever got to the point where I actually became pregnant.

We made notes, and then notes of our notes, distilling everything down to just a few words that we hoped would trigger everything else.

Evie came round when we were trying to memorise the order in which the phonic alphabet should be taught. I tried hard to push out the information that was restlessly knocking around my mind as I made her a coffee, as I leapt to move the glasses on the table out of Jakob's reach. I rinsed the clinging coffee grains from the cafetière but as they swirled down the sink in a mass of black clumps and then sediment that would not shift, I could not help but start to play the phonic sounds out in my mind, anything to distract me from the nausea that was swelling in my belly.

S. Sssssssss.

A. Aa, aa, aa, aa.

'Kit?' Evie said.

'Sorry, I'm—'

'You're miles away. I was asking how the allotment was

going now? You still go there, don't you? Maybe I could bring Jakob with me one day.'

'I haven't been there recently, actually. You know how it is. A lot going on.'

Evie leant back and gazed at me appraisingly.

'Your face is…' she stared to say and then stopped herself. 'You've started, haven't you? Induction. You and Thomas.' The words caught in her throat a little but she pushed them out.

I stopped rinsing the cafetière. The water continued to flow from the tap. I'd never noticed before how it sounded, that gushing stream; it could have been somebody shushing another.

'I should have told you.'

'Do you really think it's a good idea?' Evie said.

Her words cut through me. I turned the water off. Now the kitchen was deadly quiet.

'What do you mean by that?' My voice was dangerously low.

'Well, your history of being an out,' Evie started to say but then Jakob began to climb on to the rocking chair in the corner. It swayed unsteadily. She went to retrieve him.

She continued, Jakob on her hip. 'I just didn't think it was something that you ever wanted. That's all.'

'I thought that you might be happy for us.' I couldn't help spitting out the word: happy.

Evie sighed. 'It's not about me being happy for you. You should want to do this because you know you can. What's the financial incentive now?'

I mumbled a figure.

'Sizable. So, how are you finding it?' she asked. 'How many weeks in are you?'

'We're seven weeks in.'

'You're right in the thick of it then,' Evie said lightly. 'But you still have a way to go.' She kissed Jakob quite unselfconsciously on the head.

'Yes,' I said. I didn't trust myself to say anything more.

'And have you had any second thoughts since you started?'

'I... I...' I didn't want to admit to her how many doubts I'd had.

'It's not for everyone – sometimes you have to get halfway down the path to realise that.'

'Are you saying that I'm going to be an awful mother? Is that it?'

'Do you believe that?' Evie shot back.

I floundered.

Evie said slowly, 'You should think really carefully about whether you really want this. Whether you are up for it.'

'I think that you should leave.' The demand barked from me.

'I know it's painful to talk about, Kit,' Evie said. 'But that doesn't mean we shouldn't – there's nothing wrong with recognising a weakness. You can shoot the messenger if you want but if you don't think that you can be a good enough mother, then you probably won't be. It's not too late to change your mind.'

Each word slapped and settled deep into my core. She'd spoken aloud the very worst fear that I had not been able to admit to myself – I would not be able to do it, we would fail, I would smash our fragile happiness.

I stood there, almost paralysed, and watched her leave.

I didn't see her again until Mimi was in my arms.

NOW

I can't think about the fact that I've just left the hospital without Mimi. The arrows for the address that Evie programmed in pulse across the windscreen and direct me on.

I have no place to go, no idea of what to do but follow them.

I take the main road north and as I accelerate, the car leaps forwards.

The scenery is different here – it's rawer, more beautiful – as though we have passed by some invisible border and are in a new land. The traffic on the road has dropped off as the light begins to dwindle.

I find myself thinking of Thomas. I long for him, I crave his gentle attention, the timbre of his voice. I wish he were beside me.

For the first time, I regret leaving him today. Maybe if I had spoken to him properly, if I had forced myself to tell him truly how I felt, he would have listened, he would have come.

The directions take me to a turning where there is a sign for an island. I can see its cragginess in the distance, it sits like a ship on the sea. It's a place I've seen before, I'm sure, although I've never been here.

The sky stretches out, onwards.

It's another road that I could take. The clouds hang in tiger stripes illuminated by the dying sun.

A reflection of the sky, the land lies flat here. Everywhere there is space. Land, sky and space.

I slow the car to a crawl as I reach another turning and the directions tell me that I am almost at my destination. I take the narrow track.

This must be a lonely place to live. Devastatingly beautiful, but lonely. I haven't passed another house for a while. The road creeps round, it turns a corner and this too is familiar. I feel it in my heart, sure that this is the right place to be.

Around another bend and there's a building in the distance. Even from this far away, it makes Evie's house look slight. I drive up to the gates and when they do not open, I open the car door and step out.

There's no one there, no intercom to speak to, just solid, closed gates that show no sign of opening.

I walk right up to the gates, peer through the bars. I can still see the house in the distance; I imagine I can see a light on in there.

As I stand there staring through the gates, I notice a black globular detail in the wall. It's easy to miss. It could be something decorative, but I'm sure it's a camera. I stare into it, unblinking. And then, slowly, the gates rumble open.

I jump back into the car, press forwards. It's a long drive still to the house, each second passes painfully. This is the last move I can make and I have no way of knowing if it's a dead end or a route to the centre of a maze.

He's there to greet me when I pull up outside the door.

I recognise him immediately from the way he stands, the shape of his body, the tilt of his head.

It's too big, this house, for only one man to live in. There should be a family filling it; there should be staff, discreet in the background.

But there is only him. For a reason I can't explain, I'm sure that it's only him.

'It's Kit, isn't it?' he says.

'Jonah,' I answer back.

THEN

I swiped away the article on the Spheres I'd been reading when I heard Thomas's key in the door. It was a piece about the success of XC babies and it made me think of Jonah and his daughter, Genevieve. I had no way of knowing for sure, now I had stopped work, but Genevieve's XC should have been born by now and cleared for them to take home. I'd seen with other clients that the XC newborns were monitored for a period of time outside of the artificial womb before they were given to the parents. They needed more time to build up their microbiomes. What with that and the longer gestational periods, the XC babies being handed to their parents in photos in the article were much more developed than I remembered Jakob as a newborn in the hospital.

I'd been waiting for Thomas to return home, my skin prickling each time I heard any sound that might be him. There'd been a few false starts, when I'd risen from my chair before I realised it was just the sound of someone passing in the corridor, when the door had remained stubbornly closed under my watchful stare.

I had news. Not the news that we were hoping for, and

I wanted to tell him in person. Being on my own all day, without anyone to share it with, I could sense it multiplying inside me as the hours passed. At first it had felt containable, but it kept doubling in size, growing from two to four, four to eight, eight to sixteen. And now the information that had sprung up on my workSphere that morning was something with a shell, an outer and an inner, something alive.

I was on him before he had shaken off the outside, his bag still in hand, the skin of his coat around him. I remember the look of surprise as I embraced him. I held him hard, needing to feel something different from my liquid insides that squirmed and turned around my centre.

'I've got to go in for more tests,' I mumbled into his coat. It was just a bit too rough against my cheek, like sandpaper or calloused skin.

'Tests? What kind of tests?'

Thomas's arms were still around me but he was trying to let go of me. He wanted to speak to my face. I clung on to him tighter. It would be easier to tell him if I didn't have to look at him, if he wasn't looking at me.

'I might... I might have something wrong with me.' I was like a child. I couldn't speak in details. I could only face a vague, rounded truth.

Thomas took a breath as if he were about to speak but the air had become trapped inside him. I was aware of his pulse beating through his chest and arms.

I released him then and looked into his troubled, worried eyes.

'The induction drugs,' I said slowly in explanation, not trusting my voice not to fall apart.

*

On another day, I leapt up from my desk and went to greet him, to surprise him with the news. The news that we wanted.

But as soon as he saw my face, something changed in his. It was more complicated than any one emotion. It was cut through with despair, riddled with panic, heavy with hope.

Of course he didn't say anything of the sort, he whooped when I told him, lifted me up and swung me round. He laid his palm across my stomach. He insisted on going out to get my favourite food for dinner and kept repeating it was the best news, it was just the best news.

It was the best, it was just the best.

We were lucky, we told ourselves. And we said that because it was true.

The tests had caught the pre-cancerous cells early and the operation went smoothly. I recovered quickly.

These words make it feel contained; I know that, I like that.

Sometimes in the first moments of waking, I would forget and then remember I was pregnant. I would study myself for any sign of it and in the early days, when I would find none I could distinguish, I would catch my disappointment dropping through me like rain.

There seemed to be no time and too much time before she was born. I was impatient for her arrival and yet there was so much that we needed to do before then, that I fell into a sort of lethargy about it.

Thomas and I trailed round the Outstanding Homes for longer than we should have and so we ended up bickering and hungry from decision-making and adrenaline. We'd moved into a small house in the west quarter when I became pregnant and had been awarded the according housing credits. It was one of the newer builds with bedrooms on the ground floor and a single open living space on the first floor that would reach more light. It took us a while to decide on a property and now we just had to disagree on how to fill it.

'What's the most important thing we can give this baby?' Thomas asked me after one of these fraught afternoons.

'This sounds like one of the induction guides. What is it, safety, support...' I started to run off.

'No, seriously, what's the most important thing?'

'Love.'

'Love. Not things. Not the perfect crib. Or the most accurate heartbeat monitor. Love is the answer. We don't need all that stuff, Kit. Not really. We just feel like we do.'

'Okay,' I said. 'Love, not things. You're right.'

We kissed each other then, and I wondered how long it had been since we had last done that. It had been too long.

'But can we still get that chair?' I asked into the crease of his shoulder.

He ordered it to arrive on a Monday and it came in a huge box, which the delivery men struggled to get up the stairs to where our living quarters were on the first floor. At one point they thought it would not fit and they would have to take it back, but I insisted that they squeezed it round the corner, pleading that I wouldn't mind if there were any scuffs or wear and tear to it.

When I unwrapped it, there was no need to worry; there were layers and layers of packaging. At the centre was the golden chair, gliding lines and polished smooth to the touch.

I put it at the head of the table and imagined mealtimes with the three of us there. It seemed so real that it felt more like a memory than a daydream. But Thomas frowned when he saw it placed there, waiting.

'Don't you think it's tempting fate a little?' he said, and so I moved it into one of the cupboards, covering it with a sheet as though it were a piece of art in storage, awaiting exhibition.

I first felt Mimi move when I was standing in a queue at the supermarket. I almost dropped the box of tomatoes I was holding and looked up, grasping my stomach.

It wasn't the flurry of bubbles I'd been told to expect, but something more like a jab, a 'hey there', a jolt.

'Are you all right?' the cashier asked.

'It's just that the baby moved. It's... it's the first time.' There was a part of me that didn't want to share this with a stranger. And another that could not resist it.

'There's nothing like it,' the cashier said. She pursed her lips together as though to stop a smile from spilling out. 'Enjoy it, love. Enjoy it while it lasts.'

Her eyes glazed over with sadness, awash with memories. Then, she nodded her head, and smiled at me properly this time, although it was small, tight and fleeting.

When I could see a ripple of movement in my stomach, or thought that I could very almost see a foot outstretched and kicking me, I told myself that I would go and see Evie. I got as far as her street, but I never made it to her front door.

NOW

The distance between Mimi and me floors me now: I am on my knees.

'Easy, easy,' Jonah says. He helps me to stand and though he is slight, he takes my weight.

He is smaller than I imagined.

I have felt in the past that I know more about this man than I know about myself, although somewhere along the way I forgot he was a real person. I forgot that any of my life document clients were. They were like a book I was reading, a story I'd dip in and out of, a character on the page for the purpose of a plot.

Not real. Not wrinkled just a little around the eyes. Not wearing a jumper that has a stain on its front, which he doesn't seem to have noticed. I wonder if he did that today, at lunch, or if it's been there for a while and there was no one to tell him.

I begin to babble. 'My daughter's in hospital… my sister gave me this address. It's you, why is it you? All of this time, I've been writing—'

'I'm an admirer of your work,' he cuts in. He is thoughtful;

I am reminded of how he encouraged Genevieve when she was a young child.

'The life document – you know about me, you know who I am? But how does that link with Evie? Why did she send me to you?' I struggle to grasp each thought.

'One thing at a time.' He speaks very slowly, deliberately. It almost grates against my frantic outbursts.

'I don't know why I'm here.'

He peers at me, his head held slightly to one side. I am reminded of the robin at the roadside restaurant. 'Your daughter – Mimi.'

I almost shriek, rather than speak: 'You know about her too? You know about Mimi?'

'I learnt you'd stopped life documenting. It didn't take much to find out why.'

'You're connected with them, aren't you – OSIP? You're involved with them somehow. I need your help...'

As though I hadn't just begged, as though I weren't clawing at him desperately, he says, with a slowness: 'First things first. You must want to have a wash.'

I can't imagine what I look like to him. I am still wearing the pyjamas I wore when I climbed out of bed this morning. I am coated in Mimi's vomit. But the last thing I want to do at this moment is wash.

'I don't have time – there's no time. My daughter, she's not well—'

'You said she was in hospital. She's being cared for there?'

I can't bear to admit it but I nod, in tiny movements.

'I'm not an enforcer, Kit,' Jonah says. He has a gentle voice; I start to feel lulled by it. 'Will you come in? We can talk more, if you like. You can have a shower. You must be hungry.'

The idea of eating now revolts me. I can't imagine chewing food, I can't think of swallowing it down. All that fills my mind is that last image I have of Mimi, small on the hospital bed and growing smaller still as I ran away from her.

I want to shout, I want to shake him. I don't have time to think of myself, of being clean, of feeling nourished – I have to get back to her. Every moment that passes is another moment away from her.

But this is my only hope. I don't know why I'm here, but I know that there is no other place I should be. I meekly follow him, although on the inside, I'm churning. On the inside, I'm screaming.

Inside, the house is slightly dilapidated. Rooms that are clearly not used are full of dust and feel abandoned. Jonah leads me to the back of the house, to a large space that once must have been something grand and now has all the shabby trappings of daily life. He gestures to the sofa and hands me a bottle of water.

'No – thank you.'

But he just says, 'Drink' and continues to hold it out to me. It's a command.

I start to drink in large, noisy gulps. Water runs down my chin. I hadn't realised how thirsty I am.

'Please – sit,' he says. He points out the sofa again and then as though to encourage me, he settles in an armchair before me.

I finish the bottle of water without meaning to.

'My daughter—' I begin to say.

Jonah holds up a hand. The gesture silences me.

'First – wash. I'll get you some clean clothes. Have something to eat. I insist.'

'I've got to—' My mouth fills with all that I could lose.

'You've been rushing from one place to another all day, haven't you?' Jonah coaxes. 'You're tired, aren't you?'

'I'm… I'm—'

'If Mimi's not well, as you say, then she's in the best place she can be. There's nothing you can do but to let the doctors do their job.'

'Mimi's in hospital,' I repeat. As I say it aloud, I wonder what I am still doing here if Jonah is not able to save her. 'I should go back to her… If you can't help us, I must go.'

I am struck again by the last glimpse I had of her, surrounded by medical staff, her thin limbs decorated in tubes and drips and machines. She was almost lost amongst it all.

'I never said that.' Jonah speaks gently. 'I never said that I wouldn't help you.'

THEN

I didn't want to put Mimi down in her crib on that first day. There would be days to come when I would have given almost anything to be able to put her down, but that day I didn't want her out of my arms. She rested her head on the very crook of my arm, nestling her cheek just to the side. Her snub nose grazed against my skin. I marvelled at it.

I marvelled at every part of her.

I wondered, briefly, if I would ever be able to move again.

Thomas sat, his arm over my shoulders, balancing on the hospital bed with us. It felt as though his arms were big enough to reach the whole way around us. We stayed there, wrapped around one another, like Russian dolls, transfixed and still.

Then the door opened, and I saw Evie standing there at the entrance. She hesitated, unsure whether to step forwards or backwards. The nurse who had arrived to do some checks on Mimi tutted a little that she was in her way.

'Evie! You came!' I cried.

She was more angular than when we'd last seen each other, over a year ago. Older in a way, too. She carried herself stiffly as she walked towards us.

'Could you come back in five minutes?' I asked the nurse.

'This has to be done now,' she replied, a little sharply, but then she softened and said, 'It'll only take a jiffy.'

Evie raised her eyebrows at me but said she would come back. I wondered whether she would, but a little while later, she returned. She twisted her hands and worried the rings on her fingers; she couldn't stay still.

'There's someone here who wants to meet you,' I spoke into the blanket bundle with Mimi's delicate face at its centre. 'This is your Auntie Evie.'

Evie took a step towards us but she didn't lean in as I imagined that she might. She could not see Mimi properly from where she stood.

'Hey, why don't I go and get some drinks for us all,' Thomas said. He made a movement with his eyes in Evie's direction. He looked hopeful.

When we were alone, neither of us spoke at first.

'Why didn't you bring Jakey?' I asked in the end.

'Young children aren't allowed on labour wards,' Evie spoke mechanically.

I murmured a sound, like I should have realised that.

We fell into silence.

'How are you?' she asked instead.

'Well – I'm well,' I answered. I cringed inside. We were exchanging words like we were polite strangers. Why couldn't I tell her how I was really feeling? Excited, terrified, sore, exalted, anxious and spent. 'How are you?'

'We're both fine. Jakob's doing really well.'

'He must have grown so much,' I murmured. 'I probably wouldn't recognise him.' It was meant to be a joke but it struck the wrong chord, it sounded like a dig. We lapsed into silence again.

'Do you want to hold her?' I said, offering her up, desperate for it to be different than this taut distance between us. Mimi scrunched her face up and reached upwards without warning with one of her mittened hands.

'I'd better not. I haven't washed my hands – and Jakob's into everything at the moment.'

'There's some antibacterial...' But my voice tailed off when I saw Evie shaking her head at me. 'We've named her Mimi.'

'Mimi,' Evie repeated. 'Like Mum,' she murmured.

'Yes,' I said. She'd been known by that name as a child although no one ever called her that once she'd grown up.

Evie didn't hide the expression of disapproval on her face.

'What? What's wrong?' Tears rose up. 'Why can't you just be happy for me?'

'When we last spoke, you didn't think that you were ready to be a mother and now, and now—'

'What? Now, I am one. What's so wrong with that?'

'You know how this can end. Is that really what you want? Will you be able to go through it all?'

'Are you an enforcer now? Is that it?'

'No, that's not what this about. I'm talking to you as your sister.'

'No, you're not – you never would have treated me like this before. You're not who you were, you're not...' As I spoke, as I stumbled on my own words, I realised that I had stumbled upon a truth. 'You're not my sister any more.'

Thomas arrived back at just that moment, balancing the

three cups carefully in his hands, with a look of concentrated effort.

'I'd better go,' Evie said when she saw him.

'Don't go,' Thomas said. 'Stay for a drink.'

'I've got to go,' she said simply. She didn't offer any excuses.

She had almost got to the door when she turned back to us.

'I'm sorry if none of this is what you want to hear,' she said to me. 'It's just that you really should have thought about extractions before...'

'You're saying we shouldn't have had her,' I said.

The words came slowly, heavily.

As if in answer, Evie turned and walked from the room.

I thought I could hear her footsteps clicking along the floor, long after she had left.

NOW

I can hear Jonah's footsteps coming down the corridor.
He knocks gently on the bathroom door. 'There's clothes and a towel out here when you're ready.'

Outside I find loose grey tracksuit bottoms, a shirt that's cotton, worn and soft against my skin, a huge towel that has been folded many times.

The bathroom lights feel too bright.

As I take off my coat and peel off my stale pyjamas, I look towards the sharp mirror on the wall. I inspect every ragged detail of myself. My grey skin, my breasts sagging with the weight of useless milk. The shadows beneath my eyes are almost violet and my face is lined, haggard. My hair is matted and dull. Strands are coated in Mimi's vomit and have hardened from it; they stick out in peaks.

But beneath it all, I catch my own gaze. My eyes are furiously bright; they are burning.

THEN

Mimi's light eyes locked with mine.

'You guys are pros,' Santa told me as I guided Mimi's mouth around the dark nub of my nipple.

It hadn't felt terribly natural at first, breastfeeding, but Mimi took to it immediately, as though she were the teacher, I her pupil. Though there was something that riled me a little about the way she arched her mouth towards my breast hungrily, desperately, I followed her lead. Over time, the pain and discomfort had lessened and she latched on now with complete mastery.

'Have you heard anything from OSIP?' Santa asked, casually.

'They come round to do home visits. We have another one this week. And there's the usual examinations and sending data,' I said as lightly as I could. I didn't want to think too much about all that we had to do. 'But the IPS numbers are holding steady – they are still at ten to be Unacceptable.'

Unbelievably, three months had gone by since that day in hospital. Every morning and every night, I said a sort of prayer that we would not receive an IPS, and there had been nothing.

Nothing yet.

'It makes me feel guilty,' I admitted. 'We've just had the most enormous lot of luck. That's all it is.'

'You're doing great,' Santa reassured me. 'Enjoy it.'

Sometimes I would catch myself remembering what it was like before we had her, that I would spend a day writing, scrubbing down calls to decipher a conversation, letting my mind linger on peculiarities and ideas. It felt like a distant land to me, somewhere attractive and hazy, too far away for me to see its details. I missed it but I also knew that there was no room for it now.

Though we'd been untouched by IPSs, we were monitored so closely in the early months that there were days when my head would be swimming with it. The appointments and the examinations, the sheer amount of information that we had to gather to hand over to OSIP, it all grew day by day. The procedures had changed since Evie had had Jakob; the monitoring had intensified.

On top of the work of caring for a newborn, I was crumbling underneath these constant pressures although I knew with certainty that I couldn't let myself fall apart. I was the last pillar left, eroded, bleached, notched and withered, but still holding an enormous weight. Thomas helped as much as he could but now that he was the only one of us working, we'd naturally fallen into the pattern on weekdays of him only being around when Mimi had already been put to bed. I'd notice us mothers, waiting in queues for OSIP examinations, tapping feeding times into our goSpheres, attending classes and groups especially approved for language, social and emotional development, our heads buried, bowed towards our children. We didn't have the time, the capacity, to look up. We couldn't really see each other.

I was obsessed by Mimi and all that I needed to do around her, there was just no space left for anything else.

We were getting ready to leave Mimi for the first time. A close friend of Santa's, Marina, was babysitting for us.

'We'll be as quick as we can,' I told her. 'And we have our goSpheres with us. If there are any problems.'

I told myself that it would only be for a few hours.

I made myself remember that Marina was experienced and capable. Her son was grown-up now, he was our age. I knew Mimi would be safe in her care.

But I simply didn't want to go. I did not want to leave my daughter, who had not been parted from me since the moment she had been conceived. Every iota of my energy had been dedicated to her since she'd been born and I could not shake this mode of being. We were going to an art show of Santa's. It was meant to be 'fun'. Everyone had told me this, as the plan to leave Mimi for the evening had been formulated around me. I'd tried to explain that it was too soon, that Mimi wasn't quite ready, that I definitely wasn't, but I was damped down by their voices, their reasons and couldn't make myself heard.

'Ready to go,' Thomas said, with a smile that I could not return. It was different for him, I reminded myself, he was used to leaving her when he went to work.

'Let me check on her one last time,' I said.

I let myself into her room. The peach-yellow light of her

lamp was on, and I could see her outline in the crib. Tiny movements of her arms as she tested what way they could go, the sensation they made. She was cooing at something. I didn't dare go over to her for I was sure if I saw her face, I would never be able to leave.

There was something about the way Thomas took my hand as we walked across the road to the Tube that irked me. As though he were hurrying me on or something.

'It doesn't start till seven, don't pull at me,' I said aloud, grumpiness taking over my tone. It kept happening since Mimi was born, I would think something and then realise that I had spoken it aloud.

We arrived late, though, when Santa was halfway through giving a speech. She had stood upon a chair so she could see everyone and when saw us slip in, she stopped what she was saying and blew us a kiss.

'My son, my daughter-in-law have just arrived,' she said to the crowd, in way of an apology for her breaking off, 'having put to bed my three-month-old granddaughter!'

There was a whoop from the back of the room. And a whistle that shrieked into the air. The crowd around us were clapping, united in their applause.

They looked at Santa and then back at us. Shiny, smiling faces that for those moments seemed indistinguishable from each other.

'What an entrance,' Thomas whispered into my ear.

He didn't notice though, like I did, the few people who were not applauding.

The people that looked at us, with a pursed and judgmental stare.

The people who were thinking, why weren't we home with our daughter.

The people who might be enforcers.

NOW

I'm not an enforcer, Kit.

I remember those words as I come downstairs, hair wet, my skin smelling of soap. He'd neither denied nor confirmed his connection to OSIP but he had admitted that: *I'm not an enforcer, Kit.*

I find him in the kitchen; he is cooking. He likes cooking; I know this about him.

I watch him for a moment before he realises that I am there. He looks at what's inside the saucepan on the hob. Then he adds a splash of amber-coloured olive oil, a pinch of salt crystals that he crushes into a powder between his thumb and forefinger.

He moves quickly and bends down to a cupboard for a box of pasta, which he measures out on scales. He is methodical and measured in all that he does, I know this too. He turns to me then.

'You must be famished,' he says. 'You look like you haven't eaten properly in a month.'

I murmur something. Not an answer, not an agreement. I don't even realise that it's her name I'm saying aloud.

'Mimi.' Her name feels like it's a petal on my lips.

'Eat first. Then we'll talk,' he says.

He pours me a glass of sparkling water from a bottle in the fridge and nudges a small bowl of oversized olives towards me. His eyes are bright, a curious colour somewhere in between grey and green, not dissimilar to the shiny olives.

'Eat,' he says again.

'But OSIP—' I start to say.

'Then there's nothing we can do about it, is there?'

'But you said you could help me.'

'You want to keep her. You want to know how you can keep her,' Jonah says slowly.

'Of course. I'd do – I'd do anything.' My voice sounds cracked. I wonder if I look how I sound. 'My sister sent me here. She said she learnt something. Something that she would not tell me, something that got her son back... from them. And you, you're connected to them somehow, aren't you? I mean not directly, not openly – but I saw you reading some OSIP documents once...'

Jonah is making a study of me. His grey eyes are fixed upon my face. I gaze right back at him as though it's a test. Then he says again, 'Eat first,' and turns down the heat on the pasta so the water does not boil over.

I try to sit on one of the stools. I sit on one hand and the other I hold over my mouth because, like the boiling water, I feel that everything is about to bubble furiously and overspill. How can I wait here calmly when I don't know whether this man will help us? But I'm very aware that he's the last person I have to turn to – I have nowhere else I can run, no other possibilities. I can't annoy him or aggravate him. I can't harass or harangue. All I can do is stuff my fist into my mouth to stop me from yelling. All I can do is to sit on my hand to stop me from running away.

Jonah adds cream, pepper and smoked salmon to the pasta when it is done. He scatters pointed rocket leaves into the bowl and passes it over to me along with a fork.

I can't imagine how I will eat it all but once I start, like with the bottle of water, I find my appetite. I find that I need it. Then no forkful can hold enough. I stuff in large quantities that fill my mouth and so I have to chew hard to make it manageable.

Jonah watches me eat with something like pride. He sits on the stool opposite mine.

I'm chasing down the last string of pasta when he speaks.

'Do you think that you are a good mother?'

I stop myself. The fork clatters into the bowl.

I've come to accept over the last few months that it's my fault that she was under threat of being taken from us. Every single IPS, I could unpick and find that it was me who was wanting. Every day we were given a new chance to do better but I squandered too many of them.

Considering the IPSs, I am not sure that I am a good mother. I'm programmed to doubt myself, to unravel my every action, to obsess about how I could be better. With every interaction with OSIP, I questioned myself more and more as to whether I was good enough.

Now, after all that has happened, I have little left to give. I am unsure of how to be.

Jonah continues to search my face. I can't believe that he can wave a wand and wipe out all that has happened. Surely he won't be able to erase the path that lies before my family? But he continues to seek something within me and though I feel I am at the end, that there is nowhere left to turn, I search inside myself; I speak.

'I love her,' I say. 'I want to do the best I can for her. I want to teach her about the world, I want her to feel joy, and sadness too. I want her to feel. I want to protect her and I want to discuss things with her. I want to understand how her mind sees things. I want to see the person she'll become. That's all I know, now.'

Is that enough? Is that a good mother?

I had not stopped thinking about Mimi since the moment we handed her over to the people who would smuggle her out of the country, when she was taken from my sight.

Where is she now? I wondered. Is she still in the hospital? Has she been moved to an OSIP centre? Who was the person assigned to her care? Did they know that she adored ducks? Did they warm her milk gently so it could be considered cold but was the only way she'd have it?

Evie had been the only person I'd heard of who'd actually got their child back. There had been a few more videos popping up on the Spheres about this occurrence – reunited families in sunlit forests, smiles white and wide and polished – but Jakob was the only child outside the world of the Spheres I'd known to be returned.

I think of Mimi trussed up in a hospital bed, surrounded by strangers and wires and sterility. She must be scared. She must be wondering where I am.

'How do you know who I am?' I ask suddenly. 'Life document clients believe it's all done by computer.'

'I've made it my business to learn everything about the people that come into my life,' Jonah says. 'When life documenting started, it didn't take much digging to find out what was behind it. I'd almost left them when they found you. Like I said, I've been admiring of your work for some time.

'You have an eye for detail. The time you saw me reading the OSIP documents is a good example. That phone call with Genevieve, the one where she told me she wanted to start a family. You heard that, didn't you? And then you glimpsed documents I was reading, saw the OSIP logo?'

I nod, remembering the clicking of the young dog's paws across the kitchen floor, the hum of the cooking on the stove.

'I selected the wrong settings on my workSphere for the life document for a short period – I don't think you would have noticed if it weren't for that call. It turned the camera on. If it weren't for Genevieve's news, I wouldn't have let that slip but well... here we are. I do want to help you, Kit. I've decided. I can help you keep your daughter.'

THEN

I happily lost hours to Mimi.

    I became greedy in collecting details about her.

She was watchful like Thomas.

I liked to see what would interest her in the world. It would always be the smallest detail that I would never have guessed, I wouldn't have spotted. The feel of the silver knob of a cupboard in the sitting room. A scuffed hole in the carpet fascinated her. When we were outside, her gaze shot upwards but when I looked up all I would see was empty sky, blank clouds that merged into a wall of white. But to Mimi, it was something spectacular, something to consider.

'She's just like you,' strangers would tell me, peering into her pram; although to me she looked quite different.

She was easily quiet.

She liked it when it rained. Not being out in it, really, but the sound of it next to the window. She listened to it as though it were something physical in front of her that she could touch.

She could spend time by herself and she seemed to enjoy that just as much as playing with Thomas and me. She would look up every now and again to find me but before then she would be quite absorbed in her activity, steadied by its rhythm.

I was always there, watching and waiting, poised for when she was ready to play again.

She didn't like to sleep. She fought against it each time I put her down. Writhing against her own tiredness before all of a sudden she would drop off in a beat.

What more can I tell you of her?

That she didn't smile easily?

That she could tell when we were upset without us having said a word different?

That she would quickly find where the door was in a room.

That she wouldn't take a bottle of expressed milk unless it was warmed ever so slightly.

She mesmerised me. I was unprepared for how much I loved her, even when I hadn't slept for nights on end, even when everything in my body was telling me to sleep, when I heard her cries as a newborn, there was nothing that would stop me from rushing to her. But through it all, even when I felt so sure of who I was, what I was doing, how to soften her cries, the very particular rocking that would soothe her, I was hounded by a voice of doubt. Some nights when she would not settle in her Moses basket, I would bring her into bed with us. As soon as I cocooned myself around her, she would fall asleep. There was a large part of me that didn't want to do it; it would be an instant IPS for starters. OSIP strongly disapproved of bed-sharing. Another bit of me was merely exhausted, would do anything to comfort her and couldn't think straight about the choice I was making. And then there was, in the core of me, yet another voice that knew this was what she needed right now. To be close to me for those few hours. I could sense Thomas silently disapproving, although when I asked him, he always denied it, only saying he was worried that we were going to get into the habit of it. And I worried too. All the mixed messages and emotions and worries weighed down on me, when really I knew that sometimes she needed me close and that was all there was to it. But I was glad when in the next nights she'd settle again in her basket.

In the same way as I had first imagined her into being, sometimes she would glance over to me and I would see her long-limbed and beautiful. Her hair like a mane, her eyes dark and knowing. I would imagine her laughing with friends at a joke I would not understand. I would be able to see her creating something in front of her, making something that was just hers.

I was hungry for her. Hungry to see her become herself.

Hungry in a way that afterwards I realised was always laced with the fear that I would not see her grow up.

It seemed implausible that we'd got through the first few months without an IPS, but we did. We did. The date of her first birthday was etched in my mind; once she reached twelve months, it was probable she would not be extracted. Every day that brought us closer felt like a miracle.

After Tia and Jakob, I was so primed for OSIP that I saw them everywhere. I second-guessed everything I did. I was walking on a tight rope and waiting to fall, not feeling the thrill of being up there, of being able to balance at a dizzyingly high height.

I often would catch myself looking for Evie too. If there was anyone dark-haired nearby, my head would turn instinctively towards them. I was troubled by the thought that she might be the one to deliver the blow of an IPS.

One day, though, Evie rang to say that she and Jakob were moving up north for work. She had been promoted and could afford to live out of the quarters. It was a stilted, awkward conversation – there were no apologies and little emotion.

'The house we have is completely secluded – our only neighbour is the boatyard that's a ten-minute walk away.'

I feigned a little interest and resisted the urge to ask her why she did not ask after Mimi. I was relieved that she was moving so far away. I wondered if I would stop looking over my shoulder.

I didn't.

When Mimi turned eight months, the first change came in the OSIP regulations. The number of IPSs were altered. The minimum you could receive was reduced. They were back down to nine.

A chance was being taken away, not given.

At first, we were not overly worried. We thought it most likely that we could continue as we had been. There was no real reason for concern. After all, we hadn't received a single IPS up until then and so why would we receive one now that the threshold had changed?

Mimi had fallen ill with a sickness bug that wiped her out,

but she recovered quickly enough for it not to worry us too much. But she'd not been ill before then and we had to log it with OSIP. We did so and although I wondered briefly about how OSIP might view it, I told myself that children get ill sometimes, that we'd done everything right, by the book.

There was a confidence, almost a swagger, to us then.

I'd dressed Mimi in a white and blue stripy coat that Santa had given her and we had been on our way to the park to feed the ducks. It was, at that moment in her life, her very favourite thing to do.

I loved these passions of hers, which lasted longer and seemed more committed than most childish fancies.

She wasn't so interested in feeding the birds, as such, as watching them being fed. She gurgled when she saw them scrabbling over some pieces; she held her breath, gave an audible gasp, watching which duck would get to the food first. It was a stage, a drama of who gets and who does not.

I'd always start off next to her, in the pushchair. Then I'd retreat just a few steps back, stamping my feet to keep off the cold, perhaps suggesting that it was time to go, waiting for her attention to dwindle.

It never would, though. I would always have to call a close to the duck-watching sessions. Thomas once tried to wait her out but they had not come back for over two hours and, in the end, I had gone out to get them and called a halt to the experiment because it was time for dinner.

I'd hoped that we could drop in to pick up some things from the shops but Mimi was enraptured and so I stood by her, telling her that we would have to go soon, that we could come back tomorrow.

Of course she didn't want to leave. Of course she didn't want to go.

'Here, Meems,' I said. 'Why don't we get some food for the ducks? Get them something tasty from the shop. Maybe something for us too, huh?'

I thought if I could lure her away from the pond for long enough, she would forget about the ducks. If she were dazzled by the rows and rows and shelves of things in the little shop at the end of the road, she would let them go.

She held me in her gaze for a moment so I was quite sure that she understood what I was trying to do. *I'm not fooled by you*, the look seemed to say. Her fingers clenched a little more tightly around the bar of her pushchair and her knuckles flashed white. She looked back towards the ducks.

One of them was being chased by the others. It shook itself, ruffled its feathers indignantly, but swam on, its beak poised forwards, out of the reach of its neighbours.

'What do you think, Meems?' I tried again. 'What shall we get for the ducks? Maybe some seed bars? Or an apple? They might like an apple.'

My words ran to fill the quiet where her answers might have been.

I reached out towards her fingers, prising them one by one off the bar of her pushchair until I held her hand in mine. It was cold, and I felt in my pockets for one of her mittens and then when I found none, scolded myself for forgetting.

Mimi bleated as I blocked her view of the pond. She snatched her hand back.

'Come on, Mimi. Daddy's waiting for us to come back now. Let's say goodbye to the ducks.'

I waved at them feebly. 'Goodbye, we'll come back and see you soon,' I said, in what I hoped sounded like a final and reassuring sort of way. I started to move the pushchair and turn it away from the pond.

The duck that was being chased had swum back to the edge of the group, as they were being fed by a mother and a child a little way away from us and were distracted by the dry bread falling around them like snowflakes. At first, they did not notice his return but then they spotted him and he was driven away again. Quacks and squawks filled the air.

'Come on,' I said, laughing. 'We're going to get cold out here!'

Sometimes changing moods could shake her.

I pushed on towards one of the pathways leading off from the pond as she yelled, and kicked and struggled.

She's hungry, I thought to myself. *She's tired. I should never have brought her out here when she's due a nap and a snack. Never again*, I told myself.

'It's okay,' I said, although by now my voice was rising shrilly.

Mimi continued to shout and scream.

There was a tap on my shoulder, but I thought at first I had imagined it. Who could be tapping on my shoulder at a time like this, when they could see that I literally had my arms full with my daughter? But then it came again. An insistent, prodding tap.

I turned around and there was a small woman, dressed in tweed, well wrapped up so she appeared smaller still. She was wearing circular glasses, which she peered out of inquisitively, and her hair was cut short, almost shorn to the skull. A faded grey.

'What?' I blurted out, before I could stop myself. Her head jogged backwards as though I'd hit out at her.

'Band, *please*,' she said. She emphasised the word 'please', as though to highlight her good manners.

'My band?' I said, stupidly.

'Under the jurisdiction of OSIP, I'm issuing you an IPS at 3.04 p.m. on Tuesday 22 September for ignoring the distress of your child. Band.'

'I was not ignoring her distress. She was just getting a bit upset about leaving the park. She'll calm down in a minute.'

'I timed her crying for a period of five minutes without receiving any comfort from you.'

'Five minutes?'

'This kind of episode could have significant effects upon her stress levels if repeated over time and can lead to anxiety and depression in adulthood.'

'I know the thinking,' I couldn't stop myself from snapping back. 'But it wasn't five minutes and I was trying to calm her.'

'You can appeal if you want. But I have all the footage that supports this claim and so I would not advise it. You could be given another IPS for failing to assent. It would show a lack of understanding.'

I opened my mouth to answer back but thought better of it and held out my arm, in disbelief. She pulled my sleeve up and scanned the thin silver band and then directed the scanner at Mimi too. It made a sort of whooshing sound as it read our bands.

Mimi, for a moment, was distracted by the woman and had stopped calling for the ducks but when I looked back again, the enforcer was gone and Mimi continued to cry. The ducks swam in a swarm towards the puffs of white bread behind us.

NOW

I rush towards Jonah.

'I'll do anything. Tell me what to do.'

I mean it. There is nothing that I won't do for her.

'Your sister, Evie – she gave you this address. She didn't tell you why?' Jonah pauses for a moment as I shake my head. He speaks so softly I have to strain to listen to him. I've realised that his voice has a waver to it, a soft quality as though it has been worn away over time. 'She came here. She's been here too. She found me.'

Jonah touches his knees lightly. He threads his fingers together, interlacing them.

'She was right not to tell you anything. I can understand why she told you to come here, although, strictly speaking, she's broken the terms by doing that. But I can understand it. And due to our history,' he motions between him and me, 'I can overlook it.

'You said you would do anything for your daughter? What if I told you that you can have her, that you could keep her – but you will need to live with a lie. A lie that you would need to protect. Could you do that?'

'Of course I could – I'd do anything. I could do it.'

Suddenly, Jonah jumps up from his stool to standing in one movement. He turns and walks away from me a few paces. Behind his back, his fingers continue to interlace, in and out, rhythmically tapping over one another again and again.

He pauses at a framed picture of him and Genevieve, together. Genevieve is young, maybe three or four, bundled against him in a heap. His arm is locked around her.

'You know all about Genevieve from my life document.'

Again, he speaks so softly, his voice has such a delicate quality, that I lean in to hear.

He turns back towards me, his eyes burning.

'I love my daughter very, very much.'

I nod furiously. I'm looking, searching, for any connection between us.

'She's an XC baby,' he says. That's when I hear it. The smallest tremor, the slightest waver. It starts so imperceptibly small; a hairline crack that you might not notice at all if you weren't paying attention. 'XCs born so the mother does not have to go through induction.

'The latest science. Cutting-edge technology. It would change everything. You could have a child without any cost to its mother. If it weren't so expensive they would roll it out to everyone. Maybe it would get there one day. No more inductions. No more pain. Can you imagine that?'

I can hear him speaking these words but there's something missing. I struggle to hear it, to make myself aware of it. It's the crack. But it's widening, lengthening, deepening. There's a blackness beneath it.

'But… but…' Jonah stops entwining his fingers. They are

motionless, slack at his side. I think of a branch lying torn from the tree, its leaves shed, black and still. 'But… it didn't work.'

I look up sharply.

'It's never worked. There's never been an XC baby.'

I let the words sink into me. *There's never been an XC baby.* I can feel them prickling me, jabbing at me, insistent. Picking a scab but the skin beneath it is raw and bloodied and sore. There's a roaring in my ears, a pulse that throbs, a rushing that swarms through me.

Jonah continues to talk and his words run over me like water over stone.

'It just never worked. At times it seemed like they might be close, I think it really could happen, one day, but in the meantime they learnt that there were people who would pay, who were looking for an alternative to induction.'

'But there isn't,' I said. The words are on my lips before I know what they mean.

'That's right. Induction remains the only way to conceive today.'

'So the XCs, the XC babies they are, they have to be…'

'They are the extracted children.'

It chokes me.

Jonah fades into a blur.

I stumble from the stool as though I could wake myself from a lurid dream. That I could ground myself somehow to the swaying, skewered reality that I'm presented with.

A face sweeps into my mind. But it does not belong to

Mimi. That surprises me. I want to think of her, I want to hold her, I just want her now. If I could hold her then I could protect her from this. But another vision, a beautiful, perfect face comes to me.

It's Tia, I think of Tia. Her wide, darkly fringed eyes exploring my own. The last time that I saw her shiny, ballooning cheeks down-turning into a wail, over the shoulder of the enforcer who had plucked her from the floor. They disappeared around the corner; they were not seen again.

'Every extracted child? How can – the custodians – how do you—' There are too many questions to ask, too many insults I want to throw, too much despair; they pile into one another, they fill my mouth with revulsion.

'How do I carry on? Knowing what I know?' Jonah finishes for me. 'I've asked myself this... I... I ask myself this.'

He pauses, looks around him as though he can find an answer there. Then he catches sight of the photo of Genevieve and him when she was just a toddler. I think of the numbers, how most children are only extracted as babies.

'That's why they usually extract when they're young.'

Jonah dipped his head a little in accord.

'And all the stuff about gestational periods and building their microbiomes...'

'Yes, that's part of the cover. The reason why XCs are in essence older babies to their XC parents. And living in the quarters, birth parents do not cross paths with their child again.'

Everything was unravelling, spooling outwards, further and further.

'The compounds...'

'They don't exist.'

'Mimi,' I murmur. She'd be too old to be pass as an XC baby. Where might she have ended up if they'd taken her?

'Your daughter's around one now, isn't she?'

I nod.

'The world the way it is, there's always a market for children even if they are not newborns.'

'She'd be adopted?' The word sounds strange on my lips; I thought its use was defunct in our society.

'It happens for some people who can't afford XCs but are rich enough to be living outside of the quarters.'

'But what do they think happened to their birth family?'

'That there's been a maternal death, most commonly.'

I close my eyes; I try not to imagine it but my mind is flooded with images of Mimi, given over to strangers telling her to call them mummy and daddy, wondering where we were and why she'd been sent away. I wonder how long it would take for her to forget us.

'I didn't know when I first had her,' he murmurs. His eyes flick again to the photograph of Genevieve. 'But she got ill.'

'Genevieve?'

'I wanted to trace the genetic disorder she had. It was the only way that we could understand what we were up against. That's how I found out.'

I stare at Jonah, at the shape his mouth is making as he speaks. I start to get the sense that I'm not really here, my body is not my own. I shiver and coldness drops through me.

'Found out what?'

'You know her as Maia. Evie discovered it. When she was

going through your father's papers. That's how she got Jakob back. Genevieve was an extracted child, she was taken from a family... she was taken from your family.'

'Maia.' I whisper it. I can barely say her name but my gaze focuses on the small girl on the photograph. My eyes frantically search her familiar face. I've spent so many hours studying her, finding details for Jonah's life document, but now I'm looking for something quite different. I search for any sign of a sister I've never known.

'I can't remember her,' I admit. 'Dad told us she died when she was tiny. Just before my mother passed away.'

'She didn't die. She was extracted. She was one of the very first to be taken. And your mother committed suicide not long after that, because of the extraction. It was a huge shock, especially being one of the first. That's what really happened. Evie learnt the truth. She came to see me here.'

I'm trying to put together the words that Jonah's speaking. Everything around me feels like it's moving; the floor shifting beneath my feet, the walls distorted, at wrong angles to the floor, somehow.

My mother. She left us. She chose to leave us. There's a small voice telling me that. A photograph I have of Evie and me, taken not long after her death, lingers in my mind. We were so young.

I know so little of her. The small details that Evie would present to me were more real than any actual memories I had of my own. But now I feel close to her. It's as though I can touch the burning pain she must have felt when Maia was taken from her. I can picture her despair. It is something solid; it cast long shadows on everything around her.

'She committed suicide. Because of Maia being taken,' I repeat, dully. But still I can't absorb it. 'Why didn't Evie...? Why didn't my dad—?'

'Your father wanted to protect you from the truth. He didn't want you to grow up knowing what she had done. He thought it was better that way. And Evie wanted to protect you from that too. At first.'

'But how did she find out about Maia being Genevieve? Did Dad know that too?'

'When Genevieve got sick when she was a toddler, I started to investigate fully how the XC programme operated but I didn't get anywhere. I ended up starting a relationship with someone who worked there. That's how I learnt the truth. Because Genevieve was one of the first, they made a mistake. They didn't screen her. What happened to us would not happen now, they've learnt from their mistakes. I confronted OSIP. I had to know who Genevieve's birth family were. I had to find your family and so I could fully understand the condition she had and if it could be treated. But they refused to help me and so I had to track down your father myself. It took time, bribes, money, but I found him in the end.

'I told him it was part of a genetics study that I was running, that your family had been selected because he and your mother were able to conceive naturally. He gave samples willingly. You were still very young at the time, about five or six, I think. I discovered the rarity of her condition – neither you nor Evie are carriers.

'He was struggling with everything that had happened, raising you and Evie on his own, losing his wife and daughter.

We got talking. I don't think that he had anyone else to confide in. He told me about what had happened about Genevieve – Maia – and your mother...'

'And you listened. When all the time you had his daughter—'

'It wasn't lost on me, Kit. I'm not... proud of it. But he needed someone to talk to. And I could listen. It was the least that I could do.'

'And me... I've been writing your life document, I've been watching her, hearing her.'

'I wanted to keep you close,' Jonah said simply. 'So I could be sure you had no idea who she really was.'

I trip over myself remembering Genevieve, Maia, through the lens of the Sphere. She tumbles towards me, seemingly so close but always out of my reach.

'Does everyone know – everyone who... who has an XC?'

Jonah doesn't rush to fill the silence. 'No, not everyone. I only discovered it myself because of Genevieve getting ill. Some others may have found out but it's not general knowledge.'

'And so you were stringing Dad along, listening to him, letting him tell you everything... Did he ever find out why you were really so interested in him? Did you, did you,' I almost stumble over the words, '...introduce him to Maia?'

'No. We never met each other, only wrote. It went on for years. Sometimes I didn't hear from him for a while. It got less frequent as time went on. But I was in touch with him, right until the end. Evie found our correspondence. That was how she discovered that your sister had been extracted, and the truth of your mother's death.

'And then she came here, after Jakob was taken. Just turned up one day. Got the address from my letters. Said that she needed to get away from everything at home. And with all that had happened to her, she wanted to talk to someone who knew what your father had really gone through. She told me about Jakob, about your dad's death and learning what had happened to your mother and sister. She talked about you too. She said she didn't want you to find out, that she wanted to shield you from it. It was while she was here that she spotted a picture of Genevieve. This picture of Genevieve.'

He picked up a small, framed photo of a baby that was tucked into a corner alongside many other framed pictures of Genevieve as a child on a sideboard. It was a picture of her as a newborn, in a mass of white blankets.

'I know that—' I said suddenly. The words rush out of me. 'I know that photograph, I've seen it before.'

'Your father took the picture when Genevieve was still with you, when she was just born. He sent it to me with one of his letters. Evie was only five when she was born, she couldn't remember her clearly from then. But she had just been going through your father's photographs. She saw straightaway it was the same baby. And next to all the other photographs of Genevieve, growing up, she put it together and challenged me. I didn't deny it. I could see that she knew it was her; there was nothing I could say that would make her think otherwise. But I told her that maybe I could help her get Jakob back. That there might be a way – if she could keep Genevieve's origin a secret. He wasn't an XC or I would not have been able to help, he would have already been with his new family. He was, like your daughter, part of a quota to be adopted.'

'Sold, you mean,' I say sharply.

'Like I said,' he continues, 'to keep your daughter comes at a cost. Part of it is knowing this terrible truth, and the bigger part is hiding it. I chose to keep my daughter. I chose to live with it.'

'She's not yours,' I almost choke on the words. 'She's not your daughter.'

He speaks the next words so softly they are almost inaudible, but they are lined with a steel I recognise in myself. 'She is now.'

'So if I don't say anything, Mimi stays with us?'

'Yes,' Jonah says. 'Another child will be found.'

I swallow hard. I feel the shadow of that other family – the other mother I will be consigning to this fate.

'And all I would have to do is to stay quiet, stay out of the way?'

'Knowing what you do, you will have to become part of OSIP. That's what happened to me. Once I confronted them about Genevieve, I was forced to become part of it – if I wanted to keep her. And now she's grown up, I want her to have the chance to be a mother. I can keep it out of my public life – the work I do for them is private – but you will most probably have to become an enforcer. You will have been provided for, by OSIP, and so you will become its feeder.'

'Couldn't we just stop this? Couldn't we tell everyone what they are doing? If people knew...'

'People do know. I knew, Evie knew, there are many more. There's a reason everyone's playing along. They've all got someone to lose. And they choose them. I've seen some people come close in the years I've been working with OSIP, threatening to come clean. Their children would have been extracted, however old they were. And it doesn't stop once they're grown up. If it's not your children, it's your grandchildren.

'You will never have a day when you are not monitored – but if you play by the rules, you will keep her. Many are able to live like this. Many are able to bear it.'

'Like Evie.' Suddenly I see the past aglow with these entangled threads, they are binding weeds, strangling everything.

'Do all enforcers know?' I ask. 'Do they all know what they are doing? Do they know what they are part of?'

'Mostly not, no – but there will be a few. They will have a son or a daughter who will be taken from them if they speak up. They will be someone who knows too much but who has something to lose, a reason to stay quiet.'

'Someone like me,' I say.

'Someone like you.'

THEN

The next time it happened, we were in a play park. The time after that, we were stopped while walking over to Santa's.

Going to a playgroup. In our favourite café. The service station restaurant we happened to stop in.

Mimi became ill with another two sickness bugs and we logged them with OSIP as we had done before. The moment that we sent them through from my workSphere, an IPS sprang up immediately, for not isolating her enough.

We stopped going out after that. But she became ill again with what seemed to be another stomach flu. I took her to the hospital this time because I was worried we were not doing enough. The doctor diagnosed her with an intolerance to gluten. I asked whether we might be able to appeal against the IPS for not isolating her, as her previous illnesses were likely to be connected to her gluten intolerance, but was told that any IPS connected to health could not be appealed.

The IPSs built, they mounted. They stood upon one another's shoulders and so they seemed taller, a tower that disappeared into the clouds. We tried to be hopeful. We tried to change, be better. We tried to second-guess our mistakes, to become psychics of our own actions. We tried to not stop trying, although every day a stagnancy grew within me, a sense of hopelessness that was becoming alive.

One day, we ventured out to Marina's house as Santa was staying with her. We walked with Mimi in the pram. We'd packed every conceivable clothes change, we'd checked the pushchair several times before we left. Thomas was convinced, I remember, that nothing could go wrong. We would walk to Marina's and Mimi would sleep from the motion and then once there, we would be safe within the confines of her home. A foolproof plan.

It was bright and sunny but stingingly cold. I remember wishing I'd worn gloves; I gripped the handlebars of the pushchair tightly to warm my hands. We walked as a triangle, Mimi at its point, myself and Thomas side by side, almost pressed into one another. I found that I was holding my breath whenever someone passed, and only when they had walked past us did I let myself breathe again.

We were almost there. I could see the glossy black of Marina's front door. A car door opened and closed. I sped up as we neared the house, I wanted to be inside there now, be contained by its walls. Thomas was almost jogging alongside to keep up.

'You can stop there,' a voice said. I didn't even realise that they were speaking to us and only realised when, once we carried on, I heard, 'I said, stop.'

The winter sun shone brightly into my eyes so I could not see the enforcer clearly, or his badge, although I was now sure that it was one. I started running through checklists in my head of what they could possibly accuse us of. I looked at Mimi, who dreamt on. My eyes checked over her body, taking in her hat, still snugly planted over her head, her outside suit encasing her. She smiled in her sleep and then she shifted to one side and her face was quite still and slack.

The enforcer leant back on his heels and dug his hands into his pockets. When he looked up, I saw a sort of wolfish grin on his face for just the briefest of moments before it vanished so completely, I had to wonder if I'd imagined it. I recognised that smile, those teeth that were ever so slightly narrowed. The pale salmon lips and widened cheeks.

'Roger,' I said, quietly. The boyfriend I'd had before Thomas who I'd told I'd never have children.

He ignored me and showed us his ID. A picture of him that looked like he was trying to contain laughter, overlain with the blue, symmetrical lines of an embossed OSIP logo.

'So, how long have you been walking for today, folks?' he said. He spoke more to Thomas than me.

Roger asked us if we knew what the temperature was that day and how many miles we had covered. How long exactly we had been outside. He checked on what Mimi was wearing and so he woke her and she, flustered and disturbed, started to cry. She would not stop when I comforted her and so I took her out of her pushchair to hold her.

In her snowsuit, she felt slippery and bulky and I struggled to hold her comfortably, and all the time I could feel myself getting hotter and hotter and hotter.

'I'm sorry to do this,' Roger said. 'Looks like I'm going to have to issue you with an IPS this morning. You've been out in cold temperatures way over the prescribed time for a child this age.'

Thomas asked where we would find this information; we were unaware of it in all of our time in induction.

'I'll make sure you are sent the information,' Roger said, with a swipe. Our goSpheres chimed. 'What I suggest is you get indoors as soon as you can,' he said. 'Do you know someone close by?'

He had followed us here. Waiting until the very last minute before he revealed himself. I was sure that he knew somehow that this was where we were heading to, that he knew that we had almost made it.

He scanned my band, then Mimi's and turned to leave us, but he turned back again before he went.

'Take care now,' he said. This time, he just spoke to me.

We had run out of places that felt safe. The spaces that had once felt so normal to us were now contaminated; I had no desire to return to any of them. Breathlessness flooded through me when I imagined being back in any of them. We stopped taking Mimi to swimming lessons or to the swings. We didn't go to visit Santa any more. We wouldn't eat out, in fact, we wouldn't go out if we could help it.

In those months, we were prisoners. Our world was shrinking to the size of the walls of our house. We reached the point where we rarely left home with Mimi and one of us would venture out alone to get whatever it was that we needed; we no longer moved as a tribe of three. I'd usually be the one who would wait at home with her. I ticked off the minutes that Thomas was out, drawing the curtains, checking the chain on the door, ushering Mimi into one of the bedrooms that didn't share a wall with the corridor.

I didn't want anyone to know we were there alone.

But despite our best efforts, despite hiding away we'd somehow, effortlessly almost, reached our eighth IPS. Only one more was needed for extraction, unless we could last out the few weeks until Mimi turned one.

This meant one thing: we were no longer safe in our home.

They could visit us at any time, on any day.

All that was left to do was to wait for them to arrive.

We all woke late on our last day together. The sun was already high and the blue, unblemished sky stretched out before us like another land to explore, vast, clear and borderless.

We'd been trying to feed Mimi formula, provided by the library, trying our best to prepare her for when we'd be parted and she'd no longer be able to have breast milk from me or expressed in a bottle. We tried giving it to her just slightly warm, like how she'd take expressed milk but after just a mouthful she pursed her lips shut and refused to take a sip more.

'What if she does this with them?'

'She won't have the choice,' Thomas said and then, more gently, 'she'll be OK. It's just because it's new and she's not used to it.'

I tried to shake the mounting sense of unease about what we were about to do.

The person who was taking her to the safe house we'd never met before, we'd never meet again. He didn't introduce himself – we didn't learn his name – the only reassurance we had that he was part of the operation was that he had come at the precise time we were told – at 4.17 p.m.

My eyes sought clock faces all day but in those last few minutes, with the cake, with the candle, the rapping at first surprised me.

Thomas looked over, love written starkly all over his face. He squeezed my hand as if to say, 'It's time.' Santa busied herself with the bag we'd packed, and swept Mimi up in a close hug, whispering words into her hair that I could not make out.

When she released her, we tried to explain in our over-jolly words.

'We're going to be seeing you *really* soon.'

'It's an adventure.'

'You're going to go with this nice man – but soon we'll all be together!'

The man who was taking her paid no attention to what we were saying. He was bent over his goSphere, leant against the wall, as we made our goodbyes.

'We'll see you soon!' we chimed again, as much to reassure ourselves as her; we kept repeating it as though it would make it fact.

And as we held her to us and kissed her cheeks, it seemed as though she partly understood what was happening. I thought at first that she knew that she was leaving us. I felt it in her hug, the way she lifted her face only slightly to be kissed – it was too restrained, not in key with her usual abandon at showing and receiving love.

She looked over the shoulder of the man as she was carried out, questioning us silently in her still stare.

She didn't look away.

But then she suddenly began to scream. It was like an alarm going off inside her. She struggled and wriggled in the man's arms.

She reached towards us desperately, her fingers grasping the air, crying out for us.

Thomas clamped his arm around my shoulder, gripping me tightly.

'Mimi!' I called out.

She twisted sharply in the man's arms. He almost dropped her. He tried to keep her calm as she thrashed and shrieked but it only made her scream all the more.

It was too much to bear.

'Let her go!' I screamed, breaking free of Thomas. 'Don't hurt her! Don't hurt her like that!'

'No, Kit.' Thomas was upon me. 'We have to let her go.' He held me back and slammed our front door shut on the man grappling with our distraught daughter.

I heard her screams long after they'd gone.

NOW

Mimi gurgles as she glides back and forth on the swing, laughing.

Thomas and I stand just behind her, just a little distance between us.

She grumbles if the swing begins to lose its momentum and slows; she wants to fly high and fast.

I can't believe how quickly she has recovered. There's been no stopping her since she regained her strength. She had to stay in hospital for a few days but the doctors were pleased with her progress.

From the outside, you would not know that there was anything wrong with our picture. We are together again, us three; our daughter is well, she's thriving, she's trying to walk and then falls and then tries again. There's no lasting damage. She's lucky; we're lucky.

We are not the only family in the park, it's the first sunny day we've had after a week of sleeting rain.

There's a sense of hilarity, of laughter, in the air, from both adults and children. We've all been too long cooped up inside.

But only the children scream as they scatter across the grass, loop in and out of the playground.

Quite often now, I'll catch sight of a boy and see Jakob in him. There'll be something about the tuft of their hair, their bandy legs that will draw me to them. I have not seen him since the day we met outside their house. Though I can understand what happened between Evie and me, I find I have no impulse to see her any more. That might change, I hope that it will, but for now I live each day in the only way I can bear it and that means, for the moment, not seeing my sister.

I hear someone say my name and when I look towards the sound, I almost do not recognise the person before me.

She has dyed her hair so it is darker than I ever saw it. It's a little too black; it drains her face, pulls the colour from her lips.

'Marie,' I say. The card that I was clutching I try to fumble into my pocket, without her seeing.

'How are you?' she asks.

I cannot answer her. I reach out my hands to my side in a shrug, just as she is joined by Leo. He appears older somehow, as though more time has passed than the few years since I last saw them.

'It's Kit,' Marie says to him, unnecessarily, for it is clear he recognises me.

'My God,' Leo is saying. 'We still talk about you – about what you did for us. You were like our guardian angel. We're sorry that we just disappeared after – afterwards... we had to get away.'

'Of course,' I say. It's not enough. They look at me, at

Thomas, expectantly. This is the moment that I should introduce them but I hesitate. The silence almost turns unbearable but it is broken by Mimi crying out.

'Mama, Mama,' she repeats like a siren.

Marie and Leo's faces light up, the way everyone's does at the sight of a young child, but too quickly the light fades and dies away. Their eyes search Mimi's face, looking for another's features.

When I don't speak, Thomas does: 'This is Mimi,' he says to Marie and Leo. 'I'm Thomas.'

They lose themselves in the greetings for a moment but after that, their eyes flash with something like despair, something like envy, something like warmth and coldness, all at once.

Thomas plucks Mimi out of the swing and leaves us for a moment, the three of us, standing together and mute.

'She's lovely,' Marie says to me, in the end.

'Yes,' Leo adds. 'Beautiful.' It sounds like something they've said too many times, there's a hollow ring to it.

I try to reply, to force some words that would be appropriate from my mouth but I am empty, I have nothing.

All that I can see is Tia's smile, looking up at her mother. All I can see is her face as she was carried over the shoulder of the enforcer before she disappeared.

'Good to see you again,' Marie says.

'Yes...' Leo agrees quickly but he lets the word hang as though, like me, he knows that he should be saying more but can't bring himself to do it.

We say goodbye. We don't pretend that we will see each other again, that we would want to. I watch them leave.

They reach for one another. They take small steps as though if the other weren't there to support them, they would stumble and trip.

'Shall we go home?' Thomas asks me, returning to my side.

I know what he's really asking me: *can* we go home. He doesn't want to be here while I watch, I wait, I pounce.

I try to push Marie, Leo and Tia from my mind but they float up, stubbornly buoyant, breaking the surface of my thoughts.

'I haven't made my quota,' I murmur. I shouldn't be saying this to Thomas. The numbers are confidential.

'Mama?' Mimi says. I look down towards my daughter and let myself, for a moment, swim in her gaze. She is the reason, she is the only reason.

'Not yet,' I say to Thomas. Steel lines my voice.

I spot a mother and father who talk to each other animatedly while their son climbs the steps of the slide. His feet edge close to the drop of a stair, his hand reaches out for the bar clumsily.

I walk towards them with a purpose I do not feel, reaching into my pocket, gripping the ID I was given. The card is alien in my hand, the raised letters of OSIP embossed into its surface.

They spot me when I am just a few steps away.

ACKNOWLEDGEMENTS

Thank you to Jo Harwood, Sarah Mather, Katharine Carroll and everyone at Titan. Also thanks to Sam Matthews for fastidious copy-editing and Natasha MacKenzie for brilliant cover design.

For reading and always being encouraging, thank you Richard Ho-Yen, Celia Ho-Yen, Hanna Arnold and Alexa Weaver.

To Dan and Bee: thank you for just about everything.

This book simply would not be here without the unflagging support of two awe-inspiring women: my agent Clare Wallace and my editor Cath Trechman. Thank you for your excellent advice, patience and energy, every step of the way.

ABOUT THE AUTHOR

Polly Ho-Yen was born in Northampton and brought up in Buckinghamshire. She studied English at Birmingham University before working in publishing for several years. She was then a primary school teacher in London and while she was teaching there used to get up very early in the morning and write stories. One of those stories turned into her first novel, *Boy in the Tower*. *Boy in the Tower* was published in July 2014 by Random House Children's Publishers. It was nominated for the Carnegie Medal and shortlisted for the Blue Peter Book Award and the Waterstones Children's Book Prize. Her second novel, *Where Monsters Lie*, was published in 2016 and her third novel, *Fly Me Home*, was published in 2017. Both of these novels were also nominated for the Carnegie Medal. She now writes full-time and lives in Bristol with her husband and daughter. Find her on Twitter @bookhorse.

HOPE ISLAND

TIM MAJOR

Workaholic TV news producer Nina Scaife is determined to fight for her daughter, Laurie, after her partner Rob walks out on her. She takes Laurie to visit Rob's parents on the beautiful but remote Hope Island, to prove to her that they are still a family. But Rob's parents are wary of Nina, and the islanders are acting strangely. And as Nina struggles to reconnect with Laurie, the silent island children begin to lure her daughter away.

Meanwhile, Nina tries to resist the scoop as she is drawn to a local artists' commune, the recently unearthed archaeological site on their land, and the dead body on the beach…

'Disturbing and original, surprising and shocking, it's an excellent novel from a unique voice in the genre.' – Tim Lebbon, author of *Eden* and *The Silence* (now a Netflix original movie starring Stanley Tucci)

'Artfully written and brilliantly controlled from the first page.' – M.T. Hill, author of *Zero Bomb* and *The Breach*

'A strange and brilliantly original novel which cements Tim Major's rightful reputation as a top class writer of fantastical fiction.' – Laura Mauro, author of *Sing Your Sadness Deep*

TITANBOOKS.COM

THE SWIMMERS

MARIAN WOMACK

After the ravages of global warming, this is a place of deep jungles, strange animals, and new taxonomies. Social inequality has ravaged society, now divided into surface dwellers and people who live in the Upper Settlement, a ring perched at the edge of the planet's atmosphere. Within the surface dwellers, further divisions occur: the techies are old families, connected to the engineer tradition, builders of the Barrier, a huge wall that keeps the plastic-polluted Ocean away. They possess a much higher status than the beanies, their servants.

The novel opens after the Delivery Act has decreed all surface humans are 'equal'. Narrated by Pearl, a young techie with a thread of shuvani blood, she navigates the complex social hierarchies and monstrous, ever-changing landscape. But a radical attack close to home forces her to question what she knew about herself and the world around her.

Praise for *The Golden Key*
'An intriguing and unsettling tale… Womack brings a great sense of the uncanny to the Fens.' – Alison Littlewood, author of *A Cold Season*

'A fascinating, unsettling tale that shifts, mutates and changes meaning much like the eerie ruined house in the Fens at the centre of this weird and brilliant debut novel.' – Lisa Tuttle, author of *The Witch at Wayside Cross*

TITANBOOKS.COM

THE BOOK OF MALACHI

T.C. FARRON

Nominated for the 2020 Nommo Awards for
Speculative Fiction by Africans

Malachi, a mute thirty-year-old man, has just received
an extraordinary job offer. In exchange for six months as
a warden on a top-secret organ-farming project, Raizier
Pharmaceuticals will graft Malachi a new tongue. So Malachi
finds himself on an oilrig among warlords and mass murderers.
But are the prisoner-donors as evil as Raizier says? Do they
deserve their fate?

As doubt starts to grow, the stories of the desperate will not
be silenced – not even his own. Covertly Malachi comes
to know them, even the ones he fears, and he must make
a choice – if he wants to save one, he must save them all.
And risk everything, including himself.

'Sharp and compact but devastatingly poetic. This book packs real
power into every page.' – Charlie Human, author of *Kill Baxter*

'Thought-provoking and disturbing… This striking horror novel
is not for the faint of heart.' – *Publishers Weekly*

'Farren has created an extraordinary narrator in Malachi…
[An] intense and memorable [read].' – *SFX*

GREEN VALLEY

LOUIS GREENBERG

When Lucie Sterling's niece is abducted, she knows it won't be easy to find answers. Stanton is no ordinary city: invasive digital technology has been banned, by public vote. No surveillance state, no shadowy companies holding databases of information on private citizens, no phones tracking their every move.

Only one place stays firmly anchored in the bad old ways, in a huge bunker across town: Green Valley, where the inhabitants have retreated into the comfort of full-time virtual reality – personae non gratae to the outside world. And it's inside Green Valley, beyond the ideal virtual world it presents, that Lucie will have to go to find her missing niece.

'A smart science fiction thriller… There are strong echoes of *Black Mirror* and the works of Philip K. Dick here.' – *SFX*

'*Green Valley* is a stunning thriller, a tense story, a horror, but it's also a well-played out detective tale in a world of what could have been. Utterly brilliant.' – The Dreamcage

'The story had a real *City and the City* feel to it… An incredibly atmospheric read.' – Paperbacks and Pinot

For more fantastic fiction, author events,
exclusive excerpts, competitions, limited editions and more

VISIT OUR WEBSITE
titanbooks.com

LIKE US ON FACEBOOK
facebook.com/titanbooks

FOLLOW US ON TWITTER AND INSTAGRAM
@TitanBooks

EMAIL US
readerfeedback@titanemail.com